EMILY'S CHRISTMAS KISS

"Emily, you're a very charming, talented, and beautiful female, and I don't believe that you are on the shelf. And I'm definitely not a rake," he said in a sultry voice, putting his hand under her chin and forcing her to meet his eyes.

Emily's heart lurched as she stared into his golden-green eyes that seemed to reflect the grayness of the snow. He's not lying, she thought in a panic, and, once again, was at a complete loss.

"Do you believe me?" he asked, his hand moving from her chin to tuck a stray strand of auburn hair behind her ear.

"Lord Stratford, I'm not eligible and it's quite obvious to the world that Lady Susan and her mother are expecting an offer," she said in a wavering voice, aware of nothing save the handsome peer nestled beside her amid a winter storm.

"Lady Susan and her mother can both go to the devil," he said huskily and then leaned forward to kiss her. . . .

BOOK YOUR PLACE ON OUR WEBSITE AND MAKE THE READING CONNECTION!

We've created a customized website just for our very special readers, where you can get the inside scoop on everything that's going on with Zebra, Pinnacle and Kensington books.

When you come online, you'll have the exciting opportunity to:

- View covers of upcoming books
- Read sample chapters
- Learn about our future publishing schedule (listed by publication month *and author*)
- Find out when your favorite authors will be visiting a city near you
- Search for and order backlist books from our online catalog
- Check out author bios and background information
- Send e-mail to your favorite authors
- Meet the Kensington staff online
- Join us in weekly chats with authors, readers and other guests
- Get writing guidelines
- AND MUCH MORE!

Visit our website at
http://www.kensingtonbooks.com

EMILY'S CHRISTMAS WISH

Sharon Stancavage

ZEBRA BOOKS
Kensington Publishing Corp.
http://www.kensingtonbooks.com

ZEBRA BOOKS are published by

Kensington Publishing Corp.
850 Third Avenue
New York, NY 10022

All Kensington titles, imprints and distributed lines are available at special quantity discounts for bulk purchases for sales promotion, premiums, fund-raising, educational or institutional use.

Special book excerpts or customized printings can also be created to fit specific needs. For details, write or phone the office of the Kensington Special Sales Manager: Kensington Publishing Corp., 850 Third Avenue, New York, NY 10022. Attn. Special Sales Department. Phone: 1-800-221-2647.

Zebra and the Z logo Reg. U.S. Pat. & TM Off.

First Printing: October 2003
10 9 8 7 6 5 4 3 2 1

Printed in the United States of America

To my mother, with love and thanks.

One

"Oh Mama, what a wonderful gift," Emily exclaimed, staring at the velvet box in her hands.

Sara Winterhaven smiled fondly at her daughter, who was all but staring like a gapeseed at the pendant she was holding. "Your grandfather wanted you to have it before Christmas, so you could wear it to the local routs. I tried to explain that we didn't have any special plans for the holiday season, but he wouldn't listen. You know how he is," Sara finished dramatically, and Emily knew exactly what she meant.

Emily Winterhaven, at the advanced age of four-and-twenty, had the distinction of being the only granddaughter of the strong-willed Marquess of Rawlins. In itself, that connection did admit her into the better houses, even though Emily detested Society. What made her position even more distinctive in her grandfather's eyes was the fact that she had reached her advanced age without a single marriage proposal.

Of course, Emily herself did nothing to remedy the situation. Ever since the debacle that was her first and only Season, she actively avoided any contact with polite Society. Since that event at the age of eighteen, her hair had transformed from a short, rather loud, bright red color into a long, luxurious mane of auburn. Her eyes were still the same sparkling green and her figure, although not petite as was the current fashion, was tall and lithe. Emily had all but metamorphosed in the past six years, but was completely unaware of the change in herself.

"Did Grandfather tell you where he found the pendant?" Emily asked, still staring down at the jewel in her long, delicate fingers.

The pendant in question was the most unusual piece of jewelry that Emily had ever seen. A large, single pearl shaped like the torso of a lady was the basis of the pendant. A gold head and tail were attached, and the mermaid was holding an intricately detailed shield which had a small pearl dangling at the bottom. A crown encrusted in emeralds sat atop the mermaid's head, and two more pearls dangled from her tail. It was an odd piece, and Emily suspected that her grandfather parted with a king's ransom to purchase it.

"He picked it up in London a short time ago. He told me he found it at a small shop near White's. And he was dreadfully disappointed that you weren't feeling quite the thing and couldn't join us on the visit. The mermaid is lovely, isn't it?" Sara asked, studying Emily and noticing the drab gray gown that graced her daughter's shapely figure.

Emily looked up at her mother and gave her a brilliant smile. "It's wonderful, Mama. I'm going to write Grandfather right now and thank him," she said sincerely, rising to leave the room.

An impish smile appeared on Sara Winterhaven's face. "I have another message from your grandfather. The jeweler told him that the mermaid is very old, and will bring good luck and a blissful union to any female who wears it. So your grandfather says he expects your firstborn male heir to be named after him, since he's the one who found it," she concluded, still smiling.

"Mama, I doubt that even a charmed mermaid can find a husband for a bluestocking like me. But I will assure Grandfather that I'll definitely name my firstborn child after him. Of course, I certainly hope I don't have to name my daughter Gareth!" she exclaimed with a giggle, running her fingers over the cool surface of the lucky mermaid.

* * *

A shot rang through the cold winter air, and Nigel Manning, the Earl of Stratford, grimaced. That was Jem, his groom, putting a period to the existence of his favorite horse, Gloriana.

Gloriana was a beautiful chestnut mare, and had been his favorite mount for the past two years. She was part of a matched pair that he occasionally used for his curricle. He had an extensive stable, but Gloriana was undoubtedly his favorite, besides Diablo, who'd been scheduled to sire Gloriana's next foal.

Until the curricle overturned in a freak accident and Gloriana broke her leg. The curricle was ruined, and Nigel was more than a bit shaken himself. Of course Runaway, the other half of his matched pair and a vastly inferior horse, was uninjured.

Nigel made his way through his country home, to the library. It had been a long day and he needed a drink, he decided, flexing his fingers nervously. It was as if there was a blessed curse on the family, he mused, entering the solitude of the Manning family library. The walls were covered with literally hundreds of books, and he had personally read more than half of them. Yes, he had inherited the Manning curiosity, he thought, walking over to the decanter of port that rested unobtrusively on one of the lower shelves. Roger, his handsome and reckless younger brother, had been the one to inherit the Manning charm.

The mahogany sofa next to the fireplace seemed to beckon him, so he trod over like a man defeated and settled his long, lank frame into the cushions.

As he stared at nothing in particular, his unfashionably long, black hair once again in total disarray, he wondered what exactly he had done to deserve this run of bad luck. His hazel eyes were shrouded in worry, and he was beginning to feel much older than his two-and-thirty years.

First of all, there was the accident with Gloriana; that put him in quite the foul mood. He hated to get rid of any of his stable, and had actually tried to see if Gloriana could have her leg set. That idea earned him the unenviable reputation of acting as if he were let in the attic.

And his curricle was ruined. Which in itself wasn't necessarily the end-all of the world, but he had just had it painted and was rather pleased with the results. So he had lost his favorite mare and his most attractive rig.

Then, of course there was his father, the Marquess of Avonleigh. He wasn't the most agreeable in the first place, and, as a result of his fairly regular fits of temper, paid the highest wages in the county to their servants. Luckily, his father's valet was deaf, so he didn't have to hear the abuse that was targeted at him on a daily basis. Actually, that relationship was probably the best in the household, Nigel thought, sipping his port reflectively.

So his father was always on the disagreeable side, which he could readily handle. But now his gout had flared up, and it was rather like living with the devil himself.

To complete the picture, the fetching new scullery maid that they had recently hired—Nigel swore that they had employed everyone in the county at one time or another—was a bit on the clumsy side, and was constantly breaking dishes. That in itself didn't particularly bother Nigel, but drove his father into a fit of temper.

If I didn't detest London so heartily I'd spend the Christmas holiday there, Nigel thought, draining the glass of port. Life certainly wasn't a picnic this time of year, he decided, his head beginning to throb.

A knock at the library door brought him out of his reverie. "Yes?"

An attractive young maid appeared, this one with blond hair and a mobcap. "Begging your pardon, Lord Stratford, but Lord Avonleigh wanted me to tell you that your brother has arrived for a visit and will be joining you both for supper," she said quickly, waiting for some sort of reply.

"Very good," Nigel muttered, and wondered what sort of trouble Roger had entangled himself in. Roger, the Manning brother favored by the ladies of all ages, never made an appearance at this time of year unless something was very wrong.

Nigel stared at his empty glass and decided he definitely needed another port before facing supper with his scapegrace brother and his ailing father.

As Nigel picked at his roast leg of mutton, he began to think that he was wrong about Roger's visit. Roger was in the best of spirits, and had actually cajoled his father out of his horribly black mood. In fact, he was telling his father of his adventures in London, and the ill-tempered marquess was actually laughing with his youngest son. It's all but a miracle, Nigel thought, his head still aching a bit.

He glanced across the table and studied his younger brother. At six-and-twenty years old, Roger Manning sported the same black hair as he did, but Roger's was cut in the fashionable Brutus style. His features were classically handsome, and he had an easy charm that made him a favorite in all of the best houses. As usual, he was dressed to the nines, with a form-fitting blue waistcoat (by Weston, naturally), buff breeches, and shining Hessians. A white silk cravat was knotted loosely about his throat, completing the picture of respectability. From what Roger reported, the Incomparables of the Season were still swooning after him, even though he was a second son and didn't have any particular expectations. He had a host of friends in London, and could be found on any given night gambling at White's or escorting the beauty-of-the-moment to the theater. In short, Roger was a good-natured dandy who had the luxury of having no real responsibilities.

"What pieces of your mother's jewelry did you borrow, Roger?" the marquess asked, his voice beginning to sound a bit hostile.

Roger smiled easily. "Oh, none of consequence. I was a bit short on blunt the last time I was home, so I borrowed them for a while. Some of them ended up at the jeweler's, since I was having a run of bad luck, but I did get most of them back," he said in a cheerful voice, completely oblivious to the fact that the marquess was beginning to turn a slight shade of red.

Nigel sipped his claret and predicted his father's next move. Probably an accusation of some sort, in a loud voice that declared Roger a son unworthy of the Manning family name.

"Am I to understand that you don't have all of the jewelry you removed from this house without my permission?" the marquess asked, his skin beginning to turn red with rage.

"All but that horrible mermaid pendant. When I went back to the jeweler, he had sold it. I was a bit late coming up with the blunt and he rather got ahead of himself. I never even saw Mother wear that particular piece, you know," Roger finished, downing his claret with one long drink.

"The mermaid pendant? You sold the mermaid pendant? Have you gone mad, Roger?" the marquess practically yelled, causing Roger to wince a trifle. Nigel experienced his father's fits of temper on a daily basis, so he was rather immune.

"Father, I don't see why you're so upset. The piece was dashed ugly and I know Mother never wore it," Roger said in a level voice, glancing over at Nigel for some sort of support.

Nigel concentrated on his braised asparagus. He most certainly didn't want to get involved in this fracas.

"Don't you remember the story I told you both about the mermaid pendant? And the legend?" the marquess questioned, running his hand through his thick, gray hair in agitation.

"You'll have to refresh our memory, Father," Nigel said, his curiosity aroused. What in God's name was his father talking about? The legend? He didn't remember any sort of legend connected to any of their late mother's jewelry.

The marquess stared at both of his sons as if they were slow-tops. "I'm certain I told you the story of the mermaid pendant. It's been in your mother's family for centuries, always passed down to the eldest daughter. If she failed to produce a female heir, then it was passed to the wife of the eldest son. Are you both certain you never heard this story?" he asked, picking at his leg of mutton.

"We've never heard a word of it," Roger said, glancing over at Nigel.

The marquess was now truly agitated. He was never an easy man to know, and the gout only made matters worse. "The mermaid pendant is reputed to bring a blissful marriage to the female who wears it. But the legend also says that there will be an unending run of bad luck for the males of the family if it isn't properly passed on to the next generation," the marquess concluded, daring his sons to refute his claim.

Roger chuckled. "You can't believe a ridiculous story like that, Father! We're certainly not living in the Dark Ages and families don't have runs of bad luck because a piece of jewelry is sold," Roger concluded, certain that the discussion was over.

"Ridiculous? I think not, young man. When did you sell the mermaid?" the marquess demanded, losing complete interest in the food in front of him. His face had now turned completely red, which was an interesting contrast to his thinning gray hair and brown eyes.

Nigel sighed. This was most certainly going to be a long, difficult meal. In the end, he had no doubt that he was going to travel to the ends of the earth to retrieve the mermaid or stay at home and watch his father suffer an apoplexy in his anger over the situation.

"A little over a sennight ago. Why?" Roger asked innocently, and Nigel pitied him. He had no idea that this discussion would probably drag on until the wee hours of the morning.

"That's when my gout flared up. And Nigel, isn't that when that horrible scullery maid appeared? The one that is breaking everything she touches?"

"Actually, it is about a sennight since then," Nigel answered, beginning to wonder if his father had actually hit on the cause of their recent bad luck.

"And didn't your groom have to put down your mare today? And what about your wrecked curricle?" the marquess added in a tone that proclaimed that the pendant was the cause of all of their problems. His cheeks had returned to a more normal color, so he no longer matched his maroon waistcoat.

"Father, the mermaid has nothing to do with any of this, and I think it's best that we forget about the whole episode," Roger said calmly, and Nigel waited for his father to explode.

He didn't have to wait long. "You think we should forget about this episode? Since when do you have any authority in this house? You will do as I say, Roger, lest you forget that you are living off my sufferance. You will return to London immediately and find out who purchased the mermaid. You will then instruct the jeweler to contact that person and offer to buy the mermaid back at a very profitable price. Do I make myself clear?" the marquess said in a voice that was loud enough to be heard on the Continent.

Roger sipped his claret thoughtfully. "I can't. I actually tried to do that before I returned home and was informed that the Marquess of Rawlins purchased it as a gift for his granddaughter. He doesn't have it in his possession any longer, and I don't think we'll get much cooperation from the girl," he concluded.

"Why won't the girl sell it?" Nigel asked curiously, rather enjoying this Cheltingham tragedy that was unfolding in front of him. In fact, it was dashed more interesting than Drury Lane.

"Do you remember my first term at Oxford? And the rogues' club?" Roger replied, picking at his meat.

Nigel shook his head and the marquess commanded, "Refresh our memory."

Roger sighed audibly and sagged a bit in his chair. "The rogues' club was the most popular group at Oxford, and very few men were asked to join. As a condition of membership, you had to go through a series of tests. My test included romancing and then cutting an unexceptional young woman in her first Season," he explained as he gazed at his cold food.

"What does this have to do with the mermaid?" the Marquess asked, his voice returning to a more normal level.

Roger looked anywhere but at his father and brother. "The young woman I romanced and then cut was Emily Winterhaven. She is the granddaughter of the Marquess of Rawlins. Suffice it to say she wouldn't do a good turn for me if I were the last man on earth. And I don't blame her," he added in a soft voice.

"So, the mermaid is now in the hands of a female who detests you and we have no means of bringing it back into the family," the marquess concluded, a very pronounced frown on his forehead.

"I could steal it back," Roger said halfheartedly. His relief was apparent on his face when his father replied, "I think not."

"Why not?" Roger asked, moving the blue-and-white-patterned Dresden china plate away from him. "Then we would have the mermaid back and Emily Winterhaven would be none the wiser. We could make it appear that she lost the damnable thing," he concluded, a scowl marring his classically handsome features.

The marquess shook his head. "The mermaid can't be stolen. You have to get it back voluntarily from Miss Winterhaven or we'll be plagued with bad luck to the end of our days," he concluded in a somber voice.

Nigel leaned back a bit in his chair and sighed. I'll bet a guinea that Roger will somehow squirm his way out of this situation and I'll end up taking care of it, he thought wryly.

Roger and the marquess were up until the wee hours of the morning playing chess, or at least that's what Nigel assumed they were doing. He was alone in the library, reading Shakespeare, trying to relax, when he heard the familiar hobble-thump that marked his father's footsteps.

Moments later, the marquess appeared in the library and cordially asked, "Mind if I have a word with you, m'boy?"

Nigel cringed inwardly. Every time his father was polite to him it usually meant that he was going to ask him to do something he didn't want to do. "Sit down, Father," Nigel said in a casual voice, and noticed how difficult it was for his father to walk. Roger is the lucky one, he mused; he doesn't have to be at home and watch Father wither away day by day.

The marquess settled himself into a large, brown leather chair and appeared to study Nigel a moment before stating, "Roger and I discussed the pendant situation."

"Really," Nigel remarked, not at all surprised. He knew exactly where this discussion was leading.

"Roger is certain that Miss Winterhaven harbors quite a grudge against him, and I don't blame the poor gel. He should have been whipped for treating a young lady the way he did," the marquess said, tapping his fingers absentmindedly on his ornately carved wooden cane.

"It was quite the nine-days' wonder. You were traveling in Italy at the time, I believe," Nigel added, staring into the fire.

"Yes, I was. In any case, do you remember Cousin Harriet? We saw her fairly regularly before she was married."

"Of course. Harriet was one of my favorite cousins, even

though the connection was rather vague," Nigel replied, wondering where his father was going with the conversation.

"Harriet doesn't speak to Roger any longer. You see, she is a bosom bow of Miss Winterhaven's. After the debacle that Roger put her through, Harriet claimed that she couldn't forgive Roger. She's probably the only person who hasn't been taken in by his charm," the marquess replied, his fingers still tapping the cane.

"And?"

"And I'd like to have the mermaid pendant back in the family. I know you and Roger don't believe in the curse and think I'm a foolish old man—that's your choice. But the mermaid belonged to your mother and I know as a fact that she wanted it to stay in the family. It's obvious that Roger will sooner rot in hell before convincing Miss Winterhaven to sell it back to him, so we thought up another option," the marquess concluded, leaning back into his chair.

"So once again, as the eldest son, I have to step in and deal with the mess that Roger has created. As I've had to do my entire life," Nigel said bitterly, not daring to look at his father. He was not pleased with the situation that was being thrust on him.

The marquess sagged a bit in the chair and sighed audibly. "I know it's been difficult for you, Nigel. I haven't been much of a father since your mother died, but at least you had some time with her. Roger barely remembers her, and was left to grow into an adult without any real supervision. I know you don't want to have anything to do with this situation, and I don't blame you. I'm just asking you to consider our idea for your mother's sake," he finished somberly.

Nigel glanced over to his father, who now looked rather ashen in the firelight. His dark blue dressing gown hung on his thin form and the light made his skin look even more pale. His father was fragile and old. And since he did care deeply for him, no matter how irrational he could be, Nigel sighed and asked, "What exactly is your idea?"

"I'd like to write Harriet a note explaining what happened with the pendant and suggest, if it's not too much of a bother, that she have a small house party over the Christmas holiday. I'll ask that she invite Miss Winterhaven. You'll also be a guest at their home. That way you'll be able to get to know Miss Winterhaven and see if she can be convinced to part with the mermaid."

"Will Harriet agree to a house party? And what if Miss Winterhaven doesn't want to part with it?" Nigel asked with a sigh.

"Harriet was a great favorite of mine, so I don't think she'll balk at the idea of a party. As for Miss Winterhaven, I certainly don't expect you to force her to sell the mermaid. If this house party idea doesn't work, we'll think up another tactic," the marquess concluded, staring at Nigel expectantly.

Nigel sighed and stared back into the flames. Christmas with Harriet, her husband, and daughter might not be that horrible.

"But if you have your mind set on staying home and throwing a betrothal ball, I certainly won't stand in your way," the marquess added, with a sparkle in his eyes.

"A betrothal ball? I think not. Who have you heard that cock-and-bull story from?" Nigel demanded, sitting up in his chair.

The marquess grinned wickedly. "Lady Markston is telling everyone who will listen that her dearest Susan will be the next Countess Stratford. Didn't you know?"

"I bloody well had no idea that Susan had set her sights on marriage. I have no intention of wedding her now or in the future," Nigel said passionately. Suddenly the thought of visiting Harriet and meeting Miss Winterhaven was actually looking quite attractive.

"Then a visit to relations might be exactly what you need to cool your liaison with the younger Lady Markston," the marquess said with a smile.

"I'm not having a liaison with Susan Claredon, and I most

certainly don't plan on having one!" Nigel said passionately, then added, "So write Harriet as soon as you feel up to it. I think a visit to relations at Christmas is just what I need."

The marquess relaxed in his chair, a contented smile on his stern features. "That's a wise decision, Nigel," he said, staring into the fire.

"So Emily, what did Harriet have to say?" Sara Winterhaven asked, staring at the bit of needlepoint she was working on.

Emily sat at the pianoforte and looked blankly at the composition she was attempting to finish. Today isn't the day, she thought, and put down her pen. "Harriet is fine, Henry is fine, and Victoria has a new puppy called Wellington," Emily said, smoothing the wrinkles in her wonderfully unfashionable, high-necked brown muslin dress.

"That's all she had to say? In a letter that long?" her mother asked, still studying her needlepoint, which was a tangled mess.

"Actually, she invited me to come to their country house for the holidays. She's having a small house party and said she would be devastated if I didn't come," Emily said casually, glancing furtively at her mother. She still hadn't made up her mind on the invitation, and wanted to see her mama's reaction.

Sara smiled up at her. "Dearest, you should go see her. You've become a virtual recluse lately, and time away from the family would do you good. Plus, your father has been talking about spending the holidays with your Uncle Jon. He's invited us dozens of times, and we just can't refuse any longer. And I know that prospect doesn't appeal to you," she finished, laying the needlepoint down on her lap.

Emily sighed. Her mama was precisely right. She detested Ian and Richard, her horribly spoiled younger cousins, and was forced to endure any number of childish pranks every time she was with them. "So you wouldn't mind if I accepted the invitation?" Emily asked in a soft voice, tucking a strand of long, wavy auburn hair behind her ear.

"Not at all, dear. I'll speak to your father, of course, but I expect he'll say the same thing. You never spend any time with people your own age, and a visit to Harriet will do you a world of good," her mother concluded with all the authority of the Oracle at Delphi.

"When should I be home? I don't want to overstay my welcome," Emily asked, beginning to look forward to the trip.

Sara smiled brightly. "Well, if you decide to go see Harriet, then your father and I will more than likely go visit your Uncle Jon, and we won't be staying any longer than the Twelfth Night festivities," she concluded, a hopeful light in her steady green eyes.

"And if I decline Harriet's invitation, I'll have to visit Uncle Jon, won't I?" Emily asked in a small voice, certain of the answer.

"Unless you suddenly contract a horrible disease, yes, you'll get to spend the holiday season with your two favorite cousins," her mother replied, grinning at her.

Emily rolled her eyes toward the heavens. "Mama, I would rather spend the holidays in Newgate than spend more than a day with Ian and Richard. I have never met two more spoiled, undisciplined little boys in my life and dread spending any time at all with them!" she concluded passionately. It was obvious to everyone that Emily didn't savor the idea of a visit to Uncle Jon.

"So write Harriet that you'll be pleased to accept her invitation," her mama said evenly, noticing the look of worry on Emily's face. "And don't worry about attending a mere house party! Harriet is a bosom bow and I'm sure she won't let anything untoward happen while you're visiting her," she concluded.

Emily stared down at her hands, embarrassed that her mama knew exactly what was troubling her. Emily still didn't feel completely comfortable in any social setting since she suffered that awful humiliation at the hands of Roger Manning six years earlier. But Mama is right, she thought, the logical part of her brain winning the argument. This will be nothing more than a visit with close friends—not like a society event at all.

"And take the pendant your grandfather bought you. Harriet always loved jewelry— I'm sure she'll be green with envy over your mermaid," her mama suggested casually.

"All right. It is an unusual piece, and I'm sure Harriet will find it interesting," Emily added innocently, trying to convince herself that the visit to Harriet's house wasn't an invitation to disaster. Yes, I should take the mermaid, she thought distractedly; maybe it will bring me some luck.

Two

"Oh Emily, I'm so glad you decided to come," Harriet Langely exclaimed, enveloping Emily in a heartfelt hug.

Emily chuckled at her exuberance. "Harriet, I'm so sorry, Lady Ashton, it is wonderful to receive such a warm welcome," she said, and drew out of Harriet's embrace and actually curtsied.

Harriet laughed and pulled her beige Kashmir shawl around her shoulders. "Emily dearest, you are the scamp! No wonder little Victoria adores you. Come into the parlor and warm up while my Jenny helps your girl get you settled."

Emily smiled back warmly. The ladies had been friends for a dreadfully long time, and Harriet alone helped her weather that awful Season six years ago. As she followed her through the wainscotted halls, she decided that marriage and motherhood were definitely agreeing with Harriet. Her hair shone like spun gold, her blue eyes danced merrily, and she still had the same modest figure she did when the pair were in school. Of course, her maroon kerseymere dress was of a more stylish cut than what Emily was wearing, but Emily knew she had no touch with fashion at all.

"Would you care for some tea, Emily?" Harriet asked, closing the massive oak door behind them.

Emily gaped at the parlor. Harriet had neglected to tell her that she had become caught up in the passion for anything Egyptian, which was the current fashion. The mahogany chairs were held up by thin, delicately carved sphinxes. The sofa sported a lion's head on each arm, and, in the far corner was what appeared to be a small replica of a mummy's sarcophagus.

"Isn't it dreadful?" Harriet giggled, taking a seat on the sofa, waiting patiently for their tea to appear.

"It's rather . . . unusual," Emily managed to mutter, staring at the ornately carved female figures that formed the base of a table in the corner.

"Henry's mama has a passion, you see, and has given us all of this. She's wonderfully kind, and it would break her heart if we packed all of it up into the attic. So we've decided to live with it rather than hurt her feelings," Harriet explained, as a bland young woman walked in with the tea service.

A radiant smile broke out on Emily's face. "That's reassuring to hear. For a moment there I thought I was going to have to commit you to Bedlam."

Harriet began to pour the tea, eyeing Emily's travel-worn gown. "No, I'm not completely let in the attic yet. But where did you get that traveling dress? It's not at all the thing," Harriet remarked, handing the delicate teacup to Emily.

Emily looked down at another one of her wonderfully nondescript, high-necked brown kerseymere dresses. "Yes, I know. I have no fashion sense whatsoever. Papa ordered me to buy some decent clothes while I was here, since I can never find the time while I'm at home," Emily explained, sipping her tea.

"We'll have you rigged out properly in no time. By the by, Henry is due in at anytime. He's out riding, and Victoria is taking her afternoon nap. She was quite put out that she wasn't allowed to stay up this afternoon and wait for you," Harriet said, and Emily noticed that she actually appeared to be serene. Family life obviously agreed with her.

"And how is my favorite niece?"

"She is still enamored with Wellington, the pup of dubious heritage that actually managed to get out of his box in the stables and make it into the yard. Victoria spotted him immediately and has now officially adopted him. He has a few more relations in the stable—I don't know what's going to be done with them," she concluded.

Before Emily could ask the question that had nagged at her for the entire trip—namely, who else was going to be attending this house party—the door burst open and Henry Langely, Viscount Ashton, entered.

"Emily, how wonderful to see you," he exclaimed with a smile.

Emily looked over at the husband of her best friend and decided that he hadn't changed much since she met him during the Season. He was still on the stocky side—his hair didn't show a bit of gray and was still a rich, dark shade of brown. Of course, at two-and-thirty, Henry probably shouldn't have shown any gray at all, but with Harriet as a wife, he has more than his share of worries, Emily thought humorously. Henry was still the affable, brown-eyed lord who had captivated Harriet and endeared himself to Emily. "Lord Ashton, thank you so much for your invitation. I'm looking forward to my stay at your lovely country home," Emily replied with a grin.

"Lord Ashton! Gads, Emily, you do have a way of making a man feel ridiculous. I'll personally beat you if you don't call me Henry," he said with a grin, and sat on one of the sphinx chairs across from the sofa where the ladies were seated.

A giggle escaped from Harriet and Emily. Henry was notoriously softhearted, and didn't even like hunting. "Of course, Henry. Your wish is my command," Emily said with another giggle.

Henry relaxed in the chair and casually asked, "So, how was your trip?"

"Very uneventful. Papa keeps telling me that we're going to have a dreadful winter—he says he's been seeing all of the signs. I'm afraid to ask what the signs are, though. It is a bit chillier here," Emily commented, fixing her gaze on some of the more bizarre little Egyptian relics stuffed in every nook.

"That's what my groom keeps saying—he actually is expecting more than a bit of snow. I just hope Nigel and Aubrey get here before the weather pens us into the house," Henry commented, leaning over to get himself a cup of tea.

"Nigel and Aubrey?" Emily asked with a very pronounced frown.

"Aubrey is Henry's cousin, and Nigel is a distant cousin of mine. We've known each other since we've been children," Harriet explained, sipping her tea delicately. "Aubrey is joining us to avoid spending the holiday with his mama, who he doesn't always get on with. From what Nigel wrote, I think he's coming to escape a young woman who had decided to catch him in the parson's mousetrap," she concluded.

"Then I have something in common with both of them, since I'm escaping a visit to Uncle Jon and the demons he calls his sons," Emily said with a smile. I hope that's the extent of the house party, she thought a bit nervously. I can handle two cousins. But I'll be tempted to lock myself in the room if there are a dozen more people expected, she thought, her head spinning.

"You'll get along famously with Nigel. He's quite capable on the pianoforte—of course, not nearly as talented as you are," Henry said, draining his teacup. "You know that the music room is open to you whenever you want to play. It's far enough away from the bedrooms that you can use it without disturbing anyone," he added.

"Why, thank you, Henry. Most people are appalled when they find someone who plays for relaxation. And heaven forbid playing at night! You'd think I was having a tryst with the footman!" Emily exclaimed with a smile.

"Well, feel free to play whenever you like. Victoria is showing some interest in the pianoforte, so maybe you'll help her along," Harriet replied, her eyes wandering over to her husband.

Emily glanced at the pair and sighed with envy. It was obvious to all of the world that Henry and Harriet were deeply in love. When they looked into each other's eyes, it was as if they were the only two people in the world. It must be wonderful to be loved, Emily thought, loneliness gripping her heart like a vise.

Susan Claredon, the daughter of the Earl of Markston, studied Nigel, her intended, from across the crowded dance floor. His clothes, once again, could be improved upon, she thought, fanning herself delicately. His buff breeches fit tightly over his muscular thighs, and his gold satin waistcoat wasn't nearly as spectacular as the cerulean-and-puce waistcoat Lord Michelson was wearing. He needs a new valet, Susan decided, tucking a strand of long, blond hair behind her ear. Once again, Nigel's hair was dreadfully wild, and he looked more like a Gypsy than the future Marquess of Avonleigh. If only the old goat would stick his spoon in the wall, Susan thought with a sigh; then I could be the Marchioness Avonleigh. That's much grander than being a simple countess, which I'll have to tolerate until the old goat dies, she decided, smiling widly at Nigel from across the room.

Nigel walked slowly across the crowded room toward her, his expression grim. Susan continued to flutter her fan flirtatiously, and smoothed the wrinkles out of her gold-and-white, shot-silk gown lightly sprinkled with just enough spangles to avoid vulgarity.

"Nigel, you haven't been very attentive tonight," she admonished as he sat down next to her.

Nigel smiled weakly. "I'm sorry—I've been preoccupied with the details of the trip."

"Trip?" she asked innocently, her mind in a whirl. Was he planning their honeymoon? In Greece, perhaps, or Italy. Nigel would spend the day doing whatever Nigel did, while I'll attend glittering parties and be the toast of the Continent. Men of all shapes and sizes would love to talk to the beautiful marchioness who graced their foreign shores. Then, after

I supply him with an heir, I'll have a score of lovers, she thought wickedly, all of them dreadfully handsome.

"Yes, I'm going to spend the holiday season with a cousin of mine. I'm actually leaving tomorrow morning," he said evenly, sipping his champagne, a look of complete boredom on his angular features.

Susan's eyes bulged out of their sockets. "You're not going to be here for the holiday season? How could you, Nigel?" she said in her most convincing whine.

Nigel raised his eyebrows at her childish tone. "Susan, you know you shouldn't pout like that—you're going to get wrinkles," he commented, glancing around the room.

The pout immediately disappeared. "Will you have a special gift for me when you return?" she asked coyly, and laid her hand possessively on his muscular leg.

Nigel's eyes widened slightly as he casually took her hand in his and placed it back on her leg. "Susan, I doubt that I could ever find you a special gift," he said, and glanced toward the door. "Now you must excuse me—I've really got to call it a night," he said, getting up to leave.

Susan was in shock. It wasn't supposed to happen this way. "Have a Merry Christmas, Nigel," she said in a wounded little voice, hoping that his guilt would force him to include her in the visit to the unknown cousin.

He smiled back at her, a wide, genuine smile. "Of course, Susan. Have a Merry Christmas yourself," he replied, and casually sauntered out of the room, with Susan's glittering blue eyes boring a hole into the back to his black jacket.

Moments later, Susan could be found standing in an unobtrusive corner, smoothing the fabric of her gown and frowning distinctly at her very formidable mother.

Lady Markston, known to her bosom bows as Winifred, was a formidable lady indeed. At five-and-forty, her hair was a unique shade of brown, which the tabbies swore didn't occur in nature. Her voice was almost continually louder than everyone else's in the room and she had the stature of the

Prince Regent. Lately she had taken to wearing the most or-
nate and colorful turbans when she was out, to the horror of
everyone who encountered her. The main objective in Lady
Markston's life was getting her daughter leg-shackled as soon
as possible. Her likeliest victim was Lord Stratford, who
owned a large tract of land adjoining their property.

"Mama, what am I going to do? Nigel is leaving to spend
the holidays with some cousin," Susan whined in a most irri-
tating voice, panic apparent in her perfect blue eyes.

Winifred grunted. "What do you mean, he's leaving? What
cousin is he going to visit? Why didn't he invite you?" she
practically hissed, ignoring the cerise turban teetering precariously atop her head.

"I don't know, Mama. I don't think he's interested in me
anymore," Susan exclaimed, tears welling up in her eyes.

"You had best make sure he's still interested in you,
Susan," Winifred exclaimed, beginning a very long scold.
"How many unsuccessful Seasons have you gone through? I
won't have Society laughing because my daughter cannot
make a decent match. Stratford is unaware of the fact that you
haven't taken, and the marriage would be eminently suitable,"
she finished, glaring at her daughter.

"Well, what am I going to do, Mama?" Susan all but
wailed.

"We are going to find out which cousin he is going to visit,
and then we will arrive at their house party uninvited. I'll fab-
ricate some excuse, and you will spend the holiday with
Nigel. I expect that you'll make proper use of the time and
we'll be placing the banns before the Twelfth Night celebrations," Winifred concluded, her large breasts heaving in
agitation.

"And then I'll officially be the Countess of Stratford?"
Susan asked in a wistful voice, her tears immediately disappearing.

"You'll be a countess, my dear—you just leave everything

to your mama," Winifred said reassuringly, leading her daughter back to the festivities.

"So, tell me about Emily Winterhaven," Nigel asked casually, sipping his port. He was a trifle more relaxed this evening, and was fully prepared to leave the next morning.

Roger squirmed in his chair a bit, loosening his neck cloth. "There's not much to tell, actually," he said, turning a bit red.

Nigel smiled. I think my dearest brother is actually embarrassed over that incident, he thought distractedly. "Of course there is. You did court her actively for what, about a fortnight or more? Tell me about her," Nigel ordered, stretching his long, muscular legs out in front of him.

Roger stared at the books that lined the study walls, and appeared to study his immaculate fingernails for the longest time before replying. "Emily is actually rather nice. She has short, bright reddish hair and the most disturbing green eyes. To my knowledge, she doesn't go out in Society at all," he concluded, staring into his glass of port.

Once again, Roger surprised his older and definitely more mature brother. He actually sounds like he regrets the whole episode, Nigel thought, noticing how once again Roger was the impeccable man-about-town.

Today, Roger was wearing a buff pair of breeches with a green jacket and the most unusual green-striped waistcoat. His cravat was tied in the mathematical, and he looked as if he could walk into any drawing room.

Nigel, on the contrary, had changed into a pair of black pantaloons, his white shirt was dashed wrinkled, and he appeared to need a shave. His midnight-black hair was rather untidy, and he looked almost like a cit. But a well-dressed cit.

"Is Miss Winterhaven a harpy?" Nigel asked curiously, trying to find a reason why she was chosen to be the victim of the rogues' prank.

Roger shook his head. "Not at all."

"Is she pox-faced? Fat? Simpering?"

"No. Not at all," was Roger's reply.

"So why was Miss Winterhaven chosen to be your victim? Surely there was some reasoning behind it, or were you all just being deliberately vindictive?"

Roger couldn't look his brother in the eyes. "Miss Winterhaven is connected to trade. And she is the opposite of everything that a successful young woman in Society should be. That's why she was chosen," he finished, sipping his port.

"And what exactly does that mean?"

A deep sigh escaped Roger. "Miss Winterhaven is an atrocious dancer. She can't sing. She doesn't do watercolors or needlework. And she's the most outrageous bluestocking. She speaks several languages and used to talk about politics," he finished lamely.

"So you ruined the girl's chances in Society because she wasn't a simpering flat. Does that sum it up accurately?" Nigel said harshly, his irritation very apparent.

Roger sagged in his chair and stared at the maroon patterned Turkish carpet at his feet. "Yes, I suppose."

Nigel downed the rest of his port and stared at his brother, his eyes as black as coal. "That was a dashed selfish thing to do, Roger. You were only a child when Mama died, so you don't remember her as well as I do. She could speak more languages than Father, and they used to have long, heated arguments about what was happening in Parliament. You couldn't have shamed her more if you had tried," he finished, rising from his chair and stalking out of the room in disgust.

Nigel sighed and stared out into the dreadfully cold and drab English countryside. Small snowflakes could be seen occasionally, thick, dark clouds enveloped the sky, and the wind howled wildly around them. The carriage was warm and fairly comfortable, but, to be honest, he was dashed bored with traveling.

He glanced over at Hughes, his valet, seated across from him. He was slumped down into the upholstery, snoring. So much for witty conversation, Nigel thought wryly, craning his neck to see the house.

The country home of Henry Langely, Viscount Ashton, loomed ominously on the horizon. Harriet's daughter Victoria was playing on the frozen grass near the road, and a young woman, probably her nanny, was supervising her.

As the carriage continued toward the vast, ivy-covered house, he could see the nanny laughing with Victoria, her auburn hair falling loosely around her shoulders. He also noticed a small, brown-and-white puppy racing around their feet. The nanny laughed as freely as the child, and her whole body seemed to radiate a freedom that a firstborn son had never known.

She's incredibly beautiful, he thought, noting her tall, modest figure. Most young ladies didn't even reach his shoulders; the nanny could easily meet his eyes. Her dark blue pelisse hugged her body provocatively, and he could easily imagine her soft form pressed up against him.

As his imagination strayed, he didn't notice that the puppy, in his excitement, had begun barking furiously at his matching pair of chestnuts. The horses, a rather fidgety pair from the get-go, began to slow their pace a bit.

Before Nigel realized what was happening, the carriage was swaying precariously and he could hear his luggage falling off the back. From the window he could see little Victoria running toward the carriage, apparently yelling.

As soon as the carriage stabilized somewhat, Nigel quickly opened the door and headed out into the bleak English cold. As he went toward the front of the carriage, he could see Lawson, his driver, holding the reins tightly.

"What happened, Lawson?" he asked, unaware of the young woman sitting on the ground on the other side of the carriage, holding the puppy in her lap.

"The puppy scared the pair, m'lord. They started to rear,

and I lost control of them for a moment," Lawson said apologetically, aware of the fact that the luggage was now lying open in the dirt behind them.

"Is Wellington going to be all right?" he heard little Victoria say from the other side of the carriage.

"I think so, dear. You never told me he was afraid of horses," a soft, musical voice answered, and for one brief moment Nigel could imagine that voice whispering his name passionately into his ear. Gads, I'm daydreaming about the nanny! I must get out more, Nigel thought, running his hand distractedly through his hair as he briskly walked to the other side of the carriage to see what had happened.

She's even more beautiful than I thought, he mused, as he stared down at the nanny sitting on the ground, holding the brown-and-white puppy at her breast. Her eyes were a radiant shade of green, and her skin was the color of alabaster. Victoria hovered near her, and it was obvious that she trusted the servant entirely.

As he stood admiring the serene picture the nanny, Victoria, and the puppy made, Victoria suddenly turned and spotted him.

"Uncle Nigel," she cried exuberantly, and ran over to him and immediately threw her small arms around his long, muscular legs.

Nigel leaned over and scooped her up in his arms as if she were a toy and exclaimed, "Dearest Victoria! My, each time I see you I find you're a head taller!"

Victoria giggled as she stared at him in rapt admiration. "You're gammoning me, Uncle Nigel!" she giggled, and then turned back toward the nanny and the puppy.

"See my new puppy? His name is Wellington, and he's ever so much fun," she said, as Nigel walked over to the nanny and the puppy.

The nanny smiled hesitantly at him, which tugged at his heart even more. She doesn't even realize how beautiful she is, he mused. And she's probably too honorable to dally with me, he mentally added, giving the nanny a wide smile. "Has Wellington survived the encounter with my chestnuts?"

"We didn't know that he is rather fearful of horses. Of course, it probably doesn't help that they're so much larger than he is," Emily said in a soft voice, glancing toward the carriage. "Oh my, I'm dreadfully sorry. Wellington and I seem to have caused you to lose most of your luggage," she said apologetically.

Nigel turned and looked behind the carriage. The charming nanny was quite correct. At that very moment Hughes was trying in vain to stuff his now-dirty clothes into his trunks. The Manning Curse, he thought. Now my clothes are ruined. Why am I suffering when Roger was the one who sold the damnable mermaid, he wondered, putting Victoria back on the ground. "Well, let's have a look at the damage," he said philosophically, walking toward the catastrophe.

It was quite a sight, all of his belongings being blown about the road. He could see a nightshirt near the base of a tree, and his cravats were blown clear toward the hedgegrow.

"I'm so dreadfully sorry," Emily said, bending down and handing Wellington to Victoria, who hugged her puppy to her olive woolen pelisse.

"It wasn't your fault," Nigel said automatically, walking slowly toward Hughes. "How were you to know that the pup and my chestnuts were both a bit skittish?" he asked, a frown beginning to form on his features. How am I supposed to impress this charming young woman if all of my clothes are now covered in dirt, he wondered, thrusting his hands in the pockets of his black Polish greatcoat.

Nigel was more than amazed when the nanny, who was as well-mannered as she was alluring, actually went over to Hughes and said, "Let me help you," in that soft, sensual voice.

To his astonishment, Hughes, his very ordinary valet, gave the nanny a wide, heartfelt smile. "Thank you ever so kindly, miss," was Hughes's reply.

Nigel's jaw dropped open as the nanny began walking around the coach, picking up his unmentionables and handing them to Hughes. His face turned a slight shade of red. How ghastly, he thought, joining in the quest for his clothes.

A few moments later, all of his belongings were hastily stuffed back into the trunk, and Hughes smiled once again at the nanny, as Nigel gave him a distinctly dark look.

"Thank you ever so much for your help, miss," Hughes said, and was rewarded by a smile from the nanny.

"You're welcome," she said simply, and began to walk slowly toward the house, Victoria trailing silently behind her.

Nigel stared wistfully after her retreating form. Maybe this visit won't be a complete farce, he thought, running a hand through his hair. I'll be rid of the dashed dull Lady Susan and her harpy of a mother, and I'll be able to get to know the nanny. Henry and Harriet will probably be scandalized, but I don't really care. If I have to spend my holiday cajoling Miss Winterhaven to sell the mermaid back to the family, at least I'll be able to amuse myself elsewhere, he concluded, walking toward the front door of the house.

As the butler opened the door, one thought lingered in his mind: how does one go about seducing a respectable nanny?

Three

"Henry, you never told me that little Victoria had such an attractive nanny," Nigel said casually, staring at the truly bizarre Egyptian artifacts in the parlor.

Henry frowned at Nigel as he sipped his port. "Miss Turner? I suppose she's attractive enough—I've never really thought about it," he replied, his eyebrows raised slightly.

A relaxed smile found its way onto Nigel's face. "Of course you wouldn't notice her—you are still quite enamored of Harriet, aren't you?"

Henry smiled boyishly. "It's so dreadfully vulgar to actually admit to a *tendre* for one's wife, isn't it? I suppose I'm completely guilty of that offense, and don't pay much heed to any other females," he admitted, a trifle embarrassed.

"Well, we are family, so your secret is safe," Nigel said good-naturedly, sipping his port. "So, is Miss Winterhaven here yet?"

"Yes, she arrived a day or so ago. Harriet is having a wonderful time with her, and so is Victoria. I think you'll like her. She's much more the thing than Miss Turner," Henry added casually.

"Miss Winterhaven cannot possess the magnificent, flashing green eyes that I found on Miss Turner, or the sweet disposition. You see, I met her when Victoria's puppy spooked my bloods and found her to be utterly charming," Nigel concluded, and was rewarded by an even more severe frown from Henry.

"Miss Turner? Charming? Nigel, you've been spending much too much time in the country with your father," he concluded. Then, for good measure, he added, "But of course I'm head over heels over my wife, so I suppose I'm not an accurate judge."

Nigel leaned back a bit in the Egyptian-style chair that was painted black and accented with gilt ornaments, and studied a small, brass replica of a pyramid sitting on the mahogany sideboard to his left. "She is quite magnificent," he said softly, to no one in particular.

"Mama, Mama, look what Aunt Emily has!" Victoria proclaimed, rushing into the morning room, a lively bundle of energy in her Pomona green dress embroidered with small roses.

Harriet looked up from the Gothic that was helping her pass the time, as Victoria climbed onto the sofa next to her. Emily, wearing a very modest gray kerseymere walking dress, followed behind her daughter.

"What do you have, dearest?" Harriet asked curiously, putting the leather-bound book down on her lap.

"It's a necklace that Aunt Emily said her grandfather got her for Christmas. It's a mermaid!" Victoria exclaimed, dangling the sparkling pendant in front of her mother.

Harriet took the pearl pendant from her daughter and held it in her delicate, fair hands. *So, this is the famous Manning Mermaid,* she thought, marvelling at the workmanship. *This is the last thing I expected Nigel to have in his family,* she mused, noting the large center pearl and the crown encased in small emeralds.

"So, what do you think of it?" Emily asked, seating herself on a small mahogany chair with spiral reeding next to the gilded sofa.

"I've never seen anything quite like it," Harriet admitted, running her finger over the surface of the largest pearl.

"Wearing it would certainly help you cut a dash in Society, since it is so original," she concluded, handing it back to Emily.

Emily put the pendant over her head, and it fell onto her breast, looking rather out of place on her unexceptional gray dress. "I have no idea what possessed Grandfather to buy this piece, but I'm becoming rather fond of it," she began, then added, "Of course, it is a bit too . . . stylish for dinner, isn't it?" she asked in mock seriousness.

Harriet raised her eyebrows and replied, "Yes, I do think so," with a smile.

"Mama, did you know we saw Uncle Nigel? Wellington almost got run over by his horses, but Aunt Emily saved him. It was ever so exciting!" Victoria said, trying her hardest to act like a proper lady.

"Oh really? Was Uncle Nigel upset?" she asked, smiling down at her little girl.

"Oh no, Mama. Even though all of his clothes were all over the grounds, he didn't even lose his temper. He just kept smiling at Aunt Emily the whole time," she said seriously, which made Harriet smile.

"Is that true, Emily? Was my Cousin Nigel mooning over you?" Harriet asked, hoping upon hope that Nigel had taken a fancy to Emily. Then he could simply marry her and forget about persuading her to sell him the pendant back.

Emily blushed prettily and stared at her hands in her lap. "I think not. He was just being congenial."

"No, Aunt Emily, he really liked you. I could tell by the way he was looking at you while you were picking up his unmentionables in the dirt," Victoria exclaimed, with all the conviction a four-year-old could muster.

"His unmentionables? You were picking up his unmentionables out of the dirt?" Harriet said with a grin. This was wonderfully scandalous. Nigel was rather stiff-necked, and to have Emily traipsing after his small clothes was a deliciously silly thought.

Emily stared at a piece of lint on her dress. "Yes, well, you see, Wellington caused the horses to rear, and his trunk fell off the carriage and came open. Then, of course, the wind was rather severe this afternoon, so they were scattered about the grounds. I simply helped his valet retrieve his belongings," she explained, as if it were the most common of occurrences.

"And Nigel didn't go on about it? I mean, he didn't lose his temper?" Harriet asked with a frown. Nigel, who had been living with the marquess lately, did sound rather on edge in his letter. In fact, this sounds exactly like another example of the Manning Curse, she thought, which must be driving Nigel to drink. So why didn't he get upset? she wondered distractedly.

"No, Uncle Nigel was ever so nice to us," Victoria answered, and Harriet knew she probably should scold her daughter for being so forward. But her mother had tried to teach her manners when she was Victoria's age, and she was determined to try and teach the same thing to her daughter.

"Victoria, I have some matters I'd like to discuss with your Aunt Emily. Will you please excuse us? I believe Miss Turner is waiting for you out in the hall," Harriet said gently, and her heart strings tugged as she saw Victoria's face fall.

"Do I have to leave, Mama? I like talking with you and Aunt Emily," she said in a tiny voice, as if she were going to cry.

"Yes, you do. But I'll be up to see you later, and maybe, if you're a good girl, Aunt Emily will come by tonight to read you a bedtime story," Harriet said, glancing toward Emily.

"Will you come see me later, Aunt Emily?" Victoria asked in an even more pitiful voice, as if she were being banished to the workhouse.

"Of course, dear," Emily replied, and Victoria slowly

walked out of the morning room, her disappointment very evident.

"So, you met Nigel? What did you think of him?" Harriet asked eagerly, noticing how red Emily turned.

"He appears to be presentable enough, but of course he *is* a relation of yours. All of your family is grand, except that scoundrel Roger Manning," she commented, staring out the window.

Harriet winced slightly. Obviously, Emily was not in the mood to graciously forgive Nigel's younger brother, and she didn't particularly blame her. Roger had made her Season a debacle that was talked about long after both parties had left town. She followed Emily's gaze and looked out the window framed in heavy maroon velvet drapes. It was snowing prodigiously hard. "I've always found Nigel to be rather charming, and he's always been particularly kind to Victoria," Harriet finally concluded, studying Emily.

Emily continued to gaze out the window, a haunted look in her eyes. "Yes, he did seem to be rather charming, but I do hope you're not going to spend the holiday trying to make a match of your Cousin Nigel and me. I'm quite on the shelf and very ineligible," she stated flatly, not meeting Harriet's gaze.

I must talk to Henry about this, Harriet thought, absently twirling a loose strand of hair around her finger. Emily might be an ideal match for Nigel; I wonder what he thinks of the idea, she pondered, watching the English countryside become covered in a blanket of snow.

"And of course you do know my Cousin Nigel, Lord Stratford," Harriet said as the party seated themselves around the circular mahogany pillar-and-claw dining table.

Emily, now clad in a dark blue, merino wool dress that had a very moderate neckline adorned with a white ruffle, blushed slightly and replied, "Actually, we were never properly introduced."

Nigel, his traveling clothes more than a bit worse for the wear, cursed his damnable luck, and practically gaped at Miss Winterhaven. He had not taken a freakish liking to little Victoria's nanny. He had been dazzled by the unspoiled charm of Miss Winterhaven, the female who was ruined by his younger brother. Of course, Roger had been a trifle inaccurate in his description. Her hair wasn't short and reddish, it was auburn, long, and luxuriant. She didn't appear to be a decided bluestocking, which really didn't bother him at all in any case, and her eyes were the most magnificent green.

"Nigel? Are you attending?" Henry asked casually as Nigel gaped at Emily.

"I'm sorry, yes, Miss Winterhaven was kind enough to help retrieve my belongings after that mishap with the carriage," he said, and a slight pink tinge could be found on his cheeks.

The meal was exquisite, and Emily ate her stuffed shoulder of veal with relish, while enjoying some of Henry and Harriet's stories.

"You're very quiet, Miss Winterhaven," Nigel commented, sipping his hock, waiting eagerly for her radiant green eyes to meet his.

Emily looked up, blushing a bit. "I'm sorry, it's just that my life is rather drab, and I don't really have much to contribute," she said, blushing even more.

Harriet raised an eyebrow and said, "That's doing it up a bit brown, Emily. Your life certainly isn't drab, since not everyone spends their time in London." Harriet paused for a moment, then turned to Nigel and said softly, "Emily has spent a good part of the last few years on the Continent, studying the pianoforte. She was even invited to play for the Czar."

Nigel's eyebrows raised and he turned to Emily in surprise. "You were invited to play for the Czar? How did that come about?"

Emily picked at her creamed asparagus. "It was nothing, really. My parents and I were in Italy, and we were at some rout or another, and I played a piece that I wrote. The Czar took a liking to my music, and issued a rather vague invitation to visit him. I rather think that he was a trifle bosky at the time and was really interested in pursuing an acquaintance with my mama. Father wasn't too enthusiastic about that idea, so we never even really considered a visit," she explained, throwing Harriet a telling look.

Nigel leaned forward in his chair, all of his attention on the remarkably beautiful woman across from him. "You write your own music?" he asked in an awestruck voice, his hazel eyes large with wonder.

Blushing furiously, Emily replied, "Oh, I've written some of my own pieces, but they're very amateurish."

"That's doing it a bit too brown, Emily," Henry interjected, finishing his hock. "I've never heard anyone play as beautifully as Emily, and I've had to sit through dozens of ghastly musical evenings," he stated sagely.

Emily stared at her Dresden plate and said nothing. Finally, Harriet broke the silence by announcing, "Nigel plays, too, you see, so you needn't be embarrassed about it."

All eyes turned to Nigel, who flashed an apologetic smile. "When I was much younger, I used to play regularly, until my inestimable father proclaimed that it wasn't manly. I still play occasionally, but I was never really able to devote any time to it," he explained, his eyes resting on her perfect rosebud lips.

A sudden look of sympathy flooded Emily's luminescent green eyes, and when she looked at him it was as if they were alone at the table. "I understand completely. It's very difficult, isn't it, when Society expects us to be something we're not? I was very lucky to be indulged by my family, and, being a female with no expectations, I'm allowed much more freedom. It must be difficult for you," she remarked sympathetically, her words tugging at his heart.

"I can't believe you have no expectations, Miss Winterhaven," Nigel replied softly, his heart beating a tattoo in his chest. Miss Winterhaven was the most charming, original female; Roger must have been insane to try to ruin her, he thought, still gazing longingly at her.

Emily giggled. "You are as charming as Harriet said, Lord Stratford," she began, then added, "I'm sure Henry and Harriet will agree that I'm most assuredly on the shelf. Not only that, I'm four-and-twenty years old and my father is in trade. There are few females in polite Society who are more ineligible than I am!" she declared heartily, finishing her glass of hock.

"Emily, you can be such a widgeon!" Harriet exclaimed, frowning. "If you continue disparaging yourself, I'm going to have to have Victoria's nanny discipline you!"

Henry chuckled and glanced over at Nigel. "Dearest, you must learn to contain yourself. Nigel, are you ready to retire for our port?" he asked, glancing at the table.

"Of course, Henry," he replied, and as they left, Harriet called to Henry, "Don't be long—I thought we could play a round of whist."

"Nigel, I do believe that Emily is a regular Captain Sharp," Henry declared, as the pair of men lost their third consecutive trick.

Harriet giggled and gathered the cards up from the table and began to shuffle, the enormous Langely family diamond very prominently displayed on her delicate hand.

"We really should tell them, Harriet," Emily said in a slightly guilty tone, and smiled at her close friend.

"And what should we gentlemen know?" Henry asked in a serious voice, and Emily was certain that Henry wasn't serious at all.

As Harriet dealt the cards, she smiled benignly and replied, "Emily and I loved to play whist while we were at Miss Haversham's School for Young Ladies."

Nigel frowned at the cards in his hand, and looked hopefully at Henry. His partner was frowning as well.

Emily looked at both men and smiled. They are obviously not gamesters, she thought, since they let all and sundry know that they both have a bad hand.

The hand began, and once again, as if by some unknown forces, the ladies took another trick. Another hand was dealt. The ladies won again.

Nigel shuffled the deck and proclaimed, "Henry, I certainly hope you don't take any offense at this suggestion, but I do think the game would be more interesting if I were paired with a different player. Miss Winterhaven, would you consider forsaking your lucky streak and partnering with me?" he asked softly, and she immediately noticed the golden glow of his hazel eyes.

Emily blushed, embarrassed by the singular attention that the peer was paying her. He's just trying to be polite, Emily thought; he doesn't really care about me. He's a guest of Harriet and Henry's and wants to make the holiday as pleasant as possible, she decided, and finally replied, "If Harriet doesn't mind being paired with her husband, of course I'll be your partner."

Harriet chuckled. "I'm sorry, Nigel. You see, when we were in school, Emily and I did play whist quite regularly, and found that we were excellent partners. In the evenings, we would have competitions and fleece the other girls of chocolates and ribbons and whatever else were the stakes for the evening," she explained with a smile.

Henry frowned. "You were a Captain Sharp and you never told me? Did Miss Haversham know about this?" he demanded in mock severity.

Emily smiled at the pair who were so obviously in love with each other. They laughed and joked easily, as if they had been together their whole lives. Harriet had never looked better, and Henry wore an air of complete contentment. How I envy them, she thought a bit sadly. It's too bad I'll never be able to have that sort of relationship with a man.

"I personally suspected this sort of thing," Nigel said, loosening his cravat. "Harriet was always a very precocious little girl, always trying to lure the male members of the family into some sort of mischief."

"Harriet isn't a gamester and neither am I," Emily said, rising to Harriet's defense. "We just happen to be prodigiously good partners at whist."

Nigel smiled at the suddenly vocal Miss Winterhaven. "I congratulate you on your loyalty, Miss Winterhaven."

Emily's mind was whirling as she pretended to study her hand. What in heaven's name was he talking about? Men abhorred females who displayed any sort of bottom, she was certain of that. Roger had informed her of that numerous times, and she was careful to be very retiring when she was out in any sort of company in England. On the Continent it was different. Women could be witty and interesting and not suffer from being labeled a bluestocking.

"And it would do you well to remember that I'm just as loyal to Emily," Harriet began, and added, "She's practically family, and runs tame in our house."

Emily giggled and stared at her cards. "You make me sound like a young buck, Harriet. Run tame in your house? I think not," she said, playing her final card and winning the trick.

As Henry gathered the cards, Nigel aimed a telling look at Emily. "You're an excellent partner," he said in a soft, intimate voice that sent a very pleasant tingle up Emily's spine.

"Aunt Emily, Aunt Emily, wake up, it's snowing out," a small voice from the foot of Emily's enormous four-poster bed declared.

Emily snuggled under the covers, delightfully warm.

Henry has a marvelous house, she thought hazily. I can't feel any sort of a draft at all.

"Aunt Emily, look outside, it's snowing ever so hard!" little Victoria said, and Emily opened one eye hesitantly.

Victoria, her brown hair curled into perfect little ringlets, stood at her bedside, her blue eyes wide with anticipation. "I've never seen it snow so hard," Victoria said softly, looking anxiously toward the window.

Emily sat up in bed and smiled, still a bit groggy. "So, it is snowing, Victoria? And have you seen it snow before?" she asked, contemplating giving the child a set-down for waking her from her slumbers.

Victoria scampered away from the mahogany four-poster and pulled back the heavy blue velvet drapes. "Look outside," she said in a challenging voice, and Emily craned her neck to peer outside.

"Why, it's a blizzard," Emily exclaimed, rising out of bed and putting on her pale pink dressing robe embroidered with small flowers. She joined Victoria at the window, and they both gazed over the countryside.

Actually, Emily didn't see much of anything. Except snow. It was the first actual blizzard she had seen in her life, although her parents often told stories of particularly treacherous winters.

"Look, isn't that a carriage over there?" Victoria asked, pointing toward the road.

Emily squinted, and could see some sort of movement, far in the distance, that could have been a carriage. And it was heading toward the house. "Victoria, go tell the butler—what is his name?" she asked, a frown marring her delicate features.

"Coverdail."

"Go find Coverdail and tell him that there is a carriage coming up the drive—he'll know what to do," she finished, still staring into the bright blizzard.

Victoria toddled out of the room obediently, and Emily

knocked on the door adjoining the room next to hers. "Eliza, you slugabed, it's time to join the rest of the family downstairs," she called to her abigail, who was taking a well-deserved rest.

Instantly the door opened, and Eliza, her beautiful red hair concealed under a white mobcap, appeared. "I'm ever so sorry, Miss Emily. I must have dozed off waiting for you to wake up," she said apologetically.

Emily smiled fondly at her petite servant. "That's quite all right, Eliza. I think it's time to go downstairs, since I do believe that the family is going to be receiving visitors soon," she said, absently wondering what kind of person would be out in weather that wasn't suitable for man nor beast.

"Aubrey, deuced bad weather we're having, isn't it?" Henry asked, pouring his cousin a glass of claret.

Lord Aubrey Langely rubbed his hands together and stood closer to the warm glow of the hearth in the study. "It is dashed freakish," he lamented, staring down at his ice-covered boots melting on Henry's Aubusson carpet.

Henry handed him the claret, which Aubrey immediately downed, putting a hint of color into his pale cheeks.

At four-and-twenty, Aubrey is fast on his way to becoming a wastrel, Henry thought, sipping his drink. Once again he is dressed rather ridiculously, this time sporting a striped puce waistcoat, a cravat tied in some sort of style that was utterly unrecognizable, and a pair of buckskin breeches that belonged to a man of less sizable proportions. But, on the positive side, Aubrey is quite tolerable at cards, is fairly amiable, and the ladies find him amusing, so I suppose I should be glad of his company, Henry concluded wearily. "How was the traveling?" he asked, staring out the window, watching the snow fall like mad.

"Quite tolerable, until the snows," Aubrey replied, running his hand through his blond hair done in the fashionable Brutus style. "There were a few other carriages about, from what my coachman says, so you may be getting some unexpected visitors. The weather is making it rough going," he concluded, sitting down opposite Henry in the black armchair adorned with gilt ornaments.

"So, you've escaped your mama for the holiday season?" Henry asked casually, still rather distracted by the weather.

"Yes. We had a bit of a falling-out over some of my debts of honor, so I'd wager she's glad I'm not about to torment her constantly."

"I understand completely. That's why we're not in Brighton with the rest of the family. After the Cheltingham tragedy of last year, I simply told Mama that Victoria has been ill and needs the rest. And Harriet's family has gone to spend the holiday in Scotland! Thankfully, Victoria also gets dreadfully sick on long carriage rides, so we had to decline the invitation," he replied with a wink.

Aubrey smiled broadly at him, finally looking more the thing. His blue eyes had once again begun to sparkle with mirth, and he no longer resembled a frozen spirit of the dead. "You're very lucky to have a daughter. I simply have to get in Mama's black books before she banishes me from her entertainments. To be truthful, I'm becoming rather bored with them."

Henry stretched his aching muscles in his chair. "I hope we're a trifle more entertaining. Nigel Manning, Lord Stratford, Harriet's cousin, is also visiting, as is her bosom bow from school, Emily Winterhaven. Harriet has all sorts of activities planned, and our entire house party has been invited to Lord Blackmore's New Year's Eve masquerade. It's rather a local tradition, and Blackmore is as rich as the Golden Ball, so you won't find a better rout in the country."

Aubrey stared into the fire and commented, "I do believe spending the Christmas holiday in the country is exactly what I need to cure my blue devils. It's dashed tiring being a confirmed rake, you know," he finished wryly, a haunted look in his clear blue eyes.

"Mama, look at all the snow!" Victoria exclaimed, chasing Wellington through the freshly fallen snow.

Harriet giggled, and wrapped her cerise velvet-and-fur spencer around herself tightly. "Be careful you don't fall," she called with a laugh, and glanced toward Miss Turner, Victoria's nanny. Miss Turner was frowning prodigiously.

"Lady Ashton, this weather isn't good for the child. If she comes down with a cold, she might have to be bled," Miss Turner said seriously, rubbing her gloved hands together for warmth.

"Nonsense. A romp in the snow won't hurt Victoria," Harriet proclaimed, and turned to Emily, who was standing next to her and giggling to herself.

Once again, Emily could have shown herself to more of an advantage. Her brown redingote, which looked dashed warm, did nothing to liven her complexion or make her look anything more than a well-dressed servant. At least she has a muff, Harriet thought distractedly, squinting to see Victoria and her puppy through the thickly falling snow.

"Harriet, isn't that another carriage coming toward the house?" Emily asked, pointing toward a dim blur down the road.

Harriet squinted. "Yes, it does seem to be coming this way. Henry did mention that we might be having some additional visitors, since the weather suddenly turned so dreadful. I suppose they'll want some sort of shelter until the weather clears up," Harriet declared with a frown.

"Oh," Emily replied, her body becoming rigid with tension.

"Don't worry, Emily, they'll probably be some sort of unexceptional gentry types who will be heartily grateful for any sort of shelter. You needn't get in a tizzy every time you meet someone new in England," Harriet admonished, watching the slow progress of the carriage.

"I know. I just keep expecting everyone in the *ton* to be as awful as they were when I had my Season."

"It would be best if you forgot about that incident entirely," Harriet said, watching her daughter slide into a large drift of snow. Wellington followed after her, and all three ladies smiled. "For goodness sake, Emily, you spent more than your share of time on the Continent. I don't see why you didn't marry some sort of Italian *comte* while you were there so you didn't have to move in English Society at all," she said in a scolding tone.

"They have dreadful manners," Emily whispered with a devilish grin. "And are forever trying to take liberties."

The coach practically crawled up the drive at a snail's pace and Harriet proclaimed, "You are terribly selective, aren't you? I would have thrown Henry over in a moment if I had a bad-mannered *comte* trying to take liberties with me!"

Emily giggled, and Miss Turner, who was attempting to watch Victoria, could be heard choking a laugh herself.

"Well, I suppose we should go inside and clean ourselves up before our new guests arrive. Do you think they might decide to turn back and not seek shelter at our wonderfully inviting abode?" Harriet asked, and Emily automatically shook her head no.

"I thought not. Miss Turner, try to get Victoria and Wellington inside before the carriage arrives," she ordered, and joined Emily on their short walk back to the house.

Nigel sat alone in Henry's vast, book-lined library, sipping a glass of port. He had located a wonderfully obscure translation of Homer and was quite content to while away the afternoon reading.

Of course, Miss Winterhaven made a pretty picture, standing outside with the snow whirling about her brown redingote. Her magnificent auburn hair was held in place loosely by some combs, and she looked dashed charming, he decided, losing interest in Homer.

As Nigel contemplated Miss Winterhaven, the matter of the Manning Mermaid prickled at his conscience. No, I most certainly won't forget about the mermaid, he thought with a sigh. But how can I begin to ask Miss Winterhaven to give up a gift from her grandfather, he mused, stretching his long, well-formed legs.

"How charming to see you again, Lord Ashton," Nigel heard a female voice say faintly down the hall, and for a moment he would have bet a guinea that it was the inimitable Lady Markston. But it isn't, thank goodness, he thought, staring out the window at the blizzard. And it most certainly *was* a blizzard.

He could hear Henry mutter something in response, and then heard Emily reply very clearly, "It's my pleasure to make your acquaintance."

Then the unthinkable happened. He heard a very pronounced giggle that could have belonged to only one person.

Striding down the hall, a frown marred his less-than-classical features. As he approached the parlor door, the frown turned into a look of utter horror.

Standing in the ghastly Egyptian parlor in her traveling clothes was Lady Markston, wearing the most odious puce fur-trimmed pelisse. Standing next to her, in a buff pelisse with a large, brown muff, was her daughter, Lady Susan Claredon. Both ladies were smiling broadly at Henry, and Emily stood alone in the corner, a slight look of distress on her delicate features.

"Nigel, so good of you to join us," Henry began, loosening his cravat a trifle. "Let me introduce you to the newest members of our house party."

Susan turned and faced Nigel, her face lighting up in pure delight. "Why, Nigel, what a surprise!" she proclaimed, practically radiating happiness.

Nigel was horrified. *I left home to get rid of the harpy and her daughter* he thought, at a loss even to greet them properly. *They will drive me mad if they stay more than a night*, he mused, not at all happy with the situation.

Henry frowned. Nigel was acting like a slow-top. "Nigel, do you know Lady Markston and her daughter?" he asked, running his hand through his unruly brown hair.

Lady Markston giggled, and smiled broadly, showing off her yellowing teeth. "Do we know Lord Stratford? Why, he's practically engaged to my Susan," she proclaimed, causing almost everyone in the room to gape at her in disbelief.

Four

"Oh Mama, that's doing it up a bit too brown," Susan giggled, tossing her long, blond hair over the brown fur trim of her pelisse. She gave a deliberate glance over to Nigel and turned to Henry. "Nigel practically runs tame at our home," she said in a confidential tone, ignoring the look of horror etched on Nigel's face.

Lady Markston stared at Nigel, her displeasure very apparent. "I wasn't aware that you were acquainted with Lord Ashton," she said formally, staring at Nigel as if he were a piece of lint on her dress.

"Lord Ashton is married to my Cousin Harriet," Nigel said, taking both ladies' gloved hands and giving them the most perfunctory kiss.

"Lady Markston and her daughter are going to be joining us until the weather makes travel possible," Henry commented, running his hand through his thick brown hair.

Before anyone could reply to that pronouncement, a rather pasty-faced young maid with short, red hair and a mobcap appeared and announced, "The suites in the east wing are ready m'lord."

Henry smiled broadly and stepped forward toward his new guests. "I'm sure you'd like to freshen up after your journey, Lady Markston. Mary will show you to your rooms. I hope they meet your satisfaction," he said politely, gently moving them out of the parlor and into the hall.

"I'm sure they'll be adequate," Lady Markston replied, waiting for Susan to follow her.

Susan stood frozen in her steps, her blue eyes fixed on Nigel. "It's so good to see you again," she said in a husky voice, as her hand reached up to caress her lily-white neck.

"Of course," Nigel replied in a tone that was still noticeably frostier than the weather outside.

"Come along, Susan," Lady Markston called from the hall, and Susan's undeniably beautiful features were marred with a frown. "Excuse me, Nigel," she said in the same husky voice, then remembered her manners and turned to Emily, who was still rooted in the corner. "I look forward to seeing you at supper, Miss Hinterwaven," she said with an air of false politeness as she breezed out of the room.

Nigel leaned against the wall, a look of total disgust on his face.

"So, should I be offering you congratulations, Lord Stratford?" Emily asked in a soft voice, her eyes wide with apprehension. Lord Stratford can not be engaged to marry that female, she decided, taking an instant dislike to Susan. Lady Claredon was exactly the type who had made her short time in Society such a trial, and it would be a deuced shame if Lord Stratford were going to be leg-shackled to someone like her, she thought grimly.

"No, Miss Winterhaven, you definitely should not be offering me any such thing," he said, walking over to one of the black Egyptian chairs with ormolu supports. He eased his long form into the chair and remarked, "In fact, this is just another incident in a string of bad luck I've been having."

Emily sat down in the matching chair across from him, and leaned forward, her hands resting in her lap. "Did you have a quarrel with Lady Claredon the last time you saw her?" she asked, then blushed delicately. "I'm so terribly sorry—that really isn't any of my concern. I sound like the worst gossip."

Nigel smiled at her, and could feel the tension leaving his

body. "I'll tell you a secret, Miss Winterhaven, if you promise to keep it to yourself," he said, a wicked smile on his face.

"Of course."

"Lady Markston and her daughter both have some sort of maggot in their brains and are convinced that Susan will be the next Lady Stratford. That certainly isn't the case, and that's one of the reasons that I decided to take Harriet up on her offer. If I stayed home one more moment I'm sure Lady Markston would have put the announcement in the papers herself, just to help me along," he finished, stretching his long, muscular legs.

"Then you don't have an understanding?"

"Not at all. The truth be known, Susan is a cossetted ninnyhammer and I'm none too pleased that she's here," he concluded, then added, "You're very easy to talk to, Miss Winterhaven.

Emily blushed. "That's Hinterwaven, my lord," she replied with a deliciously feminine laugh.

"Yes, of course, Hinterwaven," he said, a relaxed smile spreading over his face. "So, Miss Hinterwaven, would you like to join me in locating Harriet to tell her the news? I believe she is acquainted with Susan, and I may need you to shield me from her blows," he said, standing up and extending his hand.

Emily placed her long, delicate fingers in his strong hand and let him help her out of the Egyptian monstrosity of a chair. "Certainly, Lord Stratford. Did you know that Harriet has gone several rounds with Gentleman Jackson? We were fond of visiting him on the days we weren't whiling our time away playing cards at White's," she said with a giggle, noticing how golden his eyes seemed in the light of the parlor.

As he tucked her arm under his, Nigel replied, "Then I most certainly need your protection. I've only stood up with Gentleman Jackson once, and he landed me a facer," he admitted, leading her out of the room.

She smiled up at him, truly enjoying his company. "You

certainly don't act like a proper English lord, if I may say so," she commented, hoping he didn't take offense.

Nigel smiled at the tall, auburn-haired beauty who was so different from the woman that Roger described. "Most proper English ladies aren't this easy to converse with," he concluded, closing the parlor door behind him.

"Lady Jersey herself proclaimed my Susan to be a diamond of the first water," Lady Markston stated, smiling placidly at her supper companions.

Nigel, clad in a simple pair of buckskin breeches, white shirt, and a brown cloth coat with brass buttons, stared into his food and said nothing. If anyone was watching him closely, they may have noticed that his eyebrows were raised and he wore a definite look of disbelief.

"Oh Mama, you do embarrass me," Susan gushed, straightening in her chair so that Nigel, as well as the handsome Lord Langely, could get a better view of her womanly charms. Her Clarence blue satin gown with gold lace trimming around the hem and neckline offered all of the gentlemen present a glance at the swell of her bosom, that in Town, would have been thought of as all the crack.

Across the table, Emily ate her *côtelettes à la provençale* silently, and wondered how Lady Claredon avoided being mistaken for a cyprian. Of course, her mother is no better, she thought, glancing down the table toward the very large and loud Lady Markston.

For dinner, Lady Markston had chosen a purple taffeta gown with a matching turban that once again barely sat on her unnaturally brown hair. A peacock feather swayed on the turban, and a large, egg-shaped ruby graced her white, freckled hand. "Nonsense, Susan," Lady Markston said, and appeared to consume an entire potato at once. "So, why haven't we met you in Town, Lord Langely?" she questioned, downing her glass of hock.

Lord Langely, looking devilishly fashionable in a blue satin coat, neck cloth tied in the Oriental, and a cerulean-and-jonquille-striped waistcoat, gave Lady Markston a warm, welcoming smile. "I can't say I've been to Almack's lately—I've had too many other matters to attend to," he said, glancing over at the fetching Lady Claredon. "If I had known you were there, Lady Claredon, I would have been dancing attendance on you every night."

Susan giggled, that annoying giggle that made Nigel visibly cringe. "You must call me Susan," she said in a sultry voice, causing her mother to frown fiercely.

"That's a grand idea," Harriet said, trying to take control of the dinner. "The weather doesn't show any signs of letting up, so we're all going to be together for quite some time. I think it would be most comfortable if we were all on a first-name basis," she proclaimed, glancing over at Henry for support.

"Yes, it would make the holiday so much more . . . festive," Henry added, delving back into his sweetbreads.

Emily continued eating, oblivious to the conversation around her. Lord Langely (who had now transformed into "Aubrey") is a sporting enough fellow, she thought, but I'll bet a guinea that he's a gamester. Lady Claredon, who now insisted that she be called Susan, was still annoying her. How could Lord Stratford be involved with a ninnyhammer like her, she thought, finishing up the food on her plate. Last of all was the flamboyant Lady Markston, who it was summarily decided would remain Lady Markston. She would drive me insane if she were my mama, Emily mused, sitting quietly at the table, drifting off into her own thoughts.

She was brought back to the present when Lady Markston proclaimed, "Oh yes, we must have a musical evening. Susan has the voice of an angel, you know."

Before Harriet could reject the idea, Henry, in a rare move, said, "Certainly, we'd love to hear her sing. It will help pass the evening."

Lady Markston beamed. "Wonderful."

Emily's heart sank. Harriet knew that she had a singing voice that would call the dead from their graves. And now Lady Markston had suggested a musical evening. There was no possible way she could escape having to sing. I could claim to be ill, she thought furtively, but that would show no breeding at all. No, it's the first night of the house party and I have to participate, she decided with a sigh, a look of resignation on her face. This was going to be a dashed long evening.

"Susan, that was lovely," Aubrey said, his blue eyes shining in admiration.

Susan had the temerity to blush, and Nigel, seated behind the pianoforte, once again rolled his eyes. That motion was not lost on Emily, who smiled at him. She was rewarded with a very forward wink that, thankfully, no one noticed.

"When we go wassailing, it's been said that my voice is the sweetest," Susan said, basking in the glow of praise.

"Do sing something else," Henry asked, casually glancing at his pocket watch.

"I wouldn't want it said that my Susan is putting herself forward," Lady Markston commented, and glanced toward Emily, who had seated herself alone in the far corner. Emily's modest bottle-green satin dress was rather unexceptional, but not completely unfashionable, and she could feel Lady Markston's look of pity. "Emily, why don't you favor us with a song? Susan and Harriet shouldn't have to do all of the entertaining this evening," she said, rather ungenerously pointing out that Emily hadn't taken her turn.

"I don't sing, Lady Markston," Emily said in a soft voice, turning a very deep shade of red.

"You don't sing? All ladies sing," Susan said, glancing over at Nigel. He was all but gaping at Emily.

"I'm sorry, I really don't sing."

"That's true, Lady Markston," Harriet quickly said, hoping

to gloss over Emily's apparent womanly deficiency. "Emily and I were at school together, and I've heard her attempts. She has other musical talents that far outweigh a pleasant voice."

"Humph, all ladies should sing. I suppose you do embroidery and watercolors then?" Lady Markston asked curiously.

Before Emily could answer, Henry jumped in to rescue her from her immediate downfall. "You know, Susan," he began, focusing all of his attention on the spoiled young beauty at his table, "I'm sure everyone would love to hear another song, if you're not too terribly exhausted."

Susan blushed prettily, basking in the attention. "Of course not, Henry," she replied, and riffled through the music, looking for another piece to showcase her angelic voice.

Emily sighed in relief. So *that's* the way it's going to be. Lady Markston has taken me in some sort of freakish dislike and is going to use my lack of womanly accomplishments to make her daughter look more attractive.

When Susan's performance ended, Emily abruptly stood up and excused herself, heading down the hall toward the warming fires in the library.

The roaring fire in the fireplace cast just enough light for Emily to start reading the ghastly Minerva Press novel she had found on one of the lower shelves. Wellington was at her feet, asleep, and she was curled up on a mahogany chair that was quite comfortable, despite its stiff back. The fire was warm, it was still snowing, and for once that evening, Emily was contented.

Nigel walked into the library a short time later, dashed tired of Lady Markston and Susan. All he really wanted was to escape from the debacle that they called a musical evening and to find some sort of book to read to get his mind off of his problems.

So when he glanced over to the warm, welcoming glow of the fireplace and saw Emily curled up in a chair, asleep, his breath was all but taken away.

Her thick mane of dark auburn hair glowed in the light of the fire, creating a golden halo around her head. Her skin was the color of porcelain, and her long, artistic fingers were wrapped around the novel that was sitting in her lap. To make the picture complete, Victoria's puppy was curled up at her feet, also oblivious to his intrusion.

Nigel stood staring at her for a long time, his heart pounding in his chest. Emily wasn't nearly as beautiful as Susan; her kind heart, the sparkle in her eyes, and the way she treated the people around her made her stand out from the usual sort of female one encountered in Society. He had no doubt that she was adored by her servants, and her personal friends were probably as fiercely loyal to her as she was to them.

The gentle rise and fall of her breasts kept him transfixed until he finally decided that it wasn't terribly proper to stand about watching someone sleep. So he decided to exit the library gracefully and leave Emily to her slumbers.

That is, until he turned and unceremoniously walked into the zebrawood inlaid writing table that he really hadn't noticed before, knocking a small wooden statue onto the floor.

"Damn," he muttered as he picked up the statue, and when he looked over at Emily, she was sitting up in her chair, regarding him with large, sleepy green eyes.

"Emily," he said with a soft, sensual smile, "I'm sorry I disturbed your rest."

Emily blushed prettily and noticed how tall and forbidding he looked in the firelight. "You must think me rather corkbrained to be dozing in the library. Actually, Lady Markston rather wore me out and I thought this was the last place I would ever encounter her," she said, still blushing.

Nigel crossed the room and seated himself in the mahogany chair opposite her, next to the fire. "Lady Markston can be a bit of a harridan, can't she? You shouldn't let her bother you, though—she just thinks she's helping her daughter," he explained, staring into the flickering depths of her green eyes.

Suddenly shy, Emily looked away and into the fire. "It's not very charitable to admit it, but I do hope the weather clears so Lady Markston and her daughter can get on with their trip," she said in a voice that was as smooth as silk.

"If you'd like, I could have a word with Lady Markston and Susan. They both tend to treat anyone who isn't a proper member of the *ton* abominably, and I'd hate to see them continue treating you badly," he said, leaning forward in his chair.

"It's very kind of you to offer, Lord Stratford," she began, and he immediately interrupted her.

"Nigel, not Lord Stratford."

"It's very kind of you to offer," she began again, glancing at him shyly, "but I'm accustomed to people like Lady Markston. Although my grandfather is a duke, my father is still connected to trade so I'm not quite respectable enough for many people. That's why I rather avoid English Society. It's different on the Continent, at least in my experience. You're judged more on your accomplishments than strictly on your birthright," she concluded, shocked at her own words.

Nigel's look was unfathomable as he replied, "It's not so much different for those of us who are fully accepted by the Upper Ten. I've been judged as Lord Stratford rather than on my own accomplishments for years, and have had all of the matchmaking mama's sending their daughters after my fortune for years. That's not a particularly pleasant experience, knowing that one's chief asset is one's blunt," he concluded, wondering why he was confiding some of his innermost thoughts to a female who was practically a stranger.

A wry, sad smile appeared on Emily's face. "I understand completely. Before I decided I didn't want to participate in Society, my only recommendation was my fortune. And my father would not sanction an alliance with a gamester in dun territory, no matter what his title," she concluded, perfectly at ease talking with Nigel.

"I think you're gammoning me, Emily. I can't believe a young woman as beautiful as you are didn't have the bucks in town begging for a dance," he said with all sincerity, completely forgetting about Roger, the mermaid pendant, and everything else except the beautiful woman in front of him.

As Emily gazed wistfully back at him, neither one noticed that Henry had joined them in the library. He coughed discreetly and brought them both out of their firelight trance.

"I should have thought I'd find you both in here—it's the only place you can be assured of refuge from Lady Markston," Henry replied, sitting down in the chair next to Nigel.

"She's usually not this bad. I don't know what kind of maggot is in her brain, but I hope she'll be more congenial tomorrow morning," Nigel replied, cursing Henry's interruption. He was enjoying his *tête-à-tête* with Emily, and didn't want it to end.

"I hope so, too. Harriet has some grand plans for tomorrow, if the weather clears. She wants the servants to drag in some of the greenery we have in the barn so we can start making ropes to decorate the house," he said casually, beginning to relax in the comfort of the library.

With a small smile, Emily stood up and replied, "Then I'd best be retiring for the evening. I know how ambitious Harriet can be, and I'm sure I'll need the rest for tomorrow's activities," she said, her eyes lingering on Nigel.

"Good evening, Emily," Nigel said in a sultry, intimate voice that caused a delicious shiver to run up Emily's spine as she left the room, Wellington trailing after her.

"Emily has Nigel's family heirloom? That's why you invited them both here for the Christmas holiday?" Henry asked incredulously, taking a helping of kippers from the bowfronted, satinwood-inlaid mahogany sideboard.

Harriet looked up guiltily from her rasher of bacon. "Yes, I know it sounds horrible, but there is an explanation," she protested, a blush staining her cheeks.

Henry joined her at the circular table inlaid with brass and stared at her intently. So intently, he failed to notice, as did Harriet, that Aubrey had come up to the door of the small breakfast room and was eavesdropping on their conversation.

"So, my dear, what is your explanation?" Henry asked, delving into his breakfast.

"Well, I wasn't sure if I should mention it at all, but when Nigel's father, the marquess, wrote, he mentioned that Roger had accidentally sold a piece of the Manning jewelry. He said it was bought by Emily's grandfather, who promptly gave it to her as an early Christmas present. The marquess would like the pendant back in the family, you see," she explained, her round morning dress of green merino wool complementing her skin color.

"And so?"

"Roger couldn't buy it back from Emily—she still detests him. So the marquess sent Nigel to buy it back from her. There's the matter of the curse, you see," she explained, as if they were discussing something as commonplace as the weather.

"The curse? Harriet, that's a Banbury story if I ever heard one," Henry proclaimed, chewing on a crisp piece of bacon.

"I know it sounds rather out of the ordinary. But the marquess claims that the family will be plagued by bad luck until the Manning Mermaid is back in the family. I thought it was a cock-and-bull story myself until Nigel started telling me all of the ghastly things that have been happening lately," Harriet finished, gazing steadily at her husband.

"Does Emily know any of this?"

"Not at all. I don't know if she'll agree to sell the pendant, since she does seem to be dashed fond of it. I do hope that Nigel isn't being solicitous to her just so she'll willingly sell him the pendant back," Harriet said, finishing up the last of her food.

Henry frowned. "I don't think so. Nigel seemed to be quite taken with Emily from the start, even though he thought that she was Miss Turner," he concluded, staring out the window. It was still snowing so hard one couldn't see much outside.

"I hope you're right," Harriet added, and was startled when, out of nowhere, Aubrey appeared.

"You both keep early hours," he proclaimed, helping himself to the food on the sideboard.

"It is the country," Henry proclaimed, not noticing the worried look on his wife's face.

How much did Aubrey hear, Harriet wondered, her blue eyes suddenly shadowed with concern. And if he did hear what we were discussing, how much will he tell Emily? Or anyone else, for that matter, she mused, her mind suddenly in a jumble.

"Aunt Emily, wake up!" a small voice from the foot of her bed said eagerly, tugging at her thick covers.

Emily opened one green eye and replied, "Victoria, my dear, I was up much later than you were last night and I would like to sleep."

"Please, Aunt Emily? The snow has turned to ice and Miss Turner won't let me go outside to play. Please, will you get up?" Victoria asked in a pleading voice, walking over to Emily's side of the enormous four-poster bed.

From the door, another voice boomed, "Victoria! There you are. How dare you bother Miss Winterhaven while she is still abed. You will come with me at once!" Miss Turner, Victoria's nanny, admonished from the doorway.

Emily let out a deep sigh and sat up in bed, propping herself up on her pillows. "Good morning, Miss Turner," Emily said in an amiable voice, pushing her loose strands of hair off of her face.

Miss Turner colored to the roots of her long, mouse-brown hair. "I'm terribly sorry for the intrusion, Miss Winterhaven. Victoria scuttled off when I wasn't looking. I do beg your pardon," she said nervously, glancing down the hall.

A gentle smile appeared on Emily's face. "I realize it's not your fault, Miss Turner, and I enjoy spending time with Victoria. Tell me, what is the rest of the house up to today?" she asked curiously, beginning to wake up more fully.

"I don't know, Miss Winterhaven," Miss Turner replied, stepping into the bedroom to collect Victoria.

"*I* know," Victoria said eagerly, still standing next to Emily's bed.

Emily smiled indulgently at the child. "Do tell, Victoria."

"Mama and Papa are still in the breakfast room with Uncle Aubrey. Lady Markston is staying in her room all day—she's recovering from the trip. Uncle Nigel is in his room, too—his valet says he has a dreadful cold. And Lady Susan is just wandering around the house and seems to be out of sorts. And she doesn't like talking to me," Victoria finished in a rush.

"Have you been pestering Lady Susan?" Miss Turner admonished, beginning to become quite cross with the child.

"No, Miss Turner. I just said good morning to her and she ignored me, as if I were a servant!" Victoria proclaimed, the picture of outraged innocence.

"You should not be bothering the guests," Miss Turner scolded, folding her hands in front of her angrily.

Victoria turned her pleading blue eyes toward Emily, who smiled sympathetically.

"She's right, Victoria. Not all adults care for children, especially if they're not accustomed to them," she explained patiently, inwardly amazed that anyone could be rude to Victoria, who was the sweetest child one could encounter.

Victoria turned a charming shade of red and looked down at the floor, quite embarrassed. A moment later, she exclaimed, "Aunt Emily, there's something in your shoes!"

Emily turned a deep shade of red, and was even more mortified when Miss Turner came over to the side of the bed and picked up her delicate kid slipper from the floor. "Why, you have rosemary in your shoe," she announced to no one in particular, a small smile appearing on her severe features.

"Yes, and thyme in the other," Emily admitted reluctantly, still a slight shade of pink.

"Why?" Victoria asked, and before Emily could answer, Miss Turner looked at her sympathetically and said, "If you don't mind, I'll explain to Victoria."

"Of course."

"Victoria," Miss Turner began, "Miss Winterhaven is practicing a fine old Christmas tradition. You see, when an unmarried young lady puts her shoes on the side of her bed, with rosemary and thyme in each shoe, the legend says that if she sleeps on her back, she'll dream of the man she is going to marry."

Victoria looked up at Emily, her eyes wide with wonder. "You were sleeping on your back when I came in. Were you dreaming about anyone?" she asked shyly.

Emily blushed and looked away. How could she tell the child that she had been dreaming about her Uncle Nigel since the moment she placed her shoes next to the bed?

Five

"You are a vision to behold," Aubrey proclaimed, staring at the blond goddess standing in front of the window of the study.

Susan tossed her artfully styled blond curls and gave him a magnificent smile. "You are much too forward, Aubrey. It's good that Mama isn't here or she would give you a dressing-down you wouldn't soon forget."

Aubrey, clad in a blue jacket with a willow-green-and-blush-colored waistcoat and buckskin breeches, seated himself on the large sofa near the fireplace. "Yes, I'm horribly forward, but you're dashed attractive, Susan, and I think you enjoy hearing accolades to your beauty."

The smile remained on Susan's face as she sat down on the small mahogany chair across from the sofa, adjusting the golden patterned Turkish shawl that covered her softly flowing gown of pale blue. "You're quite the rake, aren't you? That's why I haven't seen you around Town," she concluded, still very confident of herself.

A leisurely smile appeared on Aubrey's face. "You haven't seen me about Town because I travel in different circles than you do. I am a titled man about Town, not a young girl that hasn't taken in . . . how many Seasons have you had?" he asked, shocking Susan as he knew he would.

"That is dashed impertinent of you, sir! I demand an apology," Susan said passionately, her perfect porcelain skin becoming a bit pale at Aubrey's proclamation.

"No need to get on your high horse—I'm not planning on informing your intended of the facts. And I'm not planning to apologize. I just thought we might get on better if we realized where we stood. I still find you stunningly attractive, despite your lack of success about Town," he concluded suavely, taking a bit of snuff.

Susan was at a complete loss for words. Finally, after looking at the Aubusson carpet for the longest time, she finally said, "Please don't tell Nigel I'm not a success. Mama is expecting a spring wedding, and the truth might make him think that our marriage would be a misalliance," she concluded, unable to meet his eyes.

"Of course it would be a misalliance," Aubrey proclaimed, and smiled in delight as she raised her stunning blue eyes in protest.

"I disagree, sir! I will make a splendid marchioness some day!" she proclaimed defiantly, her eyes blazing.

"I don't doubt that," he said immediately, then added, "but not for Stratford. You don't care a farthing for him, and he isn't particularly attached to you, either."

"Sir, you have no knowledge of the situation. Nigel will offer for me before the Twelfth Night," she said, practically shouting.

"There's no need to get a feather in your bonnet. A beautiful woman like you would be bored to tears with Stratford. Why do you insist on marrying him?" he asked casually, leaning back on the sofa to study the beauty before him.

Susan stared at the carpet once again, deep in thought. Finally she replied, "Nigel is quite wealthy and has a tract of land adjoining ours. It would be a fortuitous match."

"And I am just as plump in the pocket as Stratford. Are you really so determined to spend your life with a serious member of Parliament who doesn't appreciate the fact that you are the goddess Venus incarnate? Do you really wish to be shut away in some god-awful house to rear a passel of drab children? Is that what you want, Susan?" he asked, knowing fully well that he was really trying the bounds of propriety.

Susan looked into his large blue eyes and asked in a soft, barely inaudible voice, "Does what I want matter?"

Aubrey leaned forward and used all of his rakish charm to seduce her. "What you want is of tantamount importance, Lady Susan Claredon," he declared in a serious voice that made a shiver of excitement ripple through her body.

"Will you require anything else, my lord?" Hughes asked, handing Nigel a teacup full of some sort of potion that Harriet's cook had brewed especially to cure his cold.

Nigel took the teacup filled with an extremely hot, foul-smelling liquid and sipped it slowly, a look of extreme distaste present on his pale features. "No, I don't expect I will need anything else right at this moment, Hughes. I feel dashed miserable and at any moment I fear I'll be screaming at you like my father screams at his valet. So why don't you find yourself something to eat below stairs and I'll try to rest a trifle," Nigel said, then sneezed into his handkerchief.

Hughes, his tall, thin valet, frowned noticeably. "Are you certain, my lord? Would you like a poultice from Miss Turner? The staff claims that her home remedies have helped them immensely," he said in a worried voice.

"I think not. No, I've simply caught some sort of freakish cold and need to tough it out. I'll be fine tomorrow," Nigel claimed, once again sneezing so the entire bed shook.

"As you wish, sir," Hughes replied, and left the room reluctantly. Nigel would have bet a guinea that the man was going to be back to check on him within the hour.

The olive green drapes were pulled tightly shut, but from what Hughes had told him, it was now snowing prodigiously, covering a thick layer of ice. Obviously Susan and her ghastly mama were not going to be leaving anytime in the near future.

Unfortunately, they were not the crux of his dilemma. He still had to resolve the matter of the mermaid pendant with Miss Winterhaven. That's going to be nearly impossible, he decided, pushing his damp, dark hair off his forehead. Whatever I do, Miss Winterhaven, Emily, will suspect my motives. If I befriend her, she'll believe that my only purpose was to recover the pendant. If I broach the subject now and she refuses, it could make the entire holiday uncomfortable for both of us. Then there's the fact that Roger is my younger brother. If she finds out that bit of gossip, my chances of retrieving the mermaid will be through. Of course, Father and Roger are probably having a dashed good time at home while I suffer the effects of this damnable curse. Why else would I be stricken with this miserable cold? Gads, this is an awful dilemma, he thought, staring around the empty room.

And how am I going to pass the time today? he wondered, looking around the luxuriant bedroom for some sort of book. There were none. There wasn't a newspaper to be found, or anything else that might help him while away the time. Of course, I can daydream about Emily, his mind replied, and he cursed his imagination. He had been daydreaming about Emily since the first time he saw her with that ridiculous puppy clutched to her milky white breasts.

A knock on his door brought him out of his highly improper imaginings, and he said, "Come in," confidently, before he sneezed again.

The heavy oak door opened slowly, and standing before his four-poster bed was Emily Winterhaven, as if his imagination had conjured her up for his pleasure.

Emily was wearing a very fetching cinnamon velvet morning gown with white lace at her wrists. Her long, auburn hair was pulled into a loose, thick braid, and her long, black lashes kissed her enormous green eyes. As he glanced behind her, he noticed a young woman in a white mobcap, probably her abigail, standing behind her.

"Good afternoon, Lord Stratford," Emily said in a soft

voice. "Harriet said you weren't feeling quite the thing and I thought you might care for a game of cards," she said, glancing around the room that mirrored her own.

A magnificent smile lit up Nigel's harsh features. Maybe there isn't a curse after all, he decided, propping himself up in bed a bit more. "I think a game of cards is just what I need, Emily," he said, motioning her to come toward the bed. "Why don't you have your abigail bring that small table over?" he asked, glancing toward a delicately carved mahogany table in the far corner, near the window.

"Of course. Eliza?" she asked, and in one swift move the table was next to the bed and Emily was making herself comfortable on a chair of steel with copper and brass ornaments, covered in olive velvet that matched the dressing table.

"I do appreciate your company, Emily," he began, watching her long, delicate fingers shuffle the cards. "I thought I'd go mad if I were left alone any longer."

Emily smiled. "Yes, I know. My mama was taken ill a few years ago and was terribly lonely. I realize it's rather forward of me, but I did think you might enjoy a diversion," she explained, a delicate blush coming to her cheeks.

Nigel gazed at her, enraptured by her youthful beauty. She wasn't traditionally lovely, like Susan, but her beauty seemed to emanate from within, making her immensely more desirable. "What's your pleasure?" he asked softly, noting that she turned a darker shade of red.

"I thought a game of piquet might be nice," she said, glancing over at Eliza, who had taken a seat near the door.

"Then piquet it is," he said, picking up the cards she was dealing him.

As their game began, Nigel immediately realized that piquet wasn't Emily's forte, although she was a tolerable enough player. To keep her mind off the fact that she was losing, he asked, "So, what is the rest of the party doing for amusement today?"

Emily stared at her cards, quite vexed. "I don't know. I did see Susan and Aubrey having a coze earlier, and Henry was busy with some sort of estate business. Harriet is attending to something in the kitchen, and Lady Markston is still resting from her journey."

"I do hope Susan and Aubrey get on. He seems to be an eligible enough *parti* for her," he commented, throwing down another card. His color had returned somewhat, and he noticed that the slight fever he'd had was gone. Emily was also a cure-all for his diseases, he thought, a smile dancing on his lips.

"Have you known her for a long time?"

"Ages. Her family's estate borders my ancestral home. I've been seeing her a bit more frequently to placate my father, who is convinced I should be providing him with grandchildren as soon as possible," Nigel explained, running a free hand through his long, dark, wavy locks.

Emily smiled, her face lighting up. "I understand. My grandfather is constantly haranguing me about marriage. In fact, he is so desperate for great-grandchildren that he purchased me the most unique piece of jewelry that's supposed to help one make a happy match. I don't quite understand how a mermaid pendant is going to do that, but then again, what do I know?" she said philosophically, shrugging her shoulders.

Nigel could feel the muscles in his stomach knotting. She was talking about the Manning Mermaid. The jeweler had given her grandfather some Banbury tale about the pendant, which he had repeated. "I don't think I've ever seen a mermaid pendant," he said casually, shuffling the cards.

"It's very unusual—some might even say garish. I've become quite fond of it, though," she explained, picking up her cards. "Harriet liked it, although I have no idea when I can wear it without looking horribly overdressed," Emily confessed, playing a ten of hearts.

Nigel forced himself not to frown. Emily, of course, had become fond of the pendant. That was the story of his life.

Roger had found himself in some sort of fix, which was impossible to extricate him from. What was even worse was that he didn't particularly want to buy the pendant from Emily. She's more attached to the piece than I am, he thought traitorously. "I'm sure you'll have ample opportunity to show it off during the holiday season. Harriet and Henry have any number of entertainments planned, although I don't know how this ghastly weather will affect them," he concluded, winning another hand.

Emily looked at him with a smile. "Lord Stratford," she began, and he immediately interrupted.

"Nigel. Call me Nigel."

"Nigel, then," she said with a blush, "you're a Captain Sharp yourself. Whist may not be your game, but piquet certainly is," she proclaimed, gathering up the cards.

"Don't tell me you're quitting so soon?" he asked, disappointment etched on his features.

Her lips curved up in a soft, sensual smile. "Eliza and I really should be going. If anyone realizes how long we've been closeted up here playing cards, we'll be the talk of the house. Will you be coming down for dinner?" she asked, dragging the chair back to the dressing table.

"Yes, I think so," he said with a loud sneeze. "Excuse me. I do feel markedly better, so you can tell Harriet to have a place set for me," he said, hoping to find some reason for her to stay.

Emily moved to the door, her abigail behind her, and once again favored him with a smile that made his heart lurch in his chest. "I'll see you at dinner, then," she said, disappearing through the door like a specter.

"Are you feeling more the thing?" Susan asked, her blue eyes settling on Nigel as if he were a prized bull.

Nigel sipped his sherry thoughtfully, and finally replied, "Yes, I do feel considerably better. Emily was good enough to come by and divert me with a game of piquet, which I am heartily grateful for."

Susan glared across the table at Emily, who was still wearing her cinnamon velvet dress and looked much more a member of *le beau monde*. "You visited Nigel in his room? Isn't that rather . . . indiscreet?" she asked, picking at her poached salmon.

Emily looked up, and decided that Lady Susan Claredon was not going to ruin her Christmas holiday. "I think not. My maid was in attendance for the entire visit, and I thought that Lord Stratford—I'm sorry, Nigel—might be up for a card game. I'm surprised you didn't join us, since you must know how Nigel fancies a game of piquet," she finished, sipping her sherry.

A slight red tint colored Susan's face, and Emily knew that she had touched a nerve. She was certain that Susan had no idea that Nigel liked a good game of cards.

"Miss Winterhaven, you must be the same age as my Susan. Why haven't we met you in polite Society?" Lady Markston inquired, the feather on her Pamona green turban bobbing as she spoke.

"Emily has been traveling," Harriet explained, throwing Lady Markston a dark look.

Before Lady Markston could reply, Aubrey, resplendent in a blue velvet coat with a gold satin waistcoat and a silk cravat tied in the Oriental style, interrupted. "You look lovely tonight, Susan," he began. "Will you be favoring us with some more songs later in the evening?" he asked, fingering the enormous diamond that decorated his cravat.

"Yes, that's a wonderful idea!" Lady Markston replied, eating half of her salmon in one mouthful. "There is nothing more entertaining than listening to a female with an excellent voice," she proclaimed, beaming at her daughter.

"Your daughter's talents are remarkable, Lady Markston," Harriet began, her eyes full of fire, "but we can hardly expect her to amuse us every evening," she concluded, every inch the hostess of the house party.

"Nigel, do you feel up to playing?" Henry asked casually, filling his plate with the saddle of mutton that had just arrived.

Nigel glanced over at Emily, who was staring into her plate, barely taking part in the conversation. If he didn't play, it was apparent to everyone that Susan would be singing like a canary for the entire evening, to the delight of Aubrey and Lady Markston. So he replied, "Of course," and smiled at the venomous look that he received from Lady Markston.

"Oh Nigel, you play so beautifully," Susan murmured, practically slavering over him.

Nigel looked up from the mahogany pianoforte and met Emily's clear green eyes. "I'd be interested to hear your opinion, Emily," he said softly, all but ignoring Susan in the process.

"What would Miss Winterhaven know, Nigel? The chit doesn't even move in the *ton*. How can she judge anyone's playing, for that matter?" Lady Markston asked, making it obvious to all that she did not particularly care about offending Emily.

"Lady Markston," Harriet began in a patient voice, "Emily is a dear friend of mine and I'd be gratified if you kept that fact in mind while you're at my home. She is also an accomplished musician, and has played before the Czar," she finished, glaring at Lady Markston.

There was a long pause as the entire party stared at Lady Markston. "My apologies, Miss Winterhaven," Lady Markston replied in an insincere tone, obviously hoping to placate Harriet.

"Emily?" Nigel asked in an intimate voice, staring at the beautiful young woman sitting across the room from him.

Emily blushed as the attention of the entire party turned toward her. "You play beautifully, as I'm sure everyone present would agree," she said, noting how handsome he looked sitting at the pianoforte.

"And will you play for us?" he asked, rising and walking toward her chair.

"Oh yes, do play something for us, Emily," Henry echoed, smiling at her in encouragement.

"All right," Emily said shyly, and walked over to the pianoforte and immediately became lost in her own world.

Suddenly, the unpleasantness of Lady Markston and all the uncomfortable feelings of the day disappeared as her fingers stroked the ivory keys beneath them. She played an obscure piece by Mozart from memory, and became one with the music, her body swaying with the delicate melody. Her body lost all of its stiffness, and all of the men in the room marveled at the beauty that suddenly seemed to radiate from the delicate woman at the pianoforte.

Nigel was completely entranced. He had never seen a woman play with so much passion or skill. Emily's entire being seemed to be transformed while she was at the instrument, and, try as he might, he could not tear his eyes away from the dark-haired figure before him. Her playing moved him incredibly, and he could feel his heart lurching in his breast.

When she finished, there was a brief silence; then Nigel said, "Why, Emily, you're a veritable virtuoso! No wonder you entranced the Czar." The admiration in his eyes was evident to all.

"Yes, you do play devilishly good, Emily," Aubrey added, glancing over at Susan, who was now in a full pout.

"You're very talented, Miss Winterhaven," Lady Markston conceded, and smiled over at Nigel. "And I'm sure your family must be very proud to have a musician amongst you. I know I'll be welcoming one into my family soon enough," she concluded, watching Nigel pale.

"Oh Mama, nothing is official," Susan said with a giggle, glancing toward Nigel.

Nigel smiled benignly toward both ladies and commented, "You must introduce me to this musician of yours. I had no idea Susan had met an eligible *parti*. My congratulations."

Lady Markston and Susan both paled, and Aubrey decided that it was time to strike up a closer acquaintance with Susan. "There are the most wonderful medieval tapestries in the library, Susan," he commented. "I'd be honored if you'd let me show them to you."

Lady Markston almost gasped when her daughter smiled prettily and replied, "It would be my pleasure to accompany you, Aubrey," and sauntered out of the room with him.

"So, Aubrey, why did you wish to lure me into the library?" Susan asked, smoothing the wrinkles out of her gown.

Aubrey dragged the matching mahogany chair across from Susan's seat and made himself comfortable. "I was curious about something," he replied enigmatically, drinking in her enormous blue eyes.

Susan smiled at him coyly. "And what would that be? I do hope for your sake that you're not going to suggest something improper, since I know you do have the reputation of a rake," she concluded, batting her eyelashes at him.

"If I'm such a notorious libertine, then why are you taking such pains to entice me? Could it be because the object of your matrimonial affections pays no heed to you?" he replied, immediately noticing the look of concern on her face.

"I don't know what's wrong with Nigel. He was always most attentive and now he barely notices me. Me! I could have legions of men offering for me if I only encouraged them," Susan concluded vainly, and Aubrey was certain she believed every word she said.

"I rather think that your Nigel is developing a *tendre* for Emily Winterhaven."

Susan stood up and began to pace the library. "That little nothing! How could he be interested in her? There has to be some sort of reason that he's actually paying court to that bluestocking," Susan concluded, leaning against the zebra-wood inlaid writing table.

A slow, sensual smile appeared on Aubrey's full features. "What would you say if I told you I know the reason your Nigel is bothering with the bluestocking?"

"You do? What is it?" she asked passionately, sitting back down in the mahogany chair opposite Aubrey.

Both parties were so engrossed in their conversation that neither one noticed the wide-eyed little eavesdropper standing in the hall near the open door, listening to every word they said.

"Emily has in her possession a mermaid pendant that once belonged to Nigel. He's here to buy it back. If he doesn't get it back, there's some sort of ridiculous curse that's going to fall on his family," Aubrey explained, preening under the attention of the magnificently beautiful Susan.

"A pendant? He's courting her to get the pendant? Will she sell it to him?" Susan asked in rapt attention.

"From what I gather, that's unlikely to happen."

Susan sat stiffly in her chair, a frown wrinkling her brow. Finally she asked, "Do you think Nigel would leave the party early if he got the pendant?"

Aubrey shrugged. "Possibly. From what I've heard, that is the only reason he's here."

A magnificent smile appeared on Susan's face. "Then I have the solution. We'll simply borrow the pendant from Emily and return it to Nigel, who is the rightful owner. Then Nigel can return home with me once the weather clears," she proclaimed, looking like the cat who ate the cream.

Aubrey was vastly amused. Susan was a vain, manipulative woman concerned only with her own life, and it fascinated him. He realized that her plan would probably be unsuccessful, but was anxious to hear more. "How would you go about stealing the mermaid?"

"We would simply search her room when she was busy with some sort of activity that will keep her occupied for a time. Then, after we've found it, I'll give it back to Nigel. As a Christmas present, I think," she added, relaxing in the chair.

"And if you get caught?" Aubrey asked cautiously.

Susan raised an eyebrow and looked every inch the daughter of a peer. "We won't get caught. And if we do, it won't matter. Nigel will forgive me."

Obviously she knows nothing about Stratford, Aubrey thought, studying the beauty. It was known about Town that Stratford was a rather high stickler, and who wouldn't be, after living with his father, the madman? If Susan stole the pendant and later gave it to Nigel, he would very likely be completely scandalized with her behavior, Aubrey mused, a slow smile coming onto his face. And if Nigel throws her over, then I will have a clear field for my courtship. Yes, this plan will work out very well, he concluded mentally.

"Aubrey, are you attending? What do you think?"

"I think it's a grand idea, Susan, and you're completely right. Emily Winterhaven isn't the rightful owner of the pendant, so it should be returned to Nigel. And I think it's rather shameful the way he's playing up to her so she'll eventually sell it back."

Victoria stood in the hall, her eyes as large as saucers.

"Victoria, what are you doing up?" Coverdail, the butler asked, looking down on the small eavesdropper.

"I couldn't sleep," she said weakly, and looked up into his large brown eyes.

He smiled gently and replied, "Take my hand, young lady, and I'll escort you back upstairs. And you're to stay in bed, is that clear?" he asked in mock severity, walking her down the hall.

"Yes," Victoria answered simply, a frown marring her smooth features. She was in quite a dilemma. Miss Turner had given her a lengthy lecture on tattling, and she certainly didn't want to misbehave. So, for the moment, Victoria's lips were sealed.

Six

"Papa, are you going to take us all for sleigh rides?" Victoria asked, gaping at the enormous red-and-gold sleigh behind Henry's pair of matched blacks.

Henry smiled down at his daughter, who was getting more snow-covered with every passing moment. "Of course, dear," he began, and turned to Aubrey and Nigel. "Would you both like a chance at the ribbons?"

Aubrey glanced around their small outdoor party. Miss Turner was attending Victoria. Henry and Harriet were bounding about in the snow, as was Emily. Susan was practically glued to Nigel, who looked as if he would move heaven and hell to get rid of her company. "Not today, Henry," he said casually, heartily sick and tired of the weather.

There was one advantage, he had to admit. With the exception of Susan's mother, everyone of consequence was outside. This was an ideal opportunity to filch Emily's pendant. All he had to do was make sure that her abigail was busy elsewhere, and he could stand guard while Susan searched the room. And no one would be the wiser.

"Nigel? Are you game today?" Henry asked with a smile, dusting the snow off of his dark blue greatcoat.

Nigel gazed over at Emily, who was once again in her dark blue pelisse and carried a bright white muff, her face alight with pleasure. "I think I can manage to take the ladies for a spin in your sleigh," Nigel said, still gazing longingly at Emily.

Henry smiled. "Not my sleigh. Borrowed it from Blackmore. His visitors haven't arrived yet—thought we might make use of it," Henry finished, watching Miss Turner and Victoria seat themselves in the aforementioned vehicle.

"Father knows Blackmore very well, much better than I. You're lucky to have such an amiable neighbor," Nigel commented, and walked over to the sleigh with his host.

Before Susan could tag dutifully after Nigel like a devoted puppy, Aubrey seized the opportunity to grab her arm and ask, "May I have a word?"

Sighing, Susan walked off a bit with Aubrey and replied, "Yes? This had better be important, since I hate to be away from my future husband's side."

Aubrey rolled his eyes toward the heavens, but decided to ignore that comment. "If you wish to abscond with Miss Winterhaven's mermaid, this is an ideal opportunity. I'll go inside now, and you can return to the house in a few minutes," he said, noticing how the snowflakes made her porcelain skin glisten in the daylight.

A slow smile curled her lips. "That's a devilish good idea! I'll be in after my sleigh ride," she promised, and marched right back to Nigel's side.

As Henry, Victoria, and Miss Turner rode off into the snow, Aubrey sauntered over to Harriet and Emily, glancing casually at Susan. Once again, she was hanging onto Nigel's arm as if her life depended on it. He sighed, and turned to his hostess. "Harriet, I'm really not up to romping in the snow today. I hope you won't think me ill-mannered if I go inside," he said casually.

Harriet smiled sympathetically. "Yes, I quite understand. If I had been traveling in this snow, I'm sure I wouldn't want to be out in it any longer than necessary," she replied, noticing Susan hovering over Nigel.

"I knew you'd understand," Aubrey muttered, and began to trudge toward the house.

"So, are you going to go for a sleigh ride?" Harriet asked Emily, a smile dancing on her lips.

"Undoubtedly," Emily replied, and pointed to a pair of trees in the distance. "Isn't that Henry coming round now?" she asked, and could hear the jingle of the bells on the horses' tack.

"I do believe it is. Well, at least Henry didn't overturn Blackmore's rig," Harriet commented, catching the very telling glance that Nigel was throwing toward her. "Why don't we go over and see how Nigel and Susan are holding up?" Harriet suggested.

As the ladies clopped through the knee-high snow toward the pair, Henry and his passengers pulled up next to them.

"Oh Mama, it was ever so much fun! Can we get a sleigh? Please?" Victoria chimed as Henry carried her out of the sleigh.

Harriet giggled as Henry put her daughter down in the snow and Victoria scampered over to her. "Can we, Mama?" she asked, her cheeks pink and her tiny nose running from the cold.

"We'll see," Harriet said, then turned to Emily. "Are you ready for your ride?"

Emily glanced over to Susan, who was intentionally ignoring her. "If Susan doesn't mind," she said in a soft voice, glancing over at Nigel. He looked so handsome standing next to the sled, large flakes of snow making his unfashionably long, black hair look iridescent.

"Oh, I don't mind," Susan replied, scarcely looking away from Nigel.

It was Henry who ruined all of Susan's very obvious romantic plans. He glanced over at Nigel, who looked rather miserable, and asked, "Nigel, would you mind taking Emily for her drive? My hands are dashed frozen from the trip I made."

Nigel glanced over at Emily's lithe form silhouetted against a gray sky and smiled. "Of course, Henry, my pleasure," he said with a magnificent smile that lit up his face.

Emily blushed as he held his large, capable hand out to help her into the sleigh. She felt as if her heart would burst as she placed the plaid blanket over her lap and stared at the backs of Henry's blacks, squalls of snow bursting around her.

"Are you ready, Emily?" Nigel asked with a smile, settling himself into the seat beside her.

"Yes," she replied, suddenly shy, and Nigel urged the horses forward, whisking them away from the confines of the house party.

They rode in silence for a while, each lost in thought. The snow swirled around them, making the whole scene seem rather unreal.

As they neared the edge of the forest, Nigel slowed the pair to a walk and commented, "You look very charming today, Emily."

Emily blushed. Gads, he's polite, she thought, ignoring the fact that the sleigh was rather small and that his firm, muscular thigh was pressed against her. "You're giving me a bit of Spanish coin, my lord," she said in a light voice, staring straight ahead, afraid to meet his eyes.

Nigel slowed the horses to a stop at a glade and said in a firm voice, "I most certainly am not."

Emily was at quite a loss. Why was he being so solicitous, she wondered, fairly certain that he was lying. Finally, after staring at her muff for a prodigiously long time, she said, "Then you must be the veriest of rakes, my lord, since those are the only gentlemen who make it a point to charm spinsters who are on the shelf."

If she had looked over, she would have noticed the intense look on Nigel's face. Instead she stared ahead blankly, concentrating on the horses and the white puffs coming out of their nostrils.

"Emily, you're a very charming, talented, and beautiful female, and I don't believe you're on the shelf. And I'm definitely not a rake," he said in a sultry voice, putting his hand under her chin and forcing her to meet his eyes.

Emily's heart lurched as she stared into his golden-green eyes that seemed to reflect the grayness of the snow. He's not lying, she thought in a panic, and, once again, was at a complete loss.

"Do you believe me?" he asked, his hand moving from her chin to tuck a stray strand of auburn hair behind her ear.

"Lord Stratford, I'm not eligible, and it's quite obvious to the world that Lady Susan and her mother are expecting an offer posthaste," she said in a wavering voice, aware of nothing save the handsome peer nestled beside her amid a winter storm.

"Lady Susan and her mother can both go to the devil," he said huskily, and leaned forward to kiss her.

Before Emily realized exactly what was happening, she was engulfed in his arms, returning his kisses fervently. Nothing felt more natural than to have her slim form crushed against his greatcoat, or to have her hands run through his thick, wavy hair. It was as if she had been dead for four-and-twenty years, and had suddenly come alive with the touch of his lips.

Unfortunately, Henry's blacks weren't particularly interested in standing in the snow, so, without being bidden, they began a slow walk toward the house.

Nigel broke away from Emily, who was now an even darker shade of red. Goodness, he must think I'm a doxy, she thought, staring at the white fur of her muff.

His hands on the ribbons, Nigel looked over at Emily and sighed. "I know I should really beg your pardon for accosting you, Emily, but the sad fact is that I'm not in the least bit sorry. Do you think that makes me a rake?" he said in a mock-serious voice, and was rewarded with a slight smile.

"I don't know, my lord. Do you often kiss women without their leave?" she said, smiling shyly.

"Not at all. In fact, my father has accused me of being

rather stiff-necked. Would you mind coming back to my country home and reporting that I kissed you while we were on a sleigh ride? It would do wonders for my reputation," he said with a smile, and Emily giggled.

"I think not," she said, a contented glow settling around her.

As they moved toward their starting point, Emily noticed that Susan had left, and that Henry and Harriet were in such a deep coze that they didn't even notice the sleigh approaching.

As they came to a halt, Nigel jumped out of the sleigh, and as he took her delicate hand in his, said softly, "Thank you for your company. The pleasure was very definitely mine."

Emily blushed and looked away, saying, "Thank you for the ride, Lord Stratford," her heart still pounding in her chest.

"Susan dearest, you'd best hurry," Aubrey drawled, leaning his robust form against the corridor wall outside of Emily's room.

From inside the room, Susan grumbled, "I'm not your dearest, and I'm looking as quickly as I can!"

Aubrey sighed, and leafed through the pages of the book he was holding. If any servant actually surprised them, he would simply use the book as a ruse and, he hoped, dispose of them before Susan got caught in the act of acquiring Emily's pendant.

Suddenly, he heard Susan say "Finally!" in triumph, and she appeared moments later, a smirk on her perfect rosebud lips.

"Why, Aubrey, what are you doing here? The library is on the first floor. Let me show you," she said, linking her arm in his.

From below, they could hear the rest of the party entering the house, and they both smiled in satisfaction.

"That was well-timed, Susan," he said, his eyes roving over the milky expanse of breast that her morning gown revealed.

"Wasn't it? Shall we join the others in the parlor?" she replied as they began their descent down the enormous spiral staircase.

"Henry, do you know where I can find Harriet?" Emily asked, glancing around the library, impressed by the fine selection of books.

Henry took out his gold pocket watch and glanced at it casually. "She should be in the nursery having tea with Victoria about this time," he said with a smile.

A slight frown marred Emily's brow. "Really?"

"Quite. I'm sure Harriet and Victoria would enjoy your company, if you're interested," he finished with a slight smile.

Moments later, Emily found herself walking into the nursery, only to find Miss Turner sitting on a stiff-backed mahogany chair near the window, engrossed in some sort of novel.

"Miss Turner? Can you tell me where I can find Harriet? Henry mentioned that she might be up here," Emily asked, tucking a stray strand of her auburn hair behind her ear.

"Oh, Miss Winterhaven, Lady Ashton is giving Victoria her lesson. I'm sure they wouldn't mind your company," she said with a smile, and got off her chair, motioning Emily to follow her.

Miss Turner opened the door on the other side of the room and stood aside as Emily walked in.

And promptly began to giggle.

The room was a miniature parlor, fit for entertaining children. All of the furniture was scaled much smaller, although a few of the mahogany chairs were more adult-sized. It was rather like a fairy tale, Emily thought, smiling at the pair.

Harriet and Victoria were sitting next to each other on a small mahogany couch covered in yellow, with a sofa table in front of them. The table had a full tea service on it, and it appeared that Victoria was in the process of pouring her mother another cup.

"Emily, how wonderful to see you! Won't you join our tea?" Harriet asked, waving Emily over to one of the adult-sized mahogany chairs.

Her face alight from the scene in front of her, Emily settled herself in and asked curiously, "I hope I'm not interrupting anything?"

"Oh no, Aunt Emily," Victoria broke in, trying to pronounce her words very carefully. "Mama is teaching me to be a proper lady, and I'd be ever so grateful if you helped. Would you care for a cup of tea?"

Emily was hard-pressed not to grin at the girl who was, at the age of four, trying desperately hard to act like an adult. "Yes, thank you, Victoria," she said, full of admiration for Harriet. At least she took some interest in her daughter, since many of her neighbors spent most of their time avoiding their children. Of course, she actually didn't expect anything else from Harriet.

"Thank you, Victoria," she replied as Victoria handed her the teacup, which was steaming hot.

"We were discussing Christmas traditions. Shall we test Aunt Emily?" Harriet asked her daughter with a smile.

Victoria's blue eyes brightened. "If you think it would be all right, Mama," she said primly, as if she were actually in a real parlor.

"That was nicely said, dear. Tomorrow we're going to be doing some decorating, with holly and rosemary. Emily, can you tell me why they're both used at the holiday season?" Harriet asked, sipping her tea.

Emily frowned and thought for a moment. "Well, holly is supposed to protect the house from severe weather, thunder, and lightning in the coming year. And rosemary is used in our decoration because Mary laid the Christ child's garments on a rosemary bush," she finished, intrigued by this discussion of Christmas traditions.

"Can you add anything, Victoria?" Harriet asked, watching her daughter intently.

"Some people also put a piece of holly in their beehives, and they say that the bees will sing a song in honor of baby Jesus. And if you put a sprig on your bedpost, you won't have bad dreams," Victoria concluded, sitting as straight as a soldier on the small sofa.

"Very good. And why do we eat apples on Christmas Eve?" Harriet asked.

"Oh, I know, Mama, so that we will all have good health for the following year."

Emily was all smiles, quite enjoying being part of their small family. "Do you know what we do at our home, Victoria?"

Victoria shook her head and Harriet looked on with a smile.

"Well, if a maid asks one of our manservants to bring in the holly and he doesn't, he has the most awful surprise waiting for him. The maid steals his trousers and nails them to the gate in the courtyard, to show the entire household what a spoilsport he is!" she finished with a flourish, and Victoria giggled.

"And not only that," Emily continued, "he isn't allowed to kiss any girls under the mistletoe."

"Gads, I suspect that happened only once. Our manservants would wither away and die if they were banned from using the mistletoe," Harriet lamented, still studying her daughter.

"Mama, are there many more Christmas traditions I should know?"

"Oh Victoria, there are dozens more traditions that you'll learn, but not today. Why don't you bid good afternoon to Aunt Emily and tell Miss Turner it's time for your nap," Harriet suggested, and this time Victoria didn't squabble.

She stood up, looked at Emily with her large, little-girl eyes, and said, "Thank you so much for attending our tea, Aunt Emily. I enjoyed your company very much and would be happy if you would come by again."

Once again, Emily was hard-pressed not to giggle. It was obvious that Victoria was trying very hard to be polite, but a small girl could only muster so much dignity. Finally, Emily said, "Thank you for your invitation, Victoria, and I do hope to join your party in the future."

Both ladies watched in amazement as Victoria walked out of the ridiculous little room as primly as a girl in her first Season.

"Thank you for your patience, Emily. Miss Turner thinks I'm a bit let in the attic for taking the time to teach Victoria her manners myself, but that's how my mama taught me. And I remember the wonderful talks we had, and I want Victoria to remember spending time with me, not just her nanny or governess," Harriet concluded, moving to one of the larger chairs.

"I think it's a bang-up idea. Victoria is a charming girl—you must be very proud of her."

"I am. So tell me, did you enjoy your sleigh ride with Nigel?" Harriet asked with a grin.

Emily actually blushed slightly, and stared at her hands resting in her lap.

"Is he always so . . . solicitous?"

Harriet shrugged slightly. "I don't know. Nigel is usually rather reserved until he feels comfortable with someone. Why?" Harriet asked, leaning forward, anxious to hear the answer.

"He seems to be taking a particular interest in me, when he is supposed to be entangled with Lady Susan. It's rather confusing," Emily explained, still studying her hands.

"I'm fairly certain that Nigel doesn't intend on getting leg-shackled to Lady Susan. And for you, if he's being particularly cordial, then it's probably because he finds your company enjoyable."

"Then he's not making a sport of me, the spinster who's at her last prayers?" Emily asked nervously, her large, tormented eyes meeting Harriet's.

"Nigel is definitely not making a sport of you. Just because he's English doesn't mean that he's necessarily a scoundrel, Emily," she said, a hint of uncertainty creeping into her voice.

Emily sighed. "I'm sorry, Harriet. I just have a hard time trusting unmarried men, I suppose."

"Don't worry, Emily, everything will work out right and tight," Harriet said firmly, her brow marred by the hint of a frown.

"Emily, do you have enough mistletoe for the kissing bough?" Harriet asked, glancing over to her friend.

Emily sat on the recamier on scimitar legs decorated in black-and-gold lacquer, surrounded by mistletoe. Her modestly cut, manilla-brown morning dress with fine Belgian lace at her wrists and neck made her auburn hair glow in the light of the early afternoon. "Yes, I seem to be doing fine," Emily replied, glancing around the parlor.

Harriet, Lady Markston, and Susan were all on the far side of the room, working on the ropes of holly, rosemary, bay, and fir. Lady Susan was in the process of making a number of bright red velvet bows, some of which would be used on her kissing bough. A little ways away from the trio, Miss Turner and Victoria were working on a centerpiece of evergreen branches entwined with ivy and holly for the pianoforte. Actually, Miss Turner was doing most of the work, but she didn't seem to care. Victoria was doing her best to mind her manners, which meant that she was a trifle more subdued than usual. Thankfully, Wellington, her constant canine companion, had been barred from this specific event.

"Do you need any help with the kissing bough, Aunt

Emily?" Victoria asked, glancing toward the mess that Emily had made around her.

And it was quite a sight. She had small piles of dead mistletoe that she had discarded on one side of her, and bits of wire around that. The apples were placed on the sofa table in front of her, along with the candles and ornaments that she would eventually attach. "Oh, I can always use your help, Victoria," she said, and was promptly rewarded by a bright smile.

"Miss Turner, may I go over and help Aunt Emily?" she asked seriously, and Miss Turner immediately agreed, if only to get a brief moment of respite from her duties.

Across the room, Lady Markston watched Emily and Victoria with a look of bitter disdain. "It's so sad," she commented to Harriet, a look of pity on her very obviously painted face.

Harriet frowned, glancing toward Emily and her daughter. "Pardon me, Lady Markston?"

Lady Markston shook her head slightly, causing the magenta turban complete with ostrich feathers to sway back and forth precariously. "It's so sad watching Miss Winterhaven with your daughter. She can't have her own children, so she's trying to be a mother to your little one," she said with a dramatic sigh.

Harriet didn't know quite what to reply. Lady Markston was the best *ton*, but her manners of late were leaving much to be desired. Finally, she took a deep breath and replied, "Emily could have her own children if she wanted, and takes a special interest in Victoria since she is her godmother."

"Of course," Susan chimed in, glancing over at the pair. "I know that Emily is a good friend of yours, but you do have to admit that her options are very limited. She doesn't travel in the best circles, and obviously doesn't have any expectations. It's really quite sad," she concluded with false sincerity.

Before Harriet could raise a word in defense of her friend, Lady Markston immediately said, "I'm so glad that we don't have those problems, dearest. Susan has had dozens of offers in the last few years, but decided to wait for Lord Stratford. He's been dangling after her for ages, and we expect to post the banns any day now," she concluded.

Harriet gritted her teeth, feeling less than charitable toward Lady Markston and her lovely daughter. "Really? Then I wonder why he's been spending so much time with Emily?" she asked before thinking.

Lady Markston tittered girlishly, which was a rather frightening sight. "Silly! Nigel feels sorry for her! He doesn't want her to feel uncomfortable around someone like Susan, who is obviously much more beautiful and cultured," she concluded with gusto.

"Oh Mama, you make me blush," Susan said, and Harriet decided that if the snow didn't stop, she might end up murdering one or both of the ladies.

Luckily, Miss Turner came over to consult with Harriet about Victoria's routine, rescuing her from her dreadful pair of guests.

"Excuse me for a moment, Lady Ashton," Lady Markston abruptly said to Harriet, and waddled across the room. Harriet's eyes widened in horror when she realized that Lady Markston was heading straight for Emily.

"Miss Winterhaven, you're doing the kissing bough all wrong," Lady Markston announced, somehow managing to navigate her rather robust behind onto the recamier next to Emily. "Here, let me show you," she finished, taking the bough out of Emily's hands.

Emily sighed and watched Lady Markston rework the kissing bough patiently, hoping to set a good example for Victoria. When she glanced over at the child, she was looking everywhere but at Lady Markston.

"Here, isn't this better?" she said, handing it back to Emily.

"Yes, thank you, Lady Markston," Emily replied primly, none of the dislike she felt for the lady apparent in her voice.

"You know, it's been pointed out to me that my future son-in-law has been spending a good deal of time with you. I hope

you don't misunderstand his intentions," she said confiden-
tially, a mean little gleam in her cold blue eyes.

"Intentions?" Emily asked, a bit puzzled.

A tight smile appeared on Lady Markston's thin lips. "You
must know of his relationship with Susan. They are planning
to be married after the holidays. If he's spending any time
with you, it's because he's terribly good-hearted and feels
sorry for you."

Emily's heart lurched in her chest. He doesn't like me at
all, her mind cried in agony. He's just making some sort of
game of my feelings, she thought, all of her insecurities suddenly taking over the logical part of her mind. "Really?" she
said in a soft, barely audible voice.

Lady Markston smiled broadly, certain in the knowledge
that her arrow had hit the mark. "I knew you'd understand.
You should really feel quite complimented that a fine gentleman like Lord Stratford has taken any interest in you at
all," she said, patting Emily on the leg reassuringly before she
got up and left.

Victoria looked at Emily, who was obviously quite upset.
"Don't believe her, Aunt Emily," Victoria said, her voice confident.

"Victoria, Lady Markston is a neighbor of your Uncle
Nigel's. I'm sure she knows him quite well, better than you or
I," Emily responded, staring at the kissing bough in her hand
blankly.

"Lady Claredon may want to marry Uncle Nigel, but I
don't think he wants to marry her."

Emily frowned. "And how do you know that, Victoria?"

Victoria looked away and turned away. "I can't say. But I
know Uncle Nigel doesn't like Lady Claredon as much as he
likes you. So please don't let that mean lady make you sad,"
she finished, her blue eyes large and pleading.

"I won't let Lady Markston annoy me, Victoria."

"And Aunt Emily? I don't think that Uncle Nigel is being
nice to you because he feels sorry for you."

Emily smiled softly down at the little girl with the blond hair and the innocent blue eyes. How trusting she is, Emily thought, still very disturbed by Lady Markston's words. "I don't know, Victoria. As you get older, you'll see that men don't always act or think the way ladies do," she finished, a vision of the very attentive Roger Manning in her head. With my luck, Lord Stratford will probably turn out to be as much of a rogue as Roger Manning, she thought, dreading her next meeting with Nigel.

Seven

"Having an impromptu fete was a wonderful idea!" Susan exclaimed, her eyes sparkling as much as the blue topaz necklace that graced her milky white neck.

Harriet smiled docilely, and glanced around their small ballroom. Miss Turner was commissioned to play the piano, and, although the fete only included the house party, everyone seemed to be having a grand time. Of course, she could have invited everyone in the county, but no one could have arrived, since the snow hadn't let up at all. Everyone was so busy with their various Christmas decorations that they failed to notice the fact that their finished decorations were whisked away by the servants as soon as they were completed.

The room was resplendent with garlands of bay, fir, rosemary, and pine twigs offset by perfect red silk bows. The pianoforte sported a large centerpiece of evergreen branches intertwined with ivy and holly, and Emily's kissing bough hung in the center of the room, adorned with candles, red apples, and ornaments. All in all, the room couldn't look more festive, Harriet decided, watching Henry and Lady Markston finish the dance.

"Are you both enjoying the champagne?" Harriet asked, glancing over at Lady Markston, who was now standing silently next to her daughter.

"Why, yes, you've been a most generous host," Susan said politely, her eyes fixed on Nigel. He was in the far corner of the room, talking with Emily.

"It's quite a pity about St. Thomas's Day," Lady Markston droned, her jonquille turban and gown quite out of place in the middle of the winter.

"Yes, it is," Harriet began with a smile. "On St. Thomas's Day we usually have a number of the women coming by to beg for sweets. It's grand fun, and, of course, there's also the wassailing."

Lady Markston nodded in agreement. "We always go wassailing on St. Thomas's Day at our country home—the stories I could tell you! More than one marriage has arisen from the festivities, since some of the gentlemen couldn't quite hold their ale," she finished, a sparkle of mirth in her eyes.

Before Harriet could add any of her own stories, Aubrey appeared at her side, his gold-and-puce-striped waistcoat the most colorful part of the room. "Susan, would you care to dance? I do believe Miss Turner is striking up a waltz," he said amiably, glancing at her slim figure.

For the impromptu ball, Susan had decided upon a cream underdress with an overtunic of pale blue muslin. A blue-and-gold cashmere shawl was draped around her shoulders, and she knew that she was undeniably the most attractive woman in the room. "Of course, Aubrey," she said, strolling out onto the floor with him, despite a look of censure from her mother.

"Can I get you a drink, Emily?" Nigel asked, gazing soulfully into her luminescent green eyes.

Emily smiled slightly and looked down at her gloved hands. "You'll think me the greatest widgeon, Lord Stratford," she began, and he immediately said, "Nigel." She blushed and glanced over at his shining black Hessians, desperately looking for something to focus on. "You'll think me the greatest widgeon, Nigel," she began again, "but I don't care for champagne. It gives me the most dreadful headache," she admitted shyly.

Nigel's eyes roamed over her svelte figure. She was wearing a bottle-green satin gown cut in the Grecian style that fell into folds about her slender form. A gauzy scarf of pale green was draped around her shoulders, and made her eyes seem the most improbable shade of green. "I confess, Emily, that champagne isn't a favorite of mine, either. I don't think anyone else here has the same aversion, though," he commented, watching Susan drink what must have been her eighth glass.

"I'd agree completely, but I don't doubt that was Harriet's intention. Everyone was rather on edge today, and I think she wanted to make her guests . . . relax a bit more," Emily finished, her eyes lingering on Nigel's clothes.

Tonight he wore a Spanish blue coat with a white waistcoat and black pantaloons over white silk socks. His white cravat was carefully tied, and his wild black locks had been coaxed into something that might have resembled the Brutus style, had his hair been shorter. His golden eyes focused solely on Emily, and she squirmed under his gaze.

"You look enchanting tonight," Nigel commented in the soft, lover-like tone he used when he was alone with her, and she turned an even deeper shade of red.

Emily looked up and met his eyes. "You'd best watch what you say, my lord, or your fiancée might take exception," she said, glancing over toward Susan.

"For an intelligent female, you certainly seem a bit cork-brained concerning Susan, if you don't mind me saying so. I am not and do not plan to be married to Lady Susan Claredon," he finished, and the severity in his voice made Emily firmly believe his declaration.

"Then I would suggest you speak with Lady Markston. She believes your nuptials are forthcoming," Emily said, and was rewarded by a scowl.

"Lady Markston is a bedlamite. She can keep claiming that I'm going to offer for Susan, but that won't make it happen. Would you like to waltz?" he said suddenly, noticing that Miss Turner had once again begun his dance of choice.

"I'm not the most graceful dancer," Emily admitted reluctantly.

He stood up and held his hand out for her. "It doesn't matter," he replied, and led her out to the floor.

"Look at them," Lady Markston hissed, taking the glass of champagne out of her daughter's hand.

Susan pouted. "I can have another glass of champagne if I want," she said, sounding like a spoiled child deprived of a sweet.

"You've had quite enough. Your future husband is out waltzing with a nobody and all you're doing about it is consuming more champagne than anyone else in the room! You're a grave disappointment, Susan," her mother said in dire tones, disapproval etched on her heavily painted face.

"Oh Mama, he's just toying with her. Nigel will propose—don't get on your high horse," Susan said, glancing over at Aubrey. He met her eyes across the room and smiled lazily at her.

"I think not. And don't think I don't know about the flirtation you've set up with Lord Langely. He's a rake if I ever saw one, and I most certainly don't approve of his interest."

"Yes, Mama," Susan sighed, suddenly terribly bored with this coze with her mother.

"And, at the earliest opportunity, I do expect you to remind Nigel of his duties. He's neglecting you shamelessly for that *du vieux temps* spinster and I don't like it," Lady Markston concluded, and Susan sighed, resignation written on her face.

Emily was in heaven. Nigel's strong arm was wrapped around her a trifle too tightly for propriety, but she didn't really care. The waltz Miss Turner was playing wafted through her mind, and she felt incredibly relaxed and alive at the same time.

"You're a wonderful dancer," Nigel whispered, holding her even closer.

Emily blushed. "You're giving me Spanish coin, Nigel. I'm probably the least accomplished dancer here, save Victoria."

"I think not. I can't recall a time I've enjoyed a waltz more," he said in a sultry voice, his hazel eyes gazing passionately at her.

"You know, Harriet mentioned that Henry's cousin Aubrey had something of a reputation around Town, but I think she purposely forgot to tell me that you're also quite the rake," she said, trying to keep her voice light and humorous.

Nigel chuckled and led her over toward their chairs as the waltz ended. "I must have you speak with my father. He'd be proud to hear that such a lovely young woman thought I was a rake," he said, his arm holding onto her as if his life depended on it.

Before Emily could reply, Susan appeared next to the pair, a pout on her perfect rosebud lips.

"Nigel, you've been most inattentive this evening," she exclaimed, and playfully hit him on the arm with her fan. "I demand that you dance with me," she said, licking her lips sensually.

Nigel raised an eyebrow but refused to relinquish Emily's arm. "I'm not as young as I used to be, Susan. I was rather looking forward to sitting out a set," he replied sardonically.

"Wonderful! Mama has some matters she wants to discuss with you," she exclaimed, and skillfully took Nigel's arm and began to lead him over to her mother.

Emily was hard-pressed not to giggle as Nigel mouthed an "I'm sorry," to her, as he left her standing in front of the lyre-backed mahogany chairs that sat against the ballroom walls.

"Would you care for some company?" a voice behind her asked, and Emily turned around in surprise. Aubrey was standing behind her, motioning to a chair. "Unless you'd care to dance," he said with a smile.

"I think I'll sit out this set," she replied, taking the seat

Aubrey offered and watching Henry and Harriet on the dance floor.

"I'm glad you're presently without a partner. I was afraid I was going to have to dance with Lady Markston," Aubrey said with an easy smile.

"Yes, I can see where that prospect might be a trifle daunting," she replied.

They both glanced casually around the room, and Aubrey finally commented, "I'll bet you a guinea that they don't get married."

Emily frowned. "Who? Nigel and Susan?"

"Precisely. Lady Markston is eager for the match since their property is adjacent. It's obvious that the marriage would be a misalliance, especially since Nigel seems to have developed a *tendre* for you," he concluded, and Emily's eyes widened in shock.

"A *tendre?* For me? Surely you must be wrong," she said in a soft voice, hoping that he wasn't aware that she was quite taken with Nigel.

"No, it's quite obvious, but you needn't worry. Stratford has a sterling reputation—won't try to take advantage of you or any such thing," Aubrey said casually.

Emily was speechless. Does Nigel really have a *tendre* for me? she thought, before immediately dismissing the idea as ridiculous. Peers of the realm don't court spinsters who are connected to trade unless they're polite. Very, very polite, she decided, her mind once again in a whirl.

Later that evening, after the ladies as well as Aubrey had retired, Nigel and Henry sat alone in the library, in front of the blazing fireplace.

As they sipped their respective glasses of brandy, Henry casually remarked, "Harriet wanted me to speak to you about Miss Winterhaven, Nigel."

Nigel frowned and studied his friend. Henry seemed ill at ease, and looked everywhere but at him. "Why?"

Henry continued to squirm. "Your preference for Emily has been noticed, and there have been comments made," he said vaguely, staring into the blazing embers.

"Commented on? By whom? It's no one's business what I do and who I do it with," Nigel proclaimed, his blood boiling. How dare anyone comment on my relationship with Emily, he thought angrily.

"That's not the point. It's been suggested that you're simply toying with her, since she is a spinster with no expectations, or that you're trying to get into her good graces so she'll sell you the pendant," Henry replied calmly.

"Is that what you and Harriet think? That I'm simply using Emily for my own devices?"

Henry looked into the fire. "I don't know, Nigel. Harriet and I adore Emily, but you have to admit, she isn't the type to attract the attention of the Earl of Stratford, or any other peer, for that matter."

Nigel leaned over toward Henry, his hands white around the snifter of brandy. "You know, Henry, I could call you out for making that sort of remark," he said between clenched teeth.

"Nigel, there's no need for that!" Henry exclaimed, beginning to panic. "I certainly didn't mean to slander your character—I just wanted to find out what was going on with Emily. She's practically a member of our family, and, since she is alone at our home, I feel that it's my responsibility to look after her," he finished hastily.

Nigel leaned back in his chair and sighed. "I understand, Henry. I've just been feeling waspish ever since the weather became so dashed terrible and Susan Claredon and her ghastly mother appeared. And as for your question, no, I'm not simply being nice to Emily because I feel sorry for her, since I don't particularly pity her," he concluded, his grip on his brandy loosening a bit.

"Are you trying to get in her good graces so you can get the pendant back? Harriet was terribly concerned about that—that's why I'm asking," Henry asked nervously.

"No, to be honest, I'd forgotten the dashed pendant," he confessed, finally beginning to relax.

A slow smile spread over Henry's regular features. "That's good to hear. You know, if you continue to pay court to her, there's every chance that she'll develop a *tendre* for you, and I wouldn't want to see Emily hurt," he finished in a more serious tone.

Nigel envisioned Emily willingly in his arms, her breath in his ear. "My intentions are perfectly respectable," he said in a strange tone, then added with a grin, "Would you rather have me leg-shackled to Susan Claredon? She's becoming more of a harpy as the minutes pass."

"That is quite the understatement. She appears pleasant enough, but is still tied to her mother's apron strings. Why were you courting her in the first place?"

A sigh escaped Nigel. "It wasn't actually planned. We just ended up at many of the same entertainments, and I began spending time with her since I've known her since she's been in the schoolroom. And it kept my father from badgering me about finding a suitable female to bring into the Manning family," he explained.

Henry nodded. "It happens all of the time. That's how Haversham got caught in the parson's mousetrap. One moment he was spending time with a childhood friend, the next moment her family was expecting him to post the banns. Unfortunately, he couldn't squirm out of it, and she wouldn't cry off, so now they're both miserable."

"I will not find myself leg-shackled to Susan—you can enter that in the betting books at White's, no matter what her family might be expecting."

Henry smiled gently. "That's good to hear. She would make a difficult wife. Now Emily, she's a different matter entirely. She might be of a certain age and the veriest of bluestockings, but she will be a splendid wife to some lucky cove," he proclaimed heartily.

Nigel gazed into the fire and thought of Emily and a passel of dark-haired children at her feet. "Yes, she would," he said in a soft voice, lost in his daydreams.

"Aunt Emily, can I come in?" a small voice asked from the other side of her partially closed wooden door.

Emily quickly placed the package that was going to Victoria on Christmas morning into the top drawer of the zebrawood escritoire and replied, "Of course, Victoria."

Victoria peered around the door and saw Emily, wearing a long sleeved merino gown of Devonshire brown, sitting at the escritoire on the far side of the room facing the window. She closed the door behind her and bounced over to Emily, asking pertly, "What are you doing?"

Emily smiled down at her. Victoria was, for now, the daughter she always wanted, but never quite managed to have. "Silly, what do you think I'm doing?" she replied.

Victoria glanced around the top of the writing table. There was a pair of scissors, a large variety of ribbons in red, white, green, and gold, and colored tissue paper. "Are you wrapping presents?" she asked shyly.

"You guessed my secret," Emily replied, as Victoria sat down on the freshly made bed behind her.

"What are you wrapping now?" Victoria asked, straining to see what Emily was putting in the red paper.

"A gift for Lady Markston, or at least that's who I think I'll be giving it to, since I don't think the snow is going to end anytime soon."

Victoria nodded her head in agreement. "I wish it would stop snowing and Lady Markston and Lady Claredon could leave. I don't like them very much," she finished, a bit hesitantly.

Emily made a slight clucking noise. "Victoria, you know

you should mind your tongue. It's not polite to talk about people you don't care for," she admonished, putting the final touch on the package.

"I'm sorry," Victoria said and glanced over at Emily's dressing table. "Why is there a rose on your dressing table, Aunt Emily?" she ask curiously.

Emily continued wrapping her presents and desperately hoped that Victoria didn't notice her blush. "It's another old Christmas tradition. Would you like to hear about it?"

"All right."

"Well," Emily began, "on Midsummer's Day an unmarried young lady is supposed to pick a rose. She saves the rose until Christmas morning, and if she wears it to church, her future husband will come to take it from her," she concluded, feeling dashed silly for following such an absurd tradition.

"But what if someone she doesn't like tries to take it from her? Will she still marry him?" Victoria asked curiously.

Emily smiled. "I don't know, Victoria. This is the first time I've ever saved the rose. I think a smart lady will avoid any gentleman she doesn't like at church, so then she won't have to end up leg-shackled to him," she concluded with a chuckle.

Victoria giggled and replied, "Mama hasn't told me that story yet. But today she told me about the Twelfth Night cake."

"Oh, really. What did she tell you about it?" Emily asked, placing her next gift, a belcher handkerchief for Aubrey, in a small box.

"She told me what everything in the cake means."

"Well, let's see how much you remember. What does it mean if you get the ring?"

Victoria giggled. "It means that you're going to get married. And the thimble means patience, and the button means faithfulness," she proclaimed, quite proud of herself.

"Why, you certainly remembered your lessons well. What else did your mama tell you about?" she asked, wrapping the box up in golden paper.

"She told me about the Yule log. Mama said we're very lucky because this year our Yule log is made of ash."

"And did she tell you why a Yule log made of ash is so special?" Emily asked, reaching for her next gift. This time it was a small silver comb for Lady Susan. I hope I won't have to present this gift, either, she thought, inwardly agreeing with Victoria's assessment of both ladies.

"Mama says an ash Yule log is best because Mary washed and dressed the baby Jesus for the first time by the firelight of an ash tree. Our Yule log is in the barn—Mama said we'll bring it in Christmas Eve. That's in two days!" Victoria exclaimed.

A slight cough, then a high-pitched bark interrupted their coze.

"Victoria, see who's at the door," Emily asked, covering the remaining presents on the escritoire with the tissue paper.

Victoria opened the door cautiously and cried, "Uncle Nigel! You found Wellington!"

Emily turned around in her seat, only to find Nigel standing at her door, Wellington squirming happily in his arms.

"I'm sorry to bother you, Emily, but Harriet mentioned that Wellington had been missing, and I accidentally found him locked in my bedroom. I thought I'd return him to Victoria," he finished, his eyes raking over her slender form.

Wellington continued to lick his chin, which caused him to blush most becomingly, so he handed the puppy over to Victoria.

"He likes you, Uncle Nigel, just like Aunt Emily. Maybe you should have a puppy, too!" Victoria announced.

"I have my own dog at home, Victoria. Do you have your own beast at home, Emily?" he asked casually.

Emily smiled at the handsome peer. "No—I've always wanted some sort of pet, but we travel so much that I've never really had the opportunity to have my own," she explained, noticing how gentle Nigel had been with the puppy, and how well he treated Victoria.

"I've had them all of my life, as well as the odd and assorted cat," Nigel explained, his eyes never leaving Emily.

Before Emily could reply, Victoria eagerly asked, "Could you help me train Wellington, Uncle Nigel? He's ever so smart, but I don't know what to do and neither does Miss Turner."

A warm, gentle smile flitted across Nigel's features. "Of course, Victoria, but you must promise me something."

"Anything," she replied, a wide smile on her innocent face.

"You must promise to tell me immediately if Lady Markston or Lady Claredon appear so I can, well, avoid speaking to them," he replied wryly.

Victoria giggled. "I promise, Uncle Nigel. I don't really care for them, either, but Aunt Emily says it's not proper to say so."

Nigel glanced over at Emily, who was blushing delicately. "Your Aunt Emily is perfectly right, but you see, I don't have particularly good manners, so I can admit it," he replied with a rakish grin.

Before Emily could give him a proper dressing-down in front of Victoria, he took Victoria's hand and casually remarked, "I'll see you at supper, Emily."

You are a scamp, Lord Stratford, Emily thought with a smile. And yes, I will see you at dinner and reprimand you for your odious manners in front of Victoria, she decided, wrapping her last present.

She still hadn't chosen a gift for Nigel, and was in quite a quandary. In her heart, she wanted to give him something personal and meaningful, but that wouldn't be the thing, since they really weren't that closely connected. And what does one get an earl who has everything he could possibly want?

Unfortunately, Emily didn't get the chance to give Nigel a proper dressing-down at dinner. From what Henry reported, Nigel had a bad scone and was currently in bed, recovering from its effects. Emily had no idea how one had a bad scone, and from the other side of the table, heard Harriet mutter the word "curse" to Henry. It was most curious, she thought, thoroughly disappointed that she wasn't going to be seeing Nigel that evening.

It was well past midnight when Emily sat alone in the darkened ballroom, the candelabra on the pianoforte her only light. She couldn't sleep, and was playing to relax a trifle, since she seemed to be nervous for no apparent reason.

She had just finished one of her own compositions, a desolate piece she wrote after the Roger Manning episode, when a voice at the door said, "You're quite an accomplished musician, Emily. I think I'm more impressed each time I hear you play," Nigel said.

Emily turned around and saw him standing in the shadows of the doorway, expectantly waiting for her reply. "Thank you, Nigel. I hope my playing didn't disturb you," she said softly.

Nigel walked into the room, and brought one of the numerous mahogany chairs next to the pianoforte. "Not at all. I wasn't feeling quite the thing this evening—in fact, I dozed for a while. I woke up a short time ago, and everyone else in the house is asleep, save my valet. I noticed the light from my bedroom window, and thought I'd investigate," he said, gazing intently at her ethereal form.

"I couldn't sleep, and playing usually relaxes me," Emily explained with a blush.

Nigel didn't seem to notice her embarrassment. He was busy watching the moonlight dance off her long auburn hair that hung in slight waves around her shoulders. "Yes, it used to relax me, too," he replied, entranced with the vision sitting casually in front of him.

Emily glanced over at Nigel, who looked dashed handsome in his black breeches and white shirt. He even had on a pair of brown slippers, she noted with a smile. His long, wavy black hair was wild and uncombed, but it made him look exotic somehow, like a Gypsy, she thought. "Are you feeling more the thing?" she asked softly.

"Yes, something in the scone I ate didn't agree with me at all," he replied, studying the long, graceful fingers that rested in her lap.

For some strange reason, Emily could not think of a thing to say. Nigel was looking at her with an odd expression on his face, one that made her excited and nervous all at the same time. So finally, after a long silence, she asked, "Are you looking forward to the Christmas holiday?"

Nigel smiled casually. "I was, before Susan and Lady Markston appeared."

"Yes, they can be a trial. Luckily I can disappear back into my little world and never encounter either of them again," she replied, then blushed at the audacity of her words.

"I envy you, Emily. As our nearest neighbor, it's not as easy for me to avoid them," he replied, then quickly added, "I really don't want to blither on about them. Tell me, what do you want for Christmas?"

Emily looked away as a vision of a family came into her head, with children, a dog, a cat, and a husband. That's what I want for Christmas, she thought desperately, certain that it would never happen. Not at the advanced age of four-and-twenty. "I don't know if I want anything in particular, Nigel. I received a wonderful gift from my grandfather before I came to see Harriet, though," she said, hoping to get her mind off the depressing subject of her lack of marital prospects.

"Oh really? What was it?" Nigel asked, watching the shadows from the candlelight flicker across her face.

"Well, I should tell you my grandfather is my only claim to respectability and the only reason I'm accepted in some of the better houses. He's the Marquess of Rawlins, and even though he's a bit crusty, he's the best grandfather anyone could ask for," she began, while Nigel's eyes widened in horror. "Before I left, I received the most wonderful gift from him. He picked it up in London—it's a pendant in the shape of a mermaid. It's a queer piece, but I've come to adore it, since I know Grandpapa went through quite a search to find it for me," she concluded with a smile.

"A mermaid? How unusual," he replied in a choked voice. "Would you ever sell the mermaid, say, for another pendant that was more attractive?" he asked casually, and unconsciously held his breath, waiting pensively for her answer.

Eight

"Sell my pendant? Of course not," Emily exclaimed with a frown.

Nigel sighed and shrugged. "I was just curious. I know someone who collects unusual jewelry, and would be interested in something like your mermaid. I didn't realize you were so attached to it," he replied lamely, with only one thing on his mind. The Manning Curse. He was going to have bad luck until the end of his days because he didn't have it in his heart to convince Emily to sell a gift from her beloved grandfather.

Emily tucked a long, wavy strand of hair behind her ear. "It would devastate Grandfather if I sold his gift," she replied, gazing into the flickering lights of the candelabra.

She is so incredibly beautiful, Nigel thought, studying the way the shadows fell across her high cheekbones. She doesn't care about the money she could get for the pendant, but is more concerned about her grandfather's feelings, he mused, unable to take his eyes from her shadowy figure.

Emily began to play again, a soft, lingering song of love and desperation. Her fingers glided over the ivory keys, and Nigel felt his heart lurch into his throat as he realized that he was beginning to fall in love with Miss Emily Winterhaven, a female who was firmly on the shelf. And completely right for him.

When the song reached its pinnacle, he held his breath in

awe of her talent. The silence that followed was deafening until he reached over and took her hand in his.

"You're quite a remarkable woman, Emily Winterhaven," he began in a husky voice. "Your talent is surpassed only by the kindness of your heart," he finished passionately.

Emily looked down at the ivory keys, at a complete loss for words. Her delicate mouth opened for a moment, as if she wanted to say something, but no words came out. She just gazed rapturously at him in the candlelight, her eyes large and innocent.

Nigel raised her long, delicate fingers to his lips and gently kissed her soft, porcelain skin. "I bid you good evening, dearest Emily, since I'll do much more than kiss your hand if I stay," he said huskily, gazing into the liquid pools of her eyes.

He strode rapidly out of the ballroom, his heart welling up into his throat. Nigel was positively entranced by the sole female who he was trying to connive into selling the mermaid. The Manning Curse strikes again, he thought ironically, slamming his bedroom door.

"Eliza, I'd like to wear the mermaid pendant today," Emily said, deciding that it would look perfect against her bottle-green velvet morning dress.

Eliza, being the efficient abigail that she was, quickly walked over to the portmanteau where she kept Emily's jewelry, and riffled through the satin case.

The weather had turned warmer, and now the snow was being temporarily replaced by freezing rain which, to Emily, meant that she would have to suffer through one more family meal with Susan and her mother. Which was not the most pleasant task, she decided, frowning at Eliza.

"Isn't it there?" Emily asked curiously, walking up behind Eliza.

"I can't find it, and I know it was there. I keep all of your jewels together, Miss Emily," Eliza replied in alarm. She continued riffling through the portmanteau, but to no avail.

"Then it has to be here somewhere. I'll help you look," Emily said calmly, not in the least bit concerned. Eliza was wonderfully conscientious, and Emily was certain it was just temporarily misplaced.

For the next hour, the pair searched every inch of the room for the elusive pendant. There was no trace of the mermaid pendant. Eliza was near tears. Emily was in a full-fledged panic.

Harriet, Henry, and Aubrey were in the breakfast room, enjoying a wide variety of morning fare. The enormous mahogany sideboard was filled with kippers, kidneys, sweet omelets, bacon, and poached eggs, their scents wafting alluringly out toward Emily.

She didn't notice them. Instead, she walked into the room, and, ignoring everyone, announced, "Harriet, I must have a word with you."

Harriet looked up from her poached eggs with a slight frown. "Of course, Emily," she said softly, following her friend into the hall.

"My pendant is missing. The mermaid is missing," Emily said in hushed tones, glancing suspiciously down the hallway.

Harriet relaxed a trifle, her panic subsiding. "You probably just misplaced it. Would you like me to have my abigail help you search your room?" she said in a concerned voice.

"Harriet, it's not in my room. That's why I wasn't at breakfast. Eliza and I have spent the past hour and a quarter searching the room. It's not there," Emily replied stubbornly, her eyes large and pleading.

The panic that filled Harriet gradually began to return. At first, she suspected that Emily had some sort of unpleasant confrontation with Susan or Lady Markston. But nothing like this had ever crossed her mind. "Are you sure? It couldn't have fallen off the day you showed it to me?" Harriet asked nervously, wringing her hands.

Emily shook her head. "I saw Eliza put it away that day, and I haven't worn any jewelry since."

"Is Eliza . . . trustworthy?" Harriet said hesitantly, pushing a stray lock of blond hair away from her face. The idea that the pendant was stolen was preposterous.

"Without a doubt. Eliza was born into our household, and it would be an insult to question her integrity!" Emily said passionately, then added, "And I suppose you have a house full of loyal retainers?"

Harriet nodded. "Yes."

The pair stared at each other until Harriet suggested, "Let me speak with Henry about this. If the pendant has been stolen, the thief is still in the house. You know no one has been out since this atrocious weather has hit," Harriet explained, valiantly trying to keep her wits about her.

"That's true. Talk to Henry and see what he says. I'll just die if Grandpapa's gift has been stolen," Emily said with uncharacteristic drama, and Harriet felt as if someone had hit her.

There was only one person in her home who was motivated to steal Emily's mermaid. Nigel.

As Henry approached Nigel's bedroom, he heard quite a flurry of activity, followed by a rather impolite curse. A very loud, impolite curse that involved Nigel's valet doing something with that (curse) animal.

Henry steeled himself for the inevitable confrontation, and knocked on the oak door.

"One moment," Nigel's valet said, and Henry could hear quite a bit of movement on the other side of the door.

Moments later, Hughes, Nigel's valet, opened the door a crack. To Henry's utter astonishment, he was holding Victoria's energetic puppy Wellington in his capable arms. Wellington wagged his tail at the sight of Henry, who cautiously asked, "Is Nigel available for a word?"

From inside the room, Henry heard Nigel utter another epithet before replying, "Yes, Hughes, let Henry in and be sure to get rid of that infernal animal!"

Hughes opened the door for Henry to enter, and Henry was surprised to find Nigel standing in a blue brocaded dressing gown. Nigel wasn't the earliest riser in the house, but it was past noon and he usually made an appearance downstairs by that time.

As Hughes disappeared with Wellington in his arms, Henry discovered something else. On the far side of the room, all of Nigel's shoes were haphazardly strewn across the floor. And, as Henry walked over to them, he noticed that they all bore the impressions of Wellington's teeth. "Gads, don't tell me that Wellington has developed a penchant for chewing shoes," Henry remarked with a frown.

Nigel sighed and leaned against the steel dressing table with brass and copper ornaments. "Why, yes, he actually *has* developed a taste for my footwear," Nigel said with a sigh. "Every single pair, in fact."

Henry stood gaping at the shoes in disbelief. Nigel was having the most unusual streak of bad luck. "So all of your shoes are ruined?"

"Yes, that's essentially the problem of the day. Until the next chapter in the ongoing saga of the Manning Curse," he said dispiritedly, a look of complete disgust on his face.

Henry casually walked over to the dressing table and pulled the chair away. "Do you mind if I have a seat?"

"Not at all," Nigel said, staring at all of his shoes. His ruined shoes. And boots. And slippers. "Do you know what's ironic, Henry? I spoke with Emily last night about the pendant and she said she wouldn't part with it for the world. And I really don't care. She's much more attached to the damned thing than I ever was," he finished.

Henry was now completely confused. "You told Emily you wanted to buy it? And the curse? You told her about the Manning Curse?" he asked in disbelief.

Nigel shook his head. "No, I was much more subtle than that. I just struck up a conversation and she happened to mention the mermaid. I mentioned that I know of someone who would be interested in purchasing it, and she balked like an untrained horse," he said, then paused. "And it really doesn't matter any longer. Roger caused this mess, so let him find his way out of it. I wish Emily joy of the mermaid," he concluded, looking rather haggard in the harsh afternoon light.

"So you're giving up?" Henry asked, still not quite sure what was going on.

"Most assuredly. If my father and Roger are determined to retrieve the pendant, they both have my blessings. I'll be too busy refurbishing my shoes to bother with it," he replied with a smile.

Henry was now completely confused. "Then you don't have the pendant?"

Nigel frowned, his brows furrowing together. "No, of course not. Why would I have it?"

"Emily came downstairs to breakfast in a panic this morning. The pendant is missing. Emily and her abigail searched the room, then Harriet recruited her abigail and a few maids. It's gone," he concluded, hoping Nigel wouldn't jump to the wrong conclusion.

Nigel began to pace the room. "So naturally you and Harriet thought that I nabbed it."

Henry sighed. Nigel had immediately jumped to the wrong conclusion. Well, not entirely the wrong conclusion, he thought wryly. "No, not really. Harriet wanted me to speak with you about it, that's all."

"I don't have it. In fact, I've never even seen the devilish thing. It's missing?"

"Yes," Henry began, stretching his long legs out in front of him as Nigel returned to the dressing table. "Her abigail admits she hasn't even looked at Emily's jewels for a few days, so they have no idea how long it's been gone. The mystery is that she had other, more valuable pieces in the same place, and they weren't touched. Someone was after the mermaid."

Nigel frowned. "So you both immediately thought that I was the culprit. That's not a very good compliment to my character, Henry," he said in disgust.

Henry flushed in embarrassment. "No, Nigel, it's not like that at all."

Nigel stared at his shoes strewn across the floor and said nothing for a long while. Finally he looked Henry in the eyes and said, "Henry, I have the deepest respect for Emily. She's a charming, attractive young woman with a kind heart. I could never intentionally hurt her," he said in a somber tone.

Henry studied the grave look in Nigel's eyes and realized two very important facts. First of all, Nigel didn't steal the mermaid, which was evidenced by the fact that he was still under the supposed curse. The fact that Nigel didn't have the mermaid was a vast relief to Henry, who was now able to digest the second fact he had learned that afternoon.

Nigel's eyes practically glazed over when he spoke of Emily. In fact, Henry was certain that Nigel had developed a full-fledged *tendre* for her. Which was inevitable, since they had so much in common. And Emily did look dashed attractive and charming next to Susan Claredon.

"So I suppose I'm going to have to ask for your help. I promised Harriet I'd find the mermaid for Emily," Henry said, then added, "How are your detective skills?"

"As good as anyone's, I suppose. Do you still think it's in the house?" he asked curiously, his golden eyes fixed on Henry.

"My guess is yes. As far as I know, none of the servants has left the house since the day Aubrey arrived. Emily's abigail remembers seeing it the first day of the snowstorm, but hasn't seen it since," Henry finished.

A very thoughtful expression appeared on Nigel's face. "What have you told Emily?"

"Nothing. We've convinced her to wait until the storm

breaks to call the authorities. I hope we'll be able to keep everyone in the house until we can find it," Henry concluded.

"And she's agreed?"

"For now. I'm planning on talking to all of my servants and making sure that they discreetly search all of the rooms until the mermaid is returned to its rightful owner," Henry said, rising from his seat and moving toward the door.

"I'll help in any way I can," Nigel said, following him to the door.

Henry looked over at the pile of shoes. "For now, just let me know if you hear anything about it," he said, and added with a smile, "I'll have my valet come over with some shoes, since you do seem to be in dire straits."

Nigel smiled back, his anger completely gone. "I would appreciate that. And please try to keep Wellington out of my room," he asked with a grin.

"I'll try," Henry replied, and as he walked down the hall one thought nagged at his brain. Who would want to steal Emily's mermaid?

"We're almost in the house, my lord," Henry's butler Coverdail announced, as the entire party dragged the enormous ash Yule log across the glistening oak floor.

"Henry, couldn't you have chosen a closer room? Possibly the library?" Aubrey asked, as they all heaved the log toward the parlor.

"Yes, yes, I know. Blame Harriet—she's the one who found the ash tree," Henry replied, his face beet-red from the strain.

"I think it's great fun," Susan announced as she adjusted the bright yellow plumes on her brown velvet bonnet. It matched her pelisse perfectly, and, as usual, Susan was the epitome of the fashionable London lady.

Lady Markston, who had an unfortunate back injury that prevented her from doing any sort of lifting, helped guide the enormous log into the parlor. "Just a bit more to the right, then you'll be in the door," she announced, standing far away from the straining men and ladies.

Harriet, determined that the holiday was going to be festive no matter who was at her house, had turned the parlor into a veritable forest of evergreen, holly, mistletoe, ivy, and red silk bows in every corner. The mantel was adorned with thick garlands of bay, fir, rosemary, and pine twigs accented with enormous red velvet and silk ribbons. Small cakes hung from the ceiling, just waiting for the festivities after the lighting of the Yule log. A kissing bough, much larger than the one Emily made, was positioned in the center of the room, just waiting for its candles to be lit; a veritable feast sat on the rosewood side table supported by ormolu mounts. Negus, "rack" punch, and the traditional wassail were the preferred beverages, and Harriet expected her guests to indulge themselves. A wide range of subtleties shaped like animals, ships, castles, and the Wise Men sat next to the drinks, as did mince pies, plum pudding, and a bowl of fresh apples.

As the merry group huffed and puffed and finally forced the log into the fireplace, Henry looked around the room, as if he were searching for someone. Finally he spotted Nigel on the far side of the room, frowning prodigiously at Emily, who was definitely subdued this evening.

"Nigel, I need your assistance," Henry called, as he waved the servants out of the room.

Nigel frowned even more. "Yes?"

Henry walked over to the sideboard and picked up the waiting bottle of wine. "I was wondering if you would do the honors," he asked, holding out the bottle of wine.

This was the first time that Nigel had spent the holidays with Harriet and Henry, and he fully expected Henry to do the traditional prayer. So Henry's request was more than a slight surprise. "You want me to do the prayer?" he asked incredulously.

From the other side of the room, Harriet piped in and added, "Nigel, you're a full nine months older than Henry, so it is your duty as the oldest member of our household. And I do think you'd do a much better job of it than Stephen, our head groom. At five-and-sixty he's literally the oldest member of the household, but I don't know if he could come up with an appropriate prayer," she finished, her blue eyes twinkling.

"Oh yes, Nigel, please say the Yule prayer," Susan chimed in, batting her eyelashes flirtatiously.

Nigel smiled slightly and replied, "I suppose I have no choice," and took the bottle of French wine out of Henry's hands.

Henry and Nigel took their respective places at opposite sides of the fire screen, and the rest of the party gathered around them, Emily shyly hugging the far side of the room.

"Lord, in the coming year, we ask you to bestow the gifts of health, wealth, and happiness to all of your humble servants gathered here tonight," Nigel intoned, and poured the wine three times on the log, completing the traditional Yule prayer.

Henry then lit the large ember left from last year's log and leaned over, igniting the newly blessed log. The new Yule log, which had been chosen months earlier and had been sitting in the barn, drying out, lit up immediately, dazzling the onlookers.

And so the impromptu Christmas Eve gathering began. Henry, determined that everyone was going to have a jolly good time, made sure that every glass was filled to the brim with wassail (which of course included a hearty portion of wine) and the small party was soon enlivened with a variety of games.

Aubrey, much to everyone's amazement, showed a definite penchant for diving for apples, and, as his prize, stole a kiss from Susan under the mistletoe. He also received a dark look from Lady Markston, who was obviously displeased with his behavior.

Harriet and Lady Markston were the winners of the sack

races, and everyone was glad to see that Lady Markston didn't censure the traditional family games. In fact, she seemed to enjoy the festivities as much as everyone else. But then she did drink a prodigious amount of wassail, which might have had something to do with her enthusiasm.

Henry could tell that Emily was trying her hardest to actually enjoy Christmas Eve, but her heart didn't seem to be in the festivities. But she still participated in every game, even though her mood was very subdued. It was obvious to him that she was very blue-deviled about her pendant.

It also surprised Henry that Nigel was patently ignoring Emily, instead attending to Susan's every whim. Actually, the only person who appeared to be more subdued than Emily was Aubrey. Henry watched in interest as Aubrey's eyes remained fixed to Susan.

"Come on, Emily, we're going to eat the cakes. Aren't you going to join in?" Harriet cajoled, a worried look haunting her blue eyes.

Emily smiled hesitantly. "I don't know if I'm really up to this, Harriet," she explained, her burgundy velvet gown making her look a trifle pale in the candlelight.

"You have to play, Emily," Henry explained, and gently took her arm, placing her under one of the small cakes hanging from the ceiling, and tying her hands behind her back with an old scarf.

"All right," she replied with a smile, glancing across the room at Nigel. He was having a private coze with Susan, who was standing under a cake beside him.

"Does everyone have their hands tied?" Henry asked, and a chorus of yesses was heard. "Then we'll start at the count of three. One, two, three!" he exclaimed, and everyone began their attempt at eating the cakes in front of them.

Emily was completely disinterested in the game, and just calmly stood nibbling her cake, a look of slight boredom on her pale features. Strangely enough, Emily's cake wasn't swinging back and forth like the rest. It stayed fairly still as she nibbled delicately at it, while the others struggled with their cakes.

"We have a winner!" Henry announced triumphantly, walking over to Emily, a glow of satisfaction on his face.

Emily looked over at him, a bit dazed. "I can't be the winner," she said softly. "I wasn't even trying."

Henry smiled indulgently at her. "Nonetheless, you are the winner. What would you like as your prize? A kiss under the mistletoe perhaps?" he asked, and there were giggles heard at the far side of the room. "Or do you fancy something else?" Henry asked, his brown eyes dancing with mirth.

Emily was silent as a dozen expressions flashed across her face. Finally, she softly replied, "For my prize, I would like you to kiss your wife under the kissing bough, since you certainly deserve it."

"Here, here," the others agreed, and Henry whisked his wife under the lit kissing bough and kissed her as if she were his new bride.

"Now, if everyone will relax for a moment, we're having the table set up for snapdragon," Henry announced, motioning toward a pair of servants bringing in a large mahogany table.

While the servants were preparing the room for snapdragon, Henry noticed that Susan and Nigel were still in a private coze. Lady Markston, on the other side of the room, looked as if she were ringing a peal over Aubrey. Emily, alone near the door, quietly slipped out into the hall, her dark, fringed Kashmir shawl on her arm. Henry almost went after her, but thought better of it. From the looks of things, Emily wasn't having the most pleasant evening and deserved to retire early, he decided, walking over to supervise his staff. Fortunately, no one else took notice of her absence. Or so he thought.

Nigel was enduring one of the most dreadful evenings of his entire life. If it weren't for the fact that his father was on good terms with Lord Markston (which in itself was a miracle, since his father was forever involved in some sort of brangle with everyone) he would have given dearest Susan a much-needed talking-to. In fact, he was still seriously considering that idea when Aubrey strolled over, his bright blue-and-green-striped waistcoat looking a bit tight on him.

"Nigel, can I have a word with you alone?" he asked casually, noting the possessive way Susan had her arm draped through Nigel's.

Nigel smiled brightly, relieved to have an excuse to detach Susan from him. "If you'll excuse us, Susan," he said with a smile, taking her arm away from his.

The look that Susan wore as Nigel and Aubrey walked toward the other side of the room wasn't attractive; her lip was curled into a pout, and she looked as if she were ready to throw a full-fledged tantrum.

"Sorry to bother you, Nigel, but I wanted to talk to you about Lady Susan," Aubrey said formally, thrusting his hands into his pockets.

Nigel frowned. Had Aubrey gone mad, or simply had too much Negus, he wondered, before replying, "Yes?"

"Do you both have an understanding?" Aubrey blurted out, turning a deep shade of red that made him look even more pale and foppish.

"Gads, no!" Nigel exclaimed as a look of relief flooded Aubrey's face. "Susan and her family appear to believe that I'm going to be offering for her, but that's all flummery! I have no interest in her at all," he said, emphasizing the words "at all."

"Good, I was just curious. Did you know that Emily left a few minutes ago? I think she may have been headed for the garden," Aubrey said, a sympathetic smile on his cherubic face.

"Really?" Nigel asked, glancing toward the door.

Aubrey practically grinned. Nigel did have a *tendre* for Emily, which suited his purposes marvelously. "Why don't you go see if she's all right? She seemed to be rather blue-deviled tonight," Aubrey said, glancing over at Susan, who was talking to her mother.

Nigel smiled, his features transformed. "I think I'll do just that," he replied, and strode confidently out of the room, looking for his greatcoat. The weather was still dashed bad, and he didn't want Emily to catch a chill outside.

Emily stood in the garden, the moonlight streaming onto her face, making her look rather ethereal. She held twelve sage leaves in her hands, and had been looking up at the moon, waiting to see the image of her future husband. At least that's what Mrs. Casper, one of their tenants, said would happen.

Snowflakes covered her hair and her shawl, and her hands were turning white with cold. Emily still didn't have any sort of vision. But, in retrospect, standing alone in the garden was preferable to seeing Nigel and Susan slavering over each other like they were aching to be leg-shackled.

"You're going to catch your death out here," a voice from behind her said, and Emily jumped back, startled.

She quickly turned and was facing Nigel, who held out his greatcoat for her. "Here, put this on. There are as many snowflakes on you as there are on the ground," he said, wrapping his coat around her shoulders.

"Thank you," she said, feeling very young and awkward. Why is he out here? she wondered, looking everywhere but at the handsome peer who was standing with her.

"It's a beautiful night," he said in a husky voice.

"Yes, it is," Emily replied, looking up at the yellow moon shining down on them.

Nigel studied the woman beside him. Her long, auburn hair fell like strands of fire down her shoulders, and her skin glowed like alabaster in the moonlight. Her long, delicate fingers were wrapped around his greatcoat, and her lips were trembling delicately in the cold. "You look lovely tonight, Emily," he said in a voice thick with emotion.

Emily managed a false chuckle. "Lord Stratford, you are a veritable rogue!"

Nigel put his hands on her shoulders and turned her to face him. "Emily Winterhaven, you are the most mutton-headed female I have ever had the pleasure of knowing! I am not a rogue and I'm dashed tired of telling you how beautiful you are and being fobbed off like a half-witted, unlicked cub!" he declared passionately.

Before Emily could respond to his shocking tirade (in truth, Emily was too shocked to say anything at all), Nigel wrapped his arms around her. As his lips touched hers, she was enveloped in a kiss that set her blood afire.

Nine

"Emily? Are you outside?" Harriet asked hesitantly, walking into the darkness of the garden.

There was a rustling toward the west side of the garden, on the far side of the hedge, and two figures appeared out of the moonlight.

"Harriet, shouldn't you be attending to your rout?" Emily said in a strained voice that sounded dashed odd to Harriet.

Harriet squinted. "Nigel? What are you doing out here?" she asked innocently, noting with interest that Emily had Nigel's greatcoat around her shoulders.

Nigel coughed. "I saw Emily come outside and thouqht she might need a coat," he said in a strained voice, his eyes never leaving Emily.

Emily laughed cheerily, and took hold of Harriet's arm, leading her back inside. "Actually, Lord Stratford was attempting to seduce me," she said in mock confidentiality, glancing pointedly at Nigel. "You forgot to tell him that I'm a stickler for propriety, and I was forced to give him the same set-down that I gave the comte last summer," she explained as the pair walked back into the house.

Nigel trailed behind them, his mouth dropping open as he listened to Emily's simple explanation. By the look on his face, he apparently wasn't pleased with what he was hearing.

"Do have Henry talk to him, will you?" Emily asked Harriet as they reached the doors. "You see, Lord Stratford seems to think that all women without titles are birds of paradise," she finished in a voice loud enough for Nigel to hear.

Harriet giggled. "What a Banbury tale! Nigel isn't the rake in the family at all. You have the most delicious sense of humor, Emily," she replied lightly, completely disregarding what Emily said.

The trio walked back into the Christmas Eve celebration, oblivious to the fact that Aubrey and Susan were glaring at them.

"What do you mean, you don't have my slippers?" Nigel all but bellowed at Hughes, his unflappable valet.

Hughes straightened himself to his full height and replied evenly, "Sir, as I've explained, that . . . animal ate your slippers this evening while you were at the Christmas Eve festivities."

"Dash it all! Didn't I tell you that I didn't want that cursed puppy in my room? You are certainly becoming lax in your duties, Hughes, very lax," Nigel concluded, sitting on the bed, his dressing robe wrapped tightly around him. The evening had not gone as he had planned.

A slight smile quivered on Hughes's lips. "My lord?"

Nigel sighed. His life was a Cheltingham tragedy. Emily thought he was toying with her, and he wasn't. He was being plagued by a ridiculous curse that had nothing to do with him. Susan Claredon was intent on marrying him. What else can go wrong? he wondered in disgust. "Yes, what is it?" he answered, thoroughly tired of his life.

"My lord, you did instruct me to notify you if you started sounding like the marquess. Well, pardon me for saying so, but you are doing a very remarkable impression of him," Hughes concluded, hoping that Nigel wouldn't be too angry with his observation.

To his delight, Nigel just sighed and replied, "I'm sorry, Hughes. Thank you for pointing it out to me. I'm making a mull of things, and I really have no idea how to put matters right," he concluded, staring blankly at the carpet.

"Pardon my vulgar curiosity, my lord, but does this have anything to do with Miss Winterhaven?"

Nigel looked up, quite startled. "What do you know about Miss Winterhaven?"

Hughes folded his hands together and tried to be diplomatic. "It's been noticed among the staff that you're paying singular attention to the lady in question."

Nigel sighed. "Yes, I am paying singular attention to Miss Winterhaven, but she thinks that I'm a rake," he concluded, and gave Hughes a dark look when his valet stifled a laugh.

"I'm sorry, it's just that the idea of a lady mistaking you as a rake is so . . . uncharacteristic," Hughes said, trying to hide his grin.

"Yes, I know that. But Miss Winterhaven seems to find the idea that I may . . . think highly of her completely unbelievable, since she is connected to trade and is not a peeress," he concluded, becoming more depressed by the moment. In fact, he was so depressed that he was confiding his innermost secrets and feelings to his valet, which wasn't the thing to be doing at all.

"Miss Winterhaven is a very fine lady, although she doesn't have a title," Hughes said, springing to her defense. "She is kind to all of the servants, and her abigail, a charming young girl, cannot say enough in her praise. Lady Susan and Lady Markston's staff are quite another matter entirely. Miss Winterhaven may be connected to trade, but I believe that there isn't a finer lady in this household," Hughes concluded with a slight blush at his temerity.

A slight smile reached Nigel's lips. "I'm shocked by your forwardness, Hughes! But I'm inclined to agree with you. Just because someone is born with a title doesn't necessarily mean that they're kind, generous people," he concluded with a sigh.

Before Hughes could reply, there was a slight rap on the

door, then another. Both men frowned, since it was prodigiously late to be receiving any sort of visitor.

There was another rap on the door, and Nigel shrugged slightly. "You may as well see who it is," Nigel said, his blue devils very apparent.

Hughes opened the door slightly, and his mouth dropped open in shock. The lovely Susan Claredon pushed her way past him and barged into the room, completely disregarding propriety.

Susan, clad in a frilly, pink dressing gown with pink slippers, looked as delicious as a Covent Garden bird of paradise. Her hair was still in the ringlets she wore at the festivities, and Nigel could smell the heavy perfume floating around her.

"Nigel dear, I must talk with you. Send your valet away," she said, waving her arm at Hughes.

Nigel's mouth gaped like a fish gasping for air. It was dashed forward for Susan to be visiting his bedchamber, and he would assuredly compromise her if he sent Hughes out of the room. "I think not. Hughes, please open the door while I speak with Lady Susan—I won't be accused of compromising her," he said with a frown.

Susan pouted. "Nigel, what has gotten into you?" she asked, her rosebud lips turning up most unbecomingly.

"What do you want, Lady Susan?" he said formally, walking toward the open door. He didn't want Susan to be in his room at all, and the sooner she left, the better.

Batting her eyelashes, Susan walked over to Nigel and said, "Nigel, it's Christmas. I've brought you your present." She took a small, wrapped box out of her pocket and stretched out her hand.

Truth be told, Nigel was terrified to take the package. Lady Susan had been acting dashed odd lately, and he wouldn't put it past her to give him an engagement ring. But the box looked much too large for a ring, so he reluctantly took it out of her hand. "This is quite unexpected. Wouldn't it be more the thing to exchange presents tomorrow, with the rest of the guests?"

Susan smiled angelically up at him. "I think not—this is a very special gift. Open it," she commanded, her breasts heaving in excitement.

Nigel glanced at Hughes, who simply shrugged his shoulders. The door was wide open and there was a chaperon present, so Lord Stratford couldn't be faulted for not observing the proprieties.

"I know what you wanted for Christmas, Nigel," she said in a sultry voice, "and I hope that once you open it, you'll forget all this nonsense and come home with Mama and me."

Nigel frowned. What is she talking about? he wondered, as he lifted the lid of the box. And stared in shock at the Manning Mermaid winking up at him. He was speechless.

"I know about the curse, you see, and why you're here. Everyone else might think you're being nice to Miss Winterhaven because you've formed a *tendre* for her, but I know the truth. I know you came to get the pendant back. So here it is," she announced triumphantly. "Merry Christmas," she said in a deliberately coquettish voice, and leaned closer to him, pursing her lips.

Nigel began to turn red with rage. In a controlled voice, he said, "You've stolen this from Miss Winterhaven."

"Posh, who is she? It is *your* family pendant, Nigel," she explained with a frown.

"Lady Claredon, you had no right to steal this, and I will see that it is somehow returned to Miss Winterhaven. My family concerns have nothing to do with you, nor will they ever concern you," he said in a clipped voice, opening the door even wider. "Now, I suggest you return to your room before I give you a dressing-down that you won't soon forget."

Susan's mouth dropped open, making her look like a lackwit. "But Nigel . . ." she began, only to be cut off in mid-sentence.

"Lady Claredon, you will return to your room now, and we

will never discuss this matter again. If you refuse, I'll have Hughes remove you bodily," he said, clenching his teeth in anger.

Susan looked up at him, her blue eyes large and childlike. "Good night, then," she said softly, and walked out of the bedroom, obviously defeated.

Hughes shut the door noiselessly behind her and commented, "That was well done, my lord."

Nigel went over to the bed and sat down, staring at the pendant. "I can't keep this. We have to return it to Emily," he said flatly.

"My lord, didn't you come here to retrieve the mermaid from Miss Winterhaven?" Hughes asked curiously.

"Yes, but she's quite attached to it, so I decided to hell with my father, Roger, and the curse. It's her pendant now, and I decided to let the matter drop," he finished.

"So you're going to return it?"

Nigel stared at the mermaid that seemed to be mocking him. If he kept the mermaid, his luck would probably change, and his family would be delighted. But Emily would be heartbroken, and her Christmas would be ruined.

Finally Nigel looked up at Hughes and replied, "I'm not going to return it, you are. Tomorrow, or should I say, today, when the family goes to Christmas mass. You're going to sneak into Emily's room and place it on her dressing table. Or anywhere her abigail will find it. No one needs to know about Susan's involvement, or our involvement, either. It will be our special Christmas present to Miss Winterhaven," he said softly.

"Well done, sir," Hughes said softly, and realized that his employer and friend was actually very much in love.

"Do you think it will help any, Miss Emily?" Eliza asked, staring at the small piece of Christmas cake in her hand.

"It certainly can't hurt," Emily began, and took the cake from Eliza and wrapped it in a small, white handkerchief.

"Do you really think that sleeping on a piece of Christmas cake will improve your love life?" Eliza asked with a blush.

Emily shrugged. "I just hope I don't ruin Harriet's linens," she said practically, and placed the wrapped cake under her pillow.

"Will that be all, Miss Emily?" Eliza asked, throwing back the covers and placing a warm brick at Emily's feet.

Emily crawled into bed and smiled fondly at her servant. "Yes, you can blow out the candles—I'm more than ready for some sleep," Emily said, and added, "Merry Christmas, Eliza."

Eliza took a single candle and moved to the door of her adjoining room. "Merry Christmas, Miss Emily," she said softly, leaving Emily alone.

As the moon peeped through the heavy curtains, Emily stared at the shadows that danced around the room and wondered what exactly was happening at this simple holiday house party. Was Lord Stratford really courting her? It would appear that he was, but then that's what I thought when Roger Manning was my constant companion, she mused, unable to sleep. Does Lord Stratford really think I'm a doxy who can be toyed with? Or does he actually care for my company? she wondered, her thoughts in a whirl. And what will he say when he receives my Christmas gift? Sleep would not be coming easily to Emily Winterhaven on the night before Christmas.

"We're going to church in the sleigh?" Lady Markston asked, a frown creasing her heavily painted forehead.

Standing at the front door, Henry, in his Christmas finery, refused to be daunted. "The weather is still rather impassable, Lady Markston, and Blackmore sent his sleigh over this morning. It's the only way to travel in this snow," he concluded, waving his hand toward the window.

Lady Markston gazed out the window and surveyed the situation. The ground was indeed covered with several feet of the white powder, and the trees, now covered in ice, glistened in the winter sunlight. She glanced over at Susan, who was pouting at her side, and sighed. "I suppose you're correct," she conceded, and tucked her hands into her furry brown muffler.

"Is Nigel going to be attending the service?" Susan asked coyly, flicking an invisible piece of lint off of her black velvet, fur-trimmed pelisse.

"Yes, I expect him to appear at any moment. In any case, I'll have to make a few trips with the horses since the entire party is too large to fit into the sleigh," Henry said, almost to himself, since Lady Markston and Susan were both craning their necks, looking for someone.

Moments later, Aubrey, looking all the crack in his black satin breeches, golden-striped waistcoat, and a dark green coat (obviously by Weston), strolled down the stairs, smiling at Susan. "You look as lovely as ever, Susan," he began, his eyes devouring her. "You must be so proud to be the mother of a diamond of the first water," he exclaimed, beaming at Lady Markston.

Lady Markston immediately brightened and replied, "Yes, Susan has been the toast of London for several Seasons now."

Aubrey gazed down at Susan. Her blond hair was curled into perfect ringlets and she looked incredibly angelic. "Henry," he began, "why don't I take Lady Markston and Susan now and come back with the sleigh? It will give everyone else some time to get ready, since we seem to be the only prompt members of this house party."

Henry glanced at the trio and smiled. Yes, that would be a wonderful idea. A moment away from Lady Markston was like a moment in heaven, he decided. "That's a dashed good idea, Aubrey. I'll send word to the stables to have Jem bring the sleigh up to the front door," he said with a smile. Life was suddenly improving by leaps and bounds.

Nigel was in a dashed bad mood. It was obvious to him that Emily Winterhaven thought he was a rake. And, since he had never actually tried to attract the attention of a respectable female before, he was at quite a loss about how to behave. But he did have the most delicious Christmas gift planned for her, one that he hoped would take him out of her black book. And, once the party left for church, she would have the mermaid back in her possession. Perhaps that would cure her blue devils, he thought optimistically.

"Am I presentable, Hughes?" he asked distractedly, putting on his black velvet coat.

Hughes straightened up and surveyed his employer. His mane of long, black, wavy hair had been coaxed into what could resemble a style. The velvet coat, paired with black satin breeches, an embroidered black silk waistcoat, and a crisp white shirt with ruffles at the wrist made him look a bit austere, but respectable.

Finally, after an interminably long inspection, Hughes commented, "Yes, I suppose you look well enough," with a marked absence of enthusiasm.

Nigel chuckled. "I am a trial, aren't I? It's no matter—we are in the country, mind you," he finished, walking toward the closed oak door. "You will take care of the mermaid, won't you?" he asked, his nervousness quite apparent to Hughes.

"Of course, my lord," Hughes answered stiffly.

"Very good. There will be an extra bonus for you if you can manage to get it back to Miss Winterhaven without anyone finding out the truth," Nigel said.

Hughes nodded. "Miss Winterhaven will have the mermaid back in her possession today," he assured him, as Nigel opened the door.

"Good. And Hughes?"

"Yes?"

Nigel smiled broadly. "Merry Christmas."

* * *

"What do you mean, she's already left?" Nigel asked with a frown.

Henry raised an eyebrow. "Emily left for church a quarter of an hour ago, with Miss Turner and Victoria. We're the last sleigh-full, so to speak," he finished, moving toward the door.

Nigel wasn't happy. He wanted a chance to speak privately with Emily before the church services, to apologize for his behavior in the garden. Actually, he wasn't penitent at all, for he knew that she had misread his intentions. He knew his intentions were all that were honorable, but obviously she needed some reassurance. "Then I suppose we should be leaving," he commented, following Henry out into the bright winter sun.

Nigel couldn't concentrate on the service. Reverend Something or Other was a prosy fellow, and the time ticked by more slowly than he thought possible.

Emily was down the family pew from him, looking very fetching in a Spanish fly-colored velvet pelisse, her eyes large and unbelievably green. A single rose decorated her gown, and she couldn't have looked lovelier in his eyes. Unfortunately, she refused to look at him, concentrating on the hymn book, looking up only to stare blankly at the Very Reverend Something or Other.

Nigel continued gazing dreamily at Emily, his mind drifting. Why is she wearing that faded rose? he wondered, glancing around at the congregation. If he were lucky, he would try to convince some country matron to surrender her rose for Emily, who definitely deserved something better than the rose that was, well, dying, before his eyes. Completely unable to concentrate on what was being said, Nigel spent the rest of the service scanning the crowd for females wearing roses that were actually alive.

* * *

The service ended too soon for Emily, who was dreading her first encounter with Nigel. He obviously thought she had lax morals, and believed she was ripe for a dalliance. She hoped her words to Harriet had rectified the situation, and that Nigel now realized she was completely respectable. Her glance at his face last night made her certain that he had understood her meaning, and he didn't seem to be pleased with what she had said. That must be why he's avoiding me, she thought, certain that Nigel had been waiting until the last moment to arrive at church so he didn't have to sit near her.

And her rose didn't seem to be having any effect on her situation. According to the tradition, a young woman was supposed to pluck a rose on Midsummer's Day and save it until Christmas. On Christmas Day, if she wore the rose to church, the young lady's future husband was supposed to come up to her and take the rose from her. That hadn't happened—and it isn't likely to happen, she decided, glancing around the room. Most of the parishioners had already left the small church, and their party was one of the last to leave, since the family pew was in the second row. Blackmore, who Harriet explained could be a bit of a heathen, decided to forego attending the Christmas service this year, so their party had the most prominent seats.

Emily followed Miss Turner out of the small church, still rather blue-deviled. Her pendant was gone, Nigel thought she was a doxy, and Susan Claredon looked incredibly lovely. In fact, in Emily's mind, she resembled a well-dressed scullery maid or, even worse, a poor relation.

As she walked into the brightly lit vestibule, she was startled to find Nigel there, apparently waiting for someone. Which was odd, since he had practically jumped out of his end seat at the first possible opportunity.

"Emily, may I speak with you privately for a moment?" he asked softly, his left hand carefully concealing the rose it held.

A frown marred Emily's delicate features. "I really don't think that would be proper, Lord Stratford," she replied stiffly, following him to the far end of the vestibule nonetheless.

"I'm not planning to ravish you here and now," he said with a wicked sparkle in his golden eyes.

Emily blushed, and was quite taken aback when he reached over and took the rose off of her pelisse and put it in his pocket. "May I ask what you're doing, Lord Stratford?" she asked formally, beginning to pale slightly. She was still in church, and the rose was taken from her. By a man. But Lord Stratford certainly couldn't be her future husband!

Nigel smiled as he placed the new rose on her green velvet pelisse. "Your rose was faded, and I thought you might like something more . . . festive," he said with a smile, inspecting the new red rose.

Emily looked down at it, shocked and confused. Finally, after a long silence, she formally said, "Thank you for the rose, Lord Stratford," her manners coming to her rescue.

Nigel smiled down at her, completely captivated. "You're welcome, Emily. And you must call me Nigel."

She blushed and stared at her muff. "I don't think that would be proper."

Nigel chuckled. "Yes, well, I think you realize that I'm not quite proper myself, Emily. But I would like you to call me Nigel, at least for the rest of our visit. It is Christmas, and you wouldn't deny me a favor on Christmas Day, would you?" he asked, cajoling a smile onto her face.

Emily looked up at him, a delicate pink staining her cheeks. "I suppose I can call you by your Christian name," she conceded, noticing the mischievous sparkle in his eyes.

"Thank you, Emily," he replied, taking her arm and leading her outside.

As the pair stood in the sunlight, looking for the rest of their party, he looked down at her and said, "I think you're going to have a grand Christmas, Emily—just you wait and see."

* * *

Eliza, Emily's abigail, paced the front hall nervously. Miss Emily should have been back at least a quarter of an hour ago! Instead, she was lagging at church, obviously one of the last people to be driven back to the house by Henry.

She put her small hand into the pocket of her gray dress and fingered the mermaid. "Miss Emily will be so pleased when she finds out I found the mermaid," she thought eagerly, since she knew Emily had been quite preoccupied since it turned up missing.

Eliza was highly suspicious of the way it turned up, though. Lord Stratford's valet had told her that she was wanted in the kitchen. So she went downstairs, only to find that no one had actually summoned her at all. When she returned upstairs to find Lord Stratford's valet and give him a proper dressing-down for sending her on a fool's errand, the pendant was sitting unobtrusively on the dressing table. She was so ecstatic that she completely forgot about Lord Stratford's valet.

"May I ask what business you have waiting here?" an icy female voice from behind Eliza demanded, and Eliza could sense that a scold from someone was imminent.

She turned to find the breathtakingly beautiful Lady Claredon, looking like a vision in a cream velvet dress, addressing her. "Pardon me, my lady?" Eliza asked with a stutter.

"Fool," Susan snapped, her waspish disposition very apparent. "Why are you lingering in the hall? Don't you have any other duties to perform? If you don't, I'm sure I can find something to keep you busy," she concluded, giving Eliza her haughtiest stare.

Eliza tried to keep her voice from wavering. Lady Claredon was a member of the *ton,* and she rarely was spoken to by someone with such address. "I'm waiting for Miss Emily to return, my lady," she stammered.

"Why? You should be busying yourself with something, not standing about, wasting time."

"But I have to speak with Miss Emily the moment she returns from church," Eliza began nervously, fingering the pendant in her pocket. "You see, I . . . misplaced a piece of her jewelry earlier in the week and she's been ever so blue-deviled about it. But today it turned up, and I'm sure she'll want to know about the mermaid as soon as she walks in," Eliza concluded, completely out of breath.

To her surprise, Lady Claredon paled slightly. "You located her missing piece of jewelry?" she said in a choked voice.

"Yes! It was ever so strange—it was just sitting on the dresser like it wanted to be found!" Eliza exclaimed, momentarily forgetting that she was being addressed by a personage.

"Really," Lady Claredon replied, walking off with a rather dazed expression on her face.

As Susan walked through the myriad halls, her anger began to mount. How dare he, she thought, walking toward her bedroom. Nigel is the veriest sapskull! I risk my reputation to retrieve his dashed pendant so he can leave this horrid house party and what does he do? The muttonhead gives it back to that ape leader! Why, I'd give him his congee if Mama weren't so set on our engagement, she thought traitorously, stomping into her bedroom. In one swift move, she slammed the door so vigorously that the whole house shuddered.

Ten

"Nigel, how could you?" Susan wailed, her goddess-like features remarkably transforming into those of a harridan.

Nigel frowned at her, and glanced up and down the hallway. Thankfully, no one was in sight. "What are you going on about, Susan?" he asked casually, his figure tall and imposing next to her petite stature.

"The pendant. You returned it to that . . . ape leader bluestocking that everyone thinks you have a *tendre* for! How could you give her the pendant, after all the trouble I went through for you!" she cried, her blue eyes large and pleading.

Once again, Nigel was at a loss. In all the years he had known her, Susan had never acted so . . . common. Obviously, it was time to let her know where she stood in his eyes. "Lady Claredon," he began firmly, fixing his golden gaze upon her, "the pendant is the property of Miss Winterhaven, and it was my responsibility, as a gentleman, to return it to her."

Susan's mouth dropped open, making her look rather like a dying fish. It was not an attractive pose, and Nigel was rather hard-pressed not to chuckle at the look of stupidity upon her face.

"And furthermore, you will not malign Miss Winterhaven in my presence again. You have no right to do so, Lady Claredon, and I won't hear of it any longer," he finished harshly.

"But Nigel, I did it for you," she whined, a tear falling down her cheek dramatically. "I can't believe you're being so . . . cruel to me."

Nigel glanced around the hall. Luckily, they were still alone, and almost all of the doors were closed, except down the hall. He didn't realize that Victoria and Wellington were in that room, and could hear every word that was being said. "Lady Claredon," he began, his frown very pronounced by now, "you obviously have many misconceptions concerning our acquaintance. You will always be considered a friend of the family, but never more than that. Do I make myself clear?" he asked in a clipped, irritated voice.

Tears began to roll down Susan's face as if she were on Drury Lane. "Nigel, are you jilting me? Crying off?" she sobbed, glancing around the hall.

"There is no reason to do either, since we never, at any time, had an understanding."

"But Nigel . . . I thought . . ." Susan drifted off, her sobs calming down since there was no audience to view her performance.

"I have no idea what you thought, Lady Claredon, nor do I wish to know," he said, and glared down at her, his arms folded crossed across his chest.

Susan looked up at him, her bottom lip trembling. She said nothing.

"I'll see you in the parlor when you're more composed. Harriet expects us, since everyone is going to be exchanging gifts," he said curtly, and walked stiffly away, leaving her alone in the hall. He had never expected his Christmas holiday to be so . . . complicated.

"Thank you, Aunt Emily," Victoria cried exuberantly, rushing over to Emily's seat on the edge of the parlor and enveloping her in a hug.

Emily chuckled merrily. "You're very welcome, Victoria," she said, looking down at the girl's dark-haired doll dressed as a Scottish shepherdess.

"She's ever so pretty, Aunt Emily. Did you really see people like this in Scotland?" she asked, trying very hard to pronounce "Scotland" properly.

"Yes, I did. You see, my grandpapa has an estate in Scotland, so I even know some shepherd girls. Many people think Scotland is a barbaric, backward place, but it's actually very nice," Emily explained patiently, hoping to head off the prejudice that all of the *ton* had against Scotland.

"Will you tell me some stories about Scotland later, Aunt Emily?" she asked, her blue eyes looking up entreatingly.

"Of course, dear," she replied, smiling down at her honorary niece.

As Emily glanced around the room, she was truly amazed at how sedate and family-like the entire afternoon had been. Almost all of the gifts had been exchanged, and, once again, Harriet had made sure that everyone was relaxed. So the Christmas wassail was a bit stronger than usual, and consequently, everyone was wonderfully merry.

The Christmas meal was going to be a bit less elaborate, Harriet had explained to the party earlier, since the tradition at the manor was to have a more elaborate meal on Boxing Day, with the entire staff. So the Christmas Day fare would simply be turkey, ham, stewed oysters, turnips, beets, plum pudding, fried celery, and a variety of beverages, including Regency punch and Negus.

Emily watched Nigel across the room, in a deep coze with Aubrey. Once again, Aubrey looked like a fashionable London dandy, while Nigel, in his black satin breeches, white shirt with wrist ruffles, and black, embroidered-silk waistcoat looked more like a Gypsy than a nobleman. "Or possibly an Italian poet," Emily mused with a smile, watching the revelry around her.

Lady Markston didn't seem particularly happy, and was drinking more than her share of wassail. Her daughter Susan was beside her, sampling one of the candies that she had received as a gift from Nigel. Aubrey kept glancing over at Susan, who appeared to be oblivious to him, while Nigel pointedly ignored the pair of ladies. Harriet and Henry flitted between the couples, doing their duties as proper hosts. Miss Turner watched over Victoria from the other side of the room, beaming with pride at her well-behaved charge. Victoria, unaware that anyone was paying any heed at all to her, was on the Axminster-carpeted floor near Miss Turner, working on a puzzle that Nigel had given her.

Why hasn't he opened my present? Emily wondered, staring at the small package that was still in Nigel's hands. All of the presents had been opened except the gift that Emily had given Nigel.

As Emily sat alone, lost in her thoughts, she was rather startled when Harriet's butler, Coverdail, a tall, gaunt gentleman, appeared at her side.

"Begging your pardon, Miss Winterhaven, but there is a package for you waiting at the door," he said solemnly.

Emily's eyes widened. "A package? Who is it from?" she asked, wondering if her parents decided to send her Christmas gift rather than wait to exchange gifts when they all returned home later in the month.

"I'm not privy to that information, miss. Would you follow me, please?"

"Can't you bring it in here?" she asked, still a bit dumbfounded.

"The package is rather oversized, miss—I think not," he replied stiffly, waiting for her to rise and follow him.

With a sigh, Emily put down her plate of subtleties and glided out of the room behind Coverdail.

As they moved through the halls, Emily's curiosity began to grow. What could it be? she wondered, since the mail hadn't been through in days. It couldn't be from her parents. So who was giving her the frightfully large package sitting inside the front door?

"There is your package, miss," Coverdail said formally, and swept out of the hall, leaving Emily alone.

The package was very large, almost the size of her portnanteau. A large red bow sat atop the box, and, as she leaned over to open the lid, it flew off by itself.

"Oh!" Emily exclaimed, and stepped back a few feet.

Then began to giggle.

Poking her head out of the box was the most adorable, tiny, reddish-brown puppy she had ever seen. It looked around the hall a little, then saw Emily and issued the most ridiculous little yap.

Emily giggled and went over to the box. "Why, who are you? And what are you doing in my Christmas box?" Emily asked the puppy, who was now trying to get out of the box.

The puppy yapped again, and Emily could see her little tail wagging furiously.

"I suppose I should help you out of the box," she said, picking the puppy up in her arms.

At that point, the little dog began to lick Emily's hands eagerly.

She giggled again. "You are the silliest puppy I've ever met," she replied, sitting on the glistening oak floor.

A voice from the shadows said, "Merry Christmas, Emily."

Emily looked up from the floor, completely disconcerted. "Lord Stratford—I mean, Nigel," she stuttered, turning a deep shade of red.

Nigel smiled at her and walked over to the pair. "Do you like your gift?" he asked as he sat on the floor next to her.

Emily began to stroke the puppy, completely at a loss. "I've always wanted a puppy, but because we travel so much, my parents never allowed me to have one. Thank you," she replied, staring down at the adorable ball of fur curled up happily in her lap.

Nigel looked at the package in his hands. "I thought it would be more comfortable if we exchanged presents in private. That's why I didn't open yours immediately," he explained, taking the ribbon off her gift.

"Actually, it's not much of a present," Emily said, suddenly very shy around Nigel.

As he opened the box, a mist appeared in his bright hazel eyes. He took the sheaf of papers out and replied, "You wrote this, didn't you?"

She looked at the pages of handwritten music and nodded.

Nigel glanced over at Emily, his heart filled with love. "That's a wonderful gift, Emily. Most people are appalled by the fact that I play, and you've actually given me some new music," he said, awe in his voice.

Emily shrugged a bit. "It's nothing—just a short piece I thought you might enjoy playing," she replied simply.

Once again, Nigel was consumed with the urge to lean over and kiss Emily, despite the puppy in her lap and the fact that they were sitting on the hallway floor.

"Emily, where did you go off to?" Harriet cried from down the hall, and both Emily and Nigel bounced back onto their feet.

"Over here, at the door," Emily replied, still holding the puppy in her arms.

Harriet appeared a moment later, a look of confusion on her face. "What are you doing here? And where did you get that puppy?" she asked, glancing over at Nigel, who was practically mooning over Emily.

"She—at least I *think* it's a she—is a Christmas present from Nigel," she replied, as Harriet came over and began petting the wriggling puppy.

"Oh, really?" Harriet replied, raising an eyebrow. "How did you know Emily wanted a puppy?" she asked him curiously.

Nigel shrugged. "Well, Emily spends a good deal of time playing with Victoria and Wellington, and it's obvious that she enjoys animals. And she seemed lonely at home, so I thought she might like a companion to take back with her after the holiday," he replied simply.

"This isn't a relation of Wellington's, is it? She's so small, she couldn't have come from the same litter," Emily concluded, looking into the large, brown eyes of her new pet.

"Actually, it is. She was the smallest of the litter, and there was talk that if a home couldn't be found, she would be drowned. I knew you wouldn't want that to happen, and to be honest, if you couldn't keep her, I would have," Nigel replied candidly.

Harriet looked at both of them and smiled warmly. "Why don't you put the new addition to the family in the kitchen for the night? Cook will keep her with Wellington, and you'll be able to make more arrangements tomorrow."

Emily cuddled the puppy to her breast. "I suppose she shouldn't stay in my room?"

"Wellington wasn't really house-trained when he came out of the barn, and I'd really hate to have another accident upstairs," Harriet replied.

"I'm sorry, dearest, you're being banished to the kitchens," she said softly to the puppy, who was now looking up at her with the most quizzical expression.

As Emily began walking toward the kitchen, Harriet looked over at Nigel and simply said, "If you're toying with her, I'll disown you as I've disowned Roger," and followed Emily briskly down the hall.

"Of course you must attend the New Year's masquerade at Blackmore's if you're still with us then," Henry declared, helping himself to a large portion of venison.

It was very obvious that Harriet had made the seating arrangements at the Christmas dinner table. Susan and Aubrey were paired together, as were Nigel and Emily. Lady Markston was seated next to Henry, who appeared to have the ability to converse congenially with anyone, no matter how obnoxious.

Taking another portion of stuffed ham, Lady Markston coughed delicately and replied, "I do hope the weather clears up and we can be off to my cousin's." She took a sip of her claret and added, "I hope my delicate constitution won't stop me from leaving as soon as the roads clear up, since Susan and I do so hate to impose on you so, especially during the holidays."

"It's been no trouble, no trouble at all," Henry said, finishing his third glass of port.

Across the table, Harriet was hard-pressed not to throw something at her husband. She was none too pleased to be playing the gallant hostess to Lady Markston and her horribly cossetted daughter, and was counting the moments until they finally left. But, being the gently bred lady that she was, she simply added, "Yes, Blackmore has a splendid rout—everyone who is anyone in the county attends his masquerade. It's something of a tradition, you see," she concluded, picking at her parsnips.

"A masquerade? How exciting," Susan said eagerly, glancing furtively at Nigel.

"It is on New Year's Eve, which is a sennight away, and I do expect the weather will clear up by that time," Harriet added practically, and saw a brief moment of panic cross Susan's face.

"Last year Harriet dressed as Cleopatra, and I was her escort, Marc Antony," Henry added, completely unaware that his wife was trying to discourage their uninvited guests from staying a moment longer than necessary.

"How splendid!" Aubrey exclaimed, helping himself to another serving of the stewed oysters. "I most certainly will be here for that event, so you all must help me think of an idea for a costume."

Harriet didn't miss Aubrey's intention. If the party kept discussing the masquerade, then everyone would forget about Lady Markston's departure. Of course, Aubrey didn't know that Harriet was counting the moments until her unexpected guests departed. She even had her maid check the weather every morning at dawn to see if it was possible to travel. But the weather was against her and Lady Markston and her daughter were now a part of their holiday. Unfortunately.

It wasn't long before the boned turkey, stuffed ham, stewed

oysters, turnips, beets, parsnips, and plum pudding were finished. The ladies, as usual, retired to the drawing room,
leaving the men to their port.

"I do hope you'll be attending the wedding, once we decide
on the date," Lady Markston commented, a sly smile on her
face.

Harriet frowned at her companion, and glanced toward the
other end of the room. Susan was in the corner with Emily,
leaning forward and telling her something in a very confidential manner. Probably more flummery to convince Emily
that Nigel could only fall in love with a proper lady, Harriet
thought, glancing back at Lady Markston. "Pardon me?"

"When Susan and Nigel announce their engagement, I
hope you'll be able to attend the ceremony," Lady Markston
said patiently, her hands calmly folded in her lap.

Harriet frowned, and decided to help Lady Markston out of
the delusion she was obviously suffering. "I'd be truly surprised if Nigel offers for your daughter. If anything, I'd say
he's shown a marked preference for the company of my friend
Emily," she commented airily, noting the look of consternation on Lady Markston's face.

"Oh, Nigel has always been the gallant. It's obvious that
your Miss Winterhaven is completely ineligible, and he feels
sorry for her," she concluded firmly.

"Really? And what do you make of the situation with
Henry's Cousin Aubrey?" Harriet asked, becoming more an-
noyed by the moment at this stubborn house guest who
wouldn't leave.

"What situation?" she asked innocently, looking toward the
door, waiting for the arrival of the gentlemen.

"Why, surely you've noticed that Aubrey is practically living in Susan's pocket! He's quite taken with her, you know."

Lady Markston paled a trifle, and was suddenly at a loss
for words. Luckily, the gentlemen chose that moment to re-

turn to the gathering, and Lady Markston breathed an audible sigh of relief as she saw Nigel walk over to Susan.

"Susan, Emily," Nigel said cordially, smiling at both women. *Emily looks lovely tonight,* he thought, noticing how her long auburn hair shone in the ample candlelight.

Susan smiled prettily at him, and glanced toward her mother with a look of triumph on her face.

"Susan, I do hope you don't think I'm the greatest flat, but I was wondering if you would excuse Emily and me for a moment," he said, his eyes focused only on Emily.

"But Nigel, we've barely spoken all day," Susan replied, a pout beginning to form on her perfect red lips.

Nigel smiled calmly at her. "Lady Claredon, you know I don't have anything to say to you. Emily?" he asked, holding out his arm for her.

Emily glanced at Susan, who was now glaring at her in rage. "Please excuse us," she replied, her green eyes twinkling.

The couple moved to a quiet corner of the drawing room, away from the rest of the company.

"Thank you for joining me, Emily. I just couldn't stand the idea of spending one more moment listening to Susan's flummery," he said in a rush, quite overtaken by her beauty.

Emily smiled hesitantly. "I suppose I should also thank you for getting me away from your bride-to-be," she commented casually.

Nigel rolled his eyes toward the heavens. "Does Susan still imagine that I'm going to offer for her? She is obviously as hen-witted as her mother," he finished, glaring at Susan. Something obviously had to be done.

"But your wedding will be the talk of the Season!" Emily prompted, relaxing a trifle with him.

Nigel glanced around the room, and noticed that Susan and her mother were once again in an intimate coze, and throwing disapproving looks his way. He also noticed the kissing bough on the ceiling, and decided to put an end to the speculation concerning his affections. So he took her delicate hand in his and whispered, "Come with me."

Emily followed him with a frown, as curious as the rest of the occupants of the study as to what Nigel was doing.

She had completely forgotten about the kissing bough and was stunned when Nigel stopped, and then commanded, "Look up."

Emily looked up, and turned red in embarrassment.

"Merry Christmas, Emily," he whispered, and enveloped her in a very thorough kiss that left her senses reeling.

As he released her and her confused gaze delved into his golden eyes, there was a distant cough that propelled them both back into reality.

"I haven't had the opportunity to kiss Emily under the mistletoe," Henry announced, and Nigel reluctantly let her go.

Henry then proceeded to wrap his arms around Emily and kiss her very appropriately on both cheeks, loudly wishing her a Merry Christmas. And added, "Now Aubrey, it is your turn, isn't it?" he asked with a laugh.

And so Aubrey appeared, and gave Emily a kiss much like Henry's, to Emily's complete mortification.

From across the room, Nigel smiled. It was now obvious to everyone that he favored Emily. He hoped, if he was persistent enough, she would begin to return his affection. "Perhaps," he muttered wryly.

"Nigel, do you have a moment for a word in private?" Lady Markston hissed, a frown on her very apparently painted face.

Nigel glanced around the party. Harriet was still explaining all of the Boxing Day festivities, and everyone (save Emily) appeared to have had more than their share of wassail. "Of course, Lady Markston," he replied casually, and followed her out into the hall.

Closing the door behind her, Lady Markston turned to

Nigel, her eyes blazing. "May I ask why you are so grossly using my daughter?" she demanded haughtily.

"I beg your pardon?" Nigel replied, completely confused.

"Everyone in Society is waiting for the banns to be placed, and now you're dangling after some halfwit cit, of all things. Why are you ill-using Susan?" she asked, her face red with consternation.

Nigel took a deep breath. "Lady Markston, I'm sorry if you didn't understand my relationship with Lady Claredon. I have never given her any reason to expect that I would offer for her."

"Flummery! If you don't do your duty and offer for my daughter, it will be the scandal of the Season! I will not have my family put through that humiliation," she concluded dramatically.

"Then there will be a scandal. I will not marry your daughter, and I take exception to the manner in which you referred to Miss Winterhaven. I wouldn't wed Lady Susan if she were the last available female in England," he announced.

Lady Markston paled. "You . . . blackguard! If I were a man, I would call you out!" she declared passionately.

Nigel chuckled slightly. "Lady Markston, you have no reason to have me called out. Everyone knows that Susan is a cossetted, selfish spendthrift, and that's why she didn't take during her numerous Seasons. You see, I'm not totally unaware of what is happening in London. She will never make a suitable marchioness."

"How can you speak to me this way, Nigel? Our family has been connected for years. Why, it's your father's greatest wish that our families unite to form one of the largest landholdings in the country," she explained quickly.

A small smile appeared on Nigel's harsh features. "Then I suggest that Susan start spending all of her free time with Roger. I do believe he is still eligible."

Lady Markston's large painted mouth dropped open, making her look completely ridiculous.

So as she stood gaping at him in the dimly lit hallway, Nigel made his escape. "If you'll excuse me, Lady Markston, I'd like to rejoin the party," he said, and silently opened the oak door, disappearing into the parlor. *This holiday has to improve*, he thought, looking around the room for Emily.

A while later, a very distraught Susan Claredon found herself sequestered in the library with Aubrey, completely at sixes and sevens.

"What do you need to speak with me about, dearest?" Aubrey asked with a smile. "I don't believe that you actually wanted me to show you a book," he concluded with a grin, running his hand through his hair.

"Oh Aubrey, I don't know what to do! Nigel is showing a preference for that awful ape leader, Emily Winterhaven. What can I do?" she wailed dramatically, throwing herself onto a chair.

"Do you really have such a *tendre* for Nigel that you're suffering from his lack of attentions?" he asked, seating himself in the chair next to hers.

Susan frowned, an unattractive look that added years to her age. "I don't love Nigel, you slow-top! I'm simply marrying him so I can become a marchioness," she explained.

Aubrey smiled. So he did have a chance with the vain beauty, since her affections were not engaged. Of course, he couldn't give her such a grand title, but he was definitely more tolerant than Nigel. And much more suited for the petulant young woman wailing across from him. "Do you have a plan?"

"No. Do you think I should? He'll never marry me now— he's taken that freakish liking to that drab spinster. I thought he just wanted that dashed pendant back, but as soon as I gave it to him, he gave it back to her! What am I going to do?" she wailed.

"I don't know," he said, but Aubrey had very definite ideas. He actually thought that Susan should become his bride, so he heartily encouraged the blossoming romance of Nigel and Emily.

"I know!" Susan announced, leaping out of her chair. "I'll tell Emily that the only reason Nigel is paying any heed to her is to get back that stupid pendant. Then she's bound to throw him over," she concluded with a triumphant smile.

"And Nigel will know that you told Emily, and you still won't be any closer to being his wife," he concluded quickly. Actually, her idea was rather admirable. Except that he didn't want Emily and Nigel to take a dislike to one another. He wanted to see them married.

"Then *you* can tell her. And Nigel will come running back into my waiting arms, and I'll be the most beautiful marchioness that the *ton* has ever seen," she said, wrapping a strand of her long blond hair around her finger.

Aubrey smiled. Things would be fine as long as Susan didn't divulge Nigel's secret to Emily. So he calmly said, "I'll tell Emily about the mermaid pendant when the time is right."

Susan flashed a magnificent smile and saucily said, "I knew you would do it for me," as she sauntered out the door.

Aubrey stared at the closed doors and contemplated his own plans. Yes, Susan definitely needs someone more . . . accommodating than Nigel. If she doesn't come around, I suppose I'll have to compromise her, he thought, taking a bit of snuff from his silver engraved snuffbox. And I will tell Emily Winterhaven about the pendant. When Prinny stops eating, he mused with a smile. Nigel was out of the picture and now he could make the magnificent Susan Claredon his bride.

Eleven

The Boxing Day celebration at the Ashton household was one to behold. The day began for all of the staff at approximately ten A.M., with no exception. Henry followed the tradition of his father, and of his grandfather: no servant was to work before that hour, and almost all duties were eliminated on that day of festivity.

The kitchen staff was one that was busy, but by choice. For one glorious day of the year, they were cooking the finest food for themselves and all of Henry's tenants. Cook and her minions spent the day perfecting a twelve-course meal to be enjoyed by everyone present. The boar's head was crested with rosemary and bay leaf, the oysters were stewed to perfection, the turkey was boned and roasted, and all of the vegetables were cooked until the scent filled the spacious house.

Harriet, Henry, and Victoria traditionally spent most of the day in their suites, working on the gifts for their staff. Each year they bestowed any number of presents, large and small, on the servants that shared their lives. Victoria, with the help of Miss Turner, found trinkets for the children, and delighted in helping to make Boxing Day the resounding success it always was.

Until the feast, the rest of the house party found themselves at loose ends. Emily spent the day in her room, trying to train her new unnamed puppy, without much success. Aubrey and Nigel bumped into each other in the library, and settled on a game of *vingt-et-un* to pass the time.

On the other side of the house, in Lady Markston's suite, things were hardly as tranquil. Lady Markston, wearing a tight, bosom-revealing gown of capucine with a matching feathered turban, was giving her daughter a severe dressing-down.

"And why were you closeted in the library with that fortune hunter Langely last evening?" she demanded, pacing the floor.

Susan sat on a small chair next to the bed, staring at the floor, trying to think up a reasonable explanation of why she was attending to a man other than her future husband. Of course, Nigel would rather marry that drab spinster than me, she thought bitterly.

"What do you have to say for yourself, Susan?"

Susan looked up, startled out of her reverie. "I'm sorry, Mother," she intoned in a very rehearsed voice. She had lived through dozens of these episodes with her mother.

"You are a failure as a daughter. Since your birth your only responsibility was to nab a peer. We have given you the finest dresses from Paris, the best dancing masters, your watercolors are magnificent, and no one has a more pleasing voice. Yet your Seasons have been a dismal failure and you are on the shelf just as firmly as that drab Emily Winterhaven. What are we to do with you?" she asked rhetorically, and Susan knew her mother didn't expect an answer to that question.

Strangely enough, Susan actually had an answer. While her mother was ranting, she had an idea. "Do you want me to marry Nigel?" she asked innocently, staring at the floor.

"Of course! Are you a slow-top? Think of the connections you would have if you were the next Marchioness of Avonleigh. But Nigel won't have you," she said, staring at Susan in contempt. "He told me so last night. You are a grave disappointment, Susan," Lady Markston said, shaking her head in disgust. The white plume in her turban bobbed ridiculously atop her head.

"Mother, I can always marry someone else, someone better," Susan said in a desperate voice.

"Who? A wastrel or a fortune hunter? You know very well that Nigel Manning was your last prayer."

Susan sat up straight in the chair and met her mother's eyes. "You'll see, Mother—I'll get Nigel to offer for me," she said with a confidence she certainly didn't feel. Nothing was worse than the way her mother treated her when she didn't get her way. It would be worth the sacrifice to be leg-shackled to Nigel, just to stop her mother's constant complaining.

Lady Markston raised an eyebrow as she continued to pace the room, her turban askew. "We'll discuss this at another time," she said, and motioned for Susan to leave the room.

As Susan walked to her bedroom, she knew that she had to go through with her plan. It wasn't pleasant or fair, but she had to marry Nigel. If she didn't, her mother would make her every waking moment miserable. She would be the new Countess of Stratford, and when Nigel's father stuck his spoon in the wall, the Marchioness of Avonleigh. Or I'll die trying, she thought, as she closed the door of her bedroom.

Emily walked into the ballroom and her mouth gaped open in surprise. All of London must be here, she thought, as servants of all ages and sizes, along with the rest of the house party, danced, played games, and drank some of the very abundant wassail that was sitting on a long table.

"Welcome to the party, Miss Emily," Eliza said, practically bouncing over to Emily. Her abigail was wearing her Sunday-best clothes, and looked quite fetching. Her bright red hair was neatly in place, and her face was flushed from dancing.

"Are you enjoying the Boxing Day celebration?" Emily asked with a smile, certain of the answer.

Eliza's head bobbed enthusiastically. "Oh yes—did you know that Lady Harriet, I mean, Lady Ashton, made sure that all of the servants here got a gift? She gave me this fan," Eliza replied, showing Emily a serviceable pink-and-tan fan.

"Lady Harriet is quite wonderful, isn't she? I think I should talk to Papa and see if we can make our Boxing Day a bit more festive."

Eliza continued smiling, glancing over toward a handsome young man on her left. "Our celebration is just as much fun, and doesn't seem to be as much work," Eliza replied, straightening the bodice of her pink dress.

"That is true," Emily replied, scanning the room for Nigel. She wanted to thank him for the puppy (she had been calling her "puppy" lately for want of a better name), but she didn't want anyone to think she was setting her cap for him. As if anyone would consider a spinister of four-and-twenty eligible for someone as grand as Lord Stratford, she thought, spotting Nigel on the far side of the room, talking to a throng of what was probably stable boys.

"Your gentleman friend is talking with the gents from the stable," Eliza said, glancing over at Nigel.

Emily blushed. "He isn't my gentleman friend, Eliza," she scolded weakly, looking quickly away from Nigel.

Eliza had the temerity to wink at her. "Yes, Miss Emily," she replied, and added, "Come over to the tables and play snapdragon with us."

So Emily spent the remainder of Boxing Day playing snapdragon with any number of servants, receiving dark looks of censure from the very proper Lady Markston. Emily was certain that Lady Markston was much too ladylike to stick her fingers into a fiery bowl of raisins in the first place. And she certainly wouldn't try to eat one of them without burning her fingers or her tongue, Emily thought, amazed at the talent of some of her fellow players. Her fingers were singed more than once, while some of the male servants playing had fingers that flew in and out of the bowl without touching a single flame.

As Emily continued playing snapdragon (one of her favorite parlor games since she was a child), she glanced out of the window and smiled. The weather was clearing up, and Lady Markston and her daughter would be able to go on their way. Possibly even tomorrow morning, she thought hopefully. Unless Lady Markston succumbs to some sort of illness so Susan can spend more time with Nigel, she added to herself, noting how Susan's gaze kept returning to Nigel.

But, for the moment, Nigel appeared to be ignoring Susan completely. The holiday was definitely improving for Emily.

Nigel stood across the well-lit room, relaxing against the mantel, studying Emily.

She stood in a gathering of mostly servants, his valet among them, thoroughly enjoying a game of snapdragon. Her delicate hands darted in and out of the flaming raisins, and he marveled at the fact that she didn't appear to be burning herself at all. Snapdragon was never a game that he mastered, and he watched Emily with interest. She laughed with his valet, Harriet's abigail, and a chorus of other hired hands as if she had known them all of her life. In turn, they smiled shyly back at her and appeared to be completely at ease with the very untitled Miss Winterhaven.

On the other side of the room, Henry was entertaining the stable boys with another parlor game. The rather large group of men of all ages and sizes were placing various lighted candles in a can filled with ale and trying to drink the contents. Most of the men were singeing their mustache hair and the tips of their noses, Nigel noted with a grin.

Harriet was playing the piano in the far corner, and Aubrey and Susan were sharing a stiff waltz. Susan didn't look too happy with the situation, and kept giving him marked looks across the room. He pointedly ignored them, while Aubrey occasionally flashed him a smile.

But what Nigel truly wanted to do was to go over to Emily and spend the rest of the evening with her alone. Of course,

Lady Markston would be spreading all sorts of vile gossip if I did that, he thought, glancing over to the lady in question. She was standing in a corner, and appeared to sneeze at regular intervals. She must not want to leave quite yet, he decided, and would bet Henry that Lady Markston was soon to be down with some sort of illness.

Nigel sipped his wassail, and his eyes naturally wandered back to the group playing snapdragon. Emily looked so delightful in her deep blue velvet dress, giggling like a young girl over the raisins. He could see her eyes shining from across the room, and she was undoubtedly the most beautiful and unaffected female present. Yes, she will make a splendid countess. Or a marchioness, he thought, his eyes drifting over her lithe form.

But as the evening wore on, Nigel began to thank the legendary Manning Mermaid. It was the sole cause of his acquaintance with Emily, and he was dashed grateful. He was very close to writing a very telling note to Emily's parents. I hope they won't mind their daughter marrying a peer, he thought distractedly, completely forgetting that Emily and her family were well acquainted with Roger. And his roguish ways.

The next few days were spent in a flurry of activity. Henry and Harriet separated their guests by sex, and tried to help their friends form some ideas on their costumes for the Blackmore masquerade.

Harriet was much more successful than Henry. The ladies were naturally more interested in finding a costume to suit their needs, while the gentlemen had to be coaxed a bit more. Aubrey finally relented and opted for an old uniform of one of Henry's ancestors, deciding he rather liked the look of a military man. His valet shined the tarnished medals that adorned the suit, and, in one afternoon, his costume was complete.

Henry chose something more elaborate, since he had discussed his costume with Harriet. They were once again going as Marc Antony and Cleopatra, which they had done for several fetes. Unfortunately, Henry had gained a bit in his girth, and needed some adjustments made on his very flimsy costume. Harriet was exactly the same size and shape she'd been on the day she was married, so her costume, like Aubrey's, was ready immediately. Of course, her abigail was to help her paint herself rather elaborately, so most of her work would be on the day of the masquerade itself.

Lady Markston, in a rare show of self-restraint, declared that "Since there isn't a proper *modiste* present, I will simply wear a mask and a domino. If I'm well enough to attend." Harriet was certain that Lady Markston would definitely be well enough to attend, since someone had to keep Susan at bay. As for her costume, Lady Markston was correct; there wasn't anything in the attic that would have suited someone of her girth. So, in the end, it was decided that Lady Markston should indeed wear a mask and a domino.

Then there was the question of Lady Susan's costume. Earlier in the week, while discussing the masquerade, Harriet bet Henry a shilling that Susan would decide to go to the fete dressed as Aphrodite, the Greek goddess of beauty. Henry, in all of his male innocence, declared that "No female can be that vain."

Days later, looking through the dusty trunks in the attic, Susan came upon a very sheer, completely indecent pink frock fashioned rather like a Grecian tunic. "This is it!" she squealed in delight. "I'll go to Lord Blackmore's dressed as Aphrodite!" she exclaimed, holding the sheer confection up to see if it would fit her dainty frame.

Harriet and Emily exchanged telling glances, and both ladies rolled their eyes toward the heavens. Harriet and Emily were both tired of Susan and her antics, and were counting the days until she left.

"That would be an interesting costume," Harriet commented diplomatically, staring at the costume in Susan's hands. "There is no way on this earth that Lady Markston will let her wear that costume," she whispered to Emily.

"She will look like a veritable cyprian! It will be the scandal of the year," Emily whispered back with a grin.

"I suppose we can have Blanche work on it," Susan declared, her fingers caressing the sheer material.

"Blanche, my abigail, worked with the local *modiste* for a time, before I employed her. She can work absolute miracles," Lady Markston confided with a smug smile.

"I'm going to my room to try it on. Mama, will you send Blanche posthaste?" Susan asked, walking down the narrow attic stairs.

"I'll join you, dearest," Lady Markston replied, following her down the stairs.

As soon as Lady Marston closed the attic door behind her, Emily turned to Harriet and said, "I do believe that your husband owes you a guinea."

Harriet smiled. "I couldn't convince him to bet a guinea. Henry never had any luck at all at the tables, so the most he would bet me was a shilling," she replied, opening one of the trunks in the corner. "You still haven't found anything you like?" she asked Emily with a slight sigh.

Emily shook her head, and looked into the trunk Harriet had just opened. "All of Henry's relations were, well, almost dwarfs!" she announced, and both ladies fell into a fit of the giggles.

"Dwarfs! Don't say that too loud or great, great Aunt Honoria may come back from the dead and start haunting us!" Harriet said, still giggling.

"It's true!" Emily added, riffling through the clothes. "If they weren't dwarfs they were at least much more . . . um . . . delicate than I am," she finally said, a wide smile on her face.

"Yes, well, Henry doesn't seem to have any female relations that fit your size."

Emily looked over at her friend, her eyes sparkling

wickedly. "Are you implying, Harriet, that I'm a giantess?" she asked in all seriousness.

Harriet looked over at her, momentarily worried that she had offended her friend. When she saw the smile that Emily was trying to repress, she began to giggle again. "Giantess? No, I think I'm trying to imply that Henry's ancestors were, well, elves!" she concluded with a giggle.

Emily continued to giggle as she picked up a simple, long, black-hooded cloak. "And what, may I ask, is this?" she asked, handing the garment to Harriet.

Harriet looked it over carefully. "Why, if I'm not mistaken, I do believe it's a monk's robe."

"A monk's robe? Really?"

Harriet continued to examine the merino garment. "Well, maybe not an actual monk's robe, but I do believe that there is some sort of story about one of Henry's great great grandfathers dressing up as a monk for some sort of family function or another. They say he was a bit let in the attic, but Henry has always claimed that it was done to annoy the rest of the family. I tend to agree with Henry," she concluded, handing the robe back to Emily.

"It seems to be long enough for me," Emily observed casually, a wicked gleam entering her eyes.

Harriet frowned. "You can't actually be considering going to the masquerade as a monk! We're in the country—the rustics here would be scandalized," Harriet replied, hoping to dissuade Emily from her train of thought.

Emily shrugged. "Harriet, nothing in this attic is long enough for me to wear, so any outfit will take ages to alter, if it can be altered. I could always wear a domino and a mask like Lady Markston, but that's dashed boring. And I'm certainly not going to dress up like a Greek goddess and wander about half-naked in front of a passel of strangers," she concluded, folding the monk's robe neatly.

"Emily, I'm sure my staff wouldn't mind working on a new costume for you, and they would most certainly have it done before Blackmore's rout," Harriet said weakly. She had seen the gleam in Emily's eyes before, and knew that she didn't have the slightest chance of dissuading her friend.

"I don't want your staff to go to all of that trouble. I've been trying to think up a suitable costume for days, and the only thing I felt comfortable with was a domino. I'm not young and beautiful like most of the ladies who attend these functions. In fact, I'm not even a lady. I'm just Miss Winterhaven, a spinster with no expectations. In this outfit, no one will pay any heed to me, and I'll feel much more comfortable," she concluded, walking toward the stairs.

Harriet followed her friend. "Emily, I don't see why you're still so uncomfortable in English Society," she complained, traipsing down the steps.

Emily shrugged. "I suppose I should forget about it, but I still rather dread masquerades. Don't you remember? The evening Roger Manning was going to announce our engagement was during a masquerade—you must remember how he went out of his way to humiliate me. That must be why I still dread these events, to a certain extent," Emily explained as they walked down the wainscotted halls.

Harriet *had* forgotten about Roger, Emily's humiliation at his hands, the mermaid, and the curse. All she knew was that Nigel, her favorite cousin, was quite smitten with her best friend, and that Emily appeared to favor him. The other facts had become conveniently lost among all of the holiday plans she had whirling in her mind. So Harriet calmly replied, "You'll see—you'll have the grandest time at Blackmore's masquerade, I promise."

Days later, Emily was grateful that she had chosen such a simple costume. Whatever they were doing to Susan's costume took up every waking moment of Susan and Lady Markston's time, which was quite an added bonus. Harriet was having more paste jewels applied to her costume, and the men wouldn't even mention what they were wearing. Aubrey was in seclusion with his valet, while Nigel and Henry spent a good part of their days playing cards or riding.

The weather had cleared and the roads were very nearly passable. In fact, according to Henry's groom, the roads were on their way to being perfect.

As predicted, Lady Markston had contracted some sort of malady that prevented her from traveling. So, due to her illness, Lady Markston was confined to her bed, and was only interrupted dozens of times a day by Susan and her abigail. Harriet predicted that Lady Markston would recover after the Twelfth Night celebrations. Henry declined to bet with her.

It was also the consensus that Susan and Lady Markston had given up on Nigel. He was very firmly in Emily's pocket, even though the lady in question certainly didn't realize it. Aubrey was especially pleased by that turn of events, since he could now pay court to Susan.

Until he accidentally overheard a private conversation between Lady Markston and Susan. Lady Markston's bedchamber door was left open, and Aubrey was innocently walking down the hall. Until he heard Susan's voice passionately ringing through her mother's room.

"But Mama, I *will* get Nigel to offer for me," Susan said, and Aubrey's face froze in shock. He was certain that Susan had given up on Nigel and the farcical idea of marriage to him.

"And how are you going to do that?" was Lady Markston's reply.

There was a long pause, and Aubrey could imagine the smug look on Susan's face. "Why, he's going to compromise me. Then he'll have to offer for me," she declared, as Aubrey paled.

"And when is this going to take place?" her mother asked.

"I have it all arranged. I will be hopelessly compromised tomorrow night, after the masquerade. Would you like to hear the plan? It's ever so clever," Susan said proudly.

"No, I'll have no party to it," Lady Markston said, and Aubrey heard footsteps up the stairs. So he casually walked away from the door, his face still pale. He had to make sure that he was the one who compromised Susan. But how can I do that if I don't know her plans? he wondered, his frown still in place as he retreated into his bedroom.

Emily sat in the candlelight of the music room, playing a soft tune on the pianoforte. The moonlight streamed through the open drapes, and the snow cast an eerie glow on the ground. Her puppy, finally christened with a name, was curled up underneath the instrument, fast asleep.

The scene was tranquil, but Emily felt anything but. Nigel had been distant for the past four nights, ever since the Christmas Day festivities. He must be toying with me, she thought with a sigh, her turmoil reflected in the dreadfully depressing piece of music she was playing.

She was so intent on her own musings that she didn't hear the door open behind her, or notice the shadow that fell across her music. It was only when she heard a small yip from under the pianoforte that she chanced to look behind her.

Nigel was standing in the doorway, clad simply in his breeches and a very unkempt white shirt. It was very late in the evening, well past midnight, and Emily assumed that everyone in the household was fast asleep. So she stopped playing and tightened her dressing robe around herself modestly. It certainly wasn't respectable to be alone with a gentleman in her state of undress, she realized with a slight blush.

"Nigel, I'm sorry if I disturbed you," she said softly, and when the puppy barked loudly and scampered over to him, she admonished, "Quiet, Duke!"

Nigel chuckled as he bent down to pet the puppy. "Duke? You've named your puppy after a noble title?" he said with a grin.

"Actually, since he is Wellington's brother, or sister—I still haven't really checked yet—I thought that since Wellington is a duke, that it was, well, a proper sort of name. And he—or she—seems to like it," she finished, watching Duke rolling on the floor as Nigel patted her stomach.

"I rather think that Duke is a dutchess, but I don't think she'll care," he said, picking up the puppy in his arms and walking over to the chair nearest to Emily.

As Duke continued to lick Nigel, Emily had no choice but to smile. Duke, the smallest of the litter, was by far the most affectionate puppy she had ever encountered. "Duke appears to have taken to you," she commented, watching how his large, gentle hands caressed the puppy.

"Yes, Duke is the charmer," he said, and added, "as is his mistress."

Emily blushed and looked at the ivory keys, completely confused.

"I do hope you're not vexed with me, Emily. I rather thought that if I paid you any more attention, Lady Markston would have made something scandalous out of it," he exclaimed calmly, his eyes never leaving her slim form.

Emily shrugged. "It doesn't signify. I'll be leaving Harriet's after the Twelfth Night celebrations, and I doubt that we'll really ever have any contact after that," she said in a rush, suddenly very depressed that she would very likely never see Nigel again.

"You have very little faith, Emily. I hardly think I would entrust a puppy to your care if I didn't think I'd be around to see that she was being taken care of properly," he said lightly.

"Duke will be taken care of properly," she said, staring at her hands. She was certain that Nigel was trifling with her affections.

Nigel gently put Duke on the floor, and she immediately scurried under the pianoforte. "You really must learn to take people more seriously, my dear Emily," he said softly, coming to stand next to her seat.

Emily looked up into his dark, golden eyes and said nothing.

Nigel reached down and took her hand in his, and lightly kissed it, his lips lingering on her fingers. "I suppose I should bid you good night before I kiss you and convince you even more that I'm toying with you," he said huskily, his eyes never leaving her face.

Emily blushed. "Good night, Nigel," she said softly, every fiber in her body willing him to lean over and kiss her properly.

Nigel stared at her for a very long time, and finally said, "Be sure to save all of your waltzes for me at Blackmore's masquerade."

"I'm a dreadful dancer," she reminded him, looking away from his intense gaze.

He continued to hold her hand. "You could have the grace of a milk cow and I'd still want to waltz with you."

"All right," she said softly, and felt bereft when her hand left the warm security of his.

"Good night, dearest Emily," he said, and she sighed as his tall, muscular frame disappeared into the darkness.

"Good night, Nigel," she almost whispered, her mind whirling in confusion.

Twelve

"Lady Susan? You want me to leave your silk nightdress out for you tonight?" Jane, Susan's abigail, asked, confusion written on her young face.

The nightdress in question was a frothy silk confection that was supposed to be for Lady Susan's wedding night. Jane didn't expect her to even try it on until that fateful event.

"Yes, Jane, the silk nightdress," she said, and added with a self-satisfied smirk, "and tomorrow you may offer me congratulations, since I'll undoubtedly be engaged."

Jane's jaw dropped to the floor. "Engaged? To Lord Langely?" she asked, completely surprised. The entire staff knew that Aubrey had developed a *tendre* for Susan, but thought that it was just because of the holiday season. No one actually expected him to offer for her.

"Not Aubrey—Nigel. You can be such a flat," Susan said, adjusting the bodice of her practically indecent masquerade costume.

"Really? Lord Stratford is going to offer for you?"

Susan smiled, and forgot about discretion. "Well, when he finds me in his bedroom tomorrow morning, he will be obligated, won't he?"

Horror was now etched on Jane's features. Her mistress was planning to force poor Lord Stratford into marriage, when everyone knew he was in love with the very nice Miss Winterhaven. Clearly something had to be done.

Moments later, when Susan dismissed her, Jane hurried

down to the kitchen in search of Hughes, Lord Stratford's valet. He was unavailable, and Jane thought she was at the end of her rope. Until she bumped into Gable, Lord Langely's man.

As they sat down to a very civilized tea, Jane explained the situation.

Gable checked his watch fob. "Lord Langely is due to leave for the masquerade in less than a quarter of an hour. Which gives us more than enough time to solve the problem at hand," he said reassuringly.

Jane prayed he was right.

On the other side of the house, Emily was preparing for the Blackmore masquerade. Actually, "preparation" was a harsh word. It took Eliza a scant minute to help Emily put on the severe monk's robe, complete with a voluminous hood.

"What do you think, Eliza?" she asked curiously, twirling in a circle for her maid.

"Begging your pardon, Miss Emily, but you don't look like a lady at all."

Emily giggled slightly. "That's the idea, Eliza. How can I even attempt to look proper with someone like Lady Susan attending the same rout dressed as Aphrodite? At least dressed like a monk I'll be able to be . . . inconspicuous," she concluded, peering through the hood.

Eliza frowned and finally said, "Why don't you wear your mermaid pendant? Then at least people will know you're a lady."

Emily took the sparkling pendant from Eliza and fastened it around her neck. The mermaid looked up at her, a rather tasteless medieval ornament against the dark brown wool. "It certainly looks interesting, doesn't it?" Emily asked, not too certain that she should wear the mermaid.

"It looks capital, Miss Emily," Eliza said cheerfully.

Emily shrugged slightly. "I suppose I should wear it," she acquiesced with a shrug.

The mermaid glittered merrily against the somber wool, and as Emily stared at it, she could have sworn the eyes were winking at her.

"My lord? Is something amiss?" Hughes, Nigel's valet, asked with a very definite frown.

Nigel sat on the bed, staring at his Hessians, starting to put one on his left foot. He was humming and appeared to be in the most unusual mood.

"Amiss? Not at all," Nigel replied with a smile, sliding the gleaming black boot onto his foot.

Hughes continued to frown and ran his hand through his thick brown hair. "Pardon me for mentioning it, my lord, but you do seem to be in an . . . unusual humor this evening. You usually don't appear to enjoy any evenings spent at a formal rout," Hughes commented.

Nigel stood up and casually walked over to the cheval glass mirror that rested in the corner, studying his appearance. "I'm particularly looking forward to this masquerade. Have you met Miss Winterhaven?"

"Miss Winterhaven?"

Nigel smiled broadly at his valet. "Yes, Miss Winterhaven. You found her to be . . . amiable, haven't you?"

Hughes smiled softly. "Miss Winterhaven is the kindest of ladies. I've spoken with her a number of times in the past few days. She's been trying to train her puppy, and I offered to help her. Miss Winterhaven doesn't put on any airs, and treats me with the same consideration as she treats you or Lord Ashton," he concluded quickly.

Nigel just grinned. "So *you're* the one who has taken Duke in hand? I didn't think Emily had any experience with dogs," he said, then added, "What does her abigail say about her?"

"Eliza? She adores Miss Winterhaven. Her father is as rich

as Croesus, and his staff is paid as well as any of the gentry in their district."

"I'm going to offer for her. This evening, in fact, if I can have some time alone with her," Nigel confided with a sly smile.

"Capital! Miss Winterhaven will be a grand wife, my lord, mark my words," Hughes said eagerly, now grinning himself.

"Yes, I believe she will. I plan to whisk her off into the library at the first opportunity," Nigel said, getting up and pacing about the room.

In his haste to propose, he conveniently forgot about the Manning Mermaid and Emily's prior connection with his rakish brother Roger. All he could think of was Emily and his dashed good luck at finding her.

"Emily, don't be nervous," Harriet whispered as they entered the magnificent hallway of Lord Blackmore's country estate.

As the party waited to be greeted by Lord Blackmore, Emily could feel every bone in her body cringing. She detested these large Society gatherings, and felt incredibly conspicuous.

And they reminded her of that rogue, Roger Manning. She attended her first Society masquerade with Roger, and it was there that he first told her of his eternal devotion. And many, many more lies that she had believed completely.

But she did manage to greet Lord Blackmore without incident. Their host was a dark-haired gentleman of average height wearing an outrageous red velvet jacket trimmed with white fur as his Lord of Misrule costume. As she walked toward the crush of dancers in the ballroom, she heard Lord Blackmore greet Nigel as if he were a long-lost friend, which was surprising. But then, every peer knows every other peer, Emily thought cynically, hiding in her wonderfully drab monk's robe, never straying from beside Harriet and Henry.

Harriet and Henry, who quite enjoyed dressing as Antony and Cleopatra, would have been quite unrecognizable in London. Harriet sported a long, black wig, and Henry, clad in a Roman soldier-type garb, looked dramatically different. But since they usually wore those costumes to Blackmore's yearly New Year's Eve rout, they didn't fool anyone.

Lady Susan was making quite a stir, and Emily inwardly wondered if the lady in question could make it through the evening without catching some dreadful malady. Although the snow had stopped, it was still dreadfully cold, and Lady Susan was wearing next to nothing. Which meant that the local bucks were clamoring for some sort of introduction, while Aubrey stood guard at her side.

Aubrey was clad in a regimental uniform, and looked rather dashing. He was getting more than his share of attention from the single ladies present, but considered himself Lady Susan's escort and was never far from her side.

Lord Blackmore's enormous ballroom was quite beyond Emily's expectations; in fact, it surpassed anything she had ever seen in London. Three blown-glass chandeliers hung from the vaulted ceiling, and hothouse roses intertwined with holly and mistletoe could be found in every available nook and cranny. The floor was done in the most magnificent marble Emily had ever seen, and scattered through the impressive room were a variety of partially clothed bronze sculptures. As Emily scanned the room filled with merrymakers, she noted that Greek history seemed to be a predominant theme, and that Lady Susan wasn't the only Aphrodite present at Blackmore's rout. But she is undoubtedly the most attractive, Emily conceded, following Harriet and Henry to the refreshment table.

"Quite a crush again, isn't it?" Henry commented, scanning the crowd of merrymakers.

"It always is, dear," Harriet said, then turned to Emily. "So, what do you think of Blackmore's New Year's masquerade?"

Emily smiled slightly. "It is quite overwhelming for a country rout. It seems like half of London is here!" she exclaimed.

"Yes, Blackmore spares no expense. In fact, the members of his house party usually spend the rest of the holiday resting. Until the Twelfth Night, when they all go mumming. It's quite a spectacle," Harriet replied, trying to follow Emily's gaze. "I think Nigel is still having a coze with Blackmore."

A blush stained Emily's almost-hidden cheeks. "Oh," she replied, and fingered the mermaid dangling on her breast nervously.

"Aubrey certainly has taken quite a liking to Lady Susan. Much to the annoyance of her mother," Henry observed, handing each lady a glass of ratafia.

Harriet chuckled. "It would serve Lady Markston right if Aubrey offered for her. Everyone knows she's only after Nigel for his blunt," she observed, adjusting her long, black wig slightly.

Henry smiled warmly at her and had the audacity to wink. "Remember to save me the waltz at midnight," he said mysteriously.

"What's so special about the waltz at midnight?" Emily asked innocently, failing to notice that Nigel, looking spectacularly dashing in his black domino and half-mask, was walking toward their party from the other side of the immense ballroom.

A brilliant smile lit up Harriet's face. "Emily! You mean you forgot one of Miss Haversham's old wives' tales?" she said merrily.

"Yes. There's one about waltzing at midnight?"

"Miss Haversham always said that on the eve of the new year you will marry the person you're dancing with at midnight," Harriet said breathlessly, trying to adjust her wig more.

"I don't remember that," Emily protested, noting how Henry kept his arm possessively around Harriet.

"Well, Harriet and I have been waltzing together at midnight every New Year's Eve since we've been together, and look at us!" Henry said with a wide smile, and Emily couldn't help but grin.

"But you're already married," Emily protested, so engrossed in their conversation that she momentarily forgot about feeling ill at ease.

"That's a mere technicality, Emily!" Henry protested, and kissed Harriet gingerly on her very painted cheek.

Emily giggled as a deep, masculine voice behind her said, "Then I must make sure I'm dancing at midnight with the right person."

She turned and looked into Nigel's golden-green eyes, once again momentarily confused. Why does he keep pretending he has a *tendre* for me? she wondered, grateful that she was practically hidden in her monk's robe.

"I should say so. I wouldn't want you leg-shackled to the wrong chit," Henry said casually, glancing across the crowded room at Lady Susan. Aubrey was gallantly at her side, and Lady Markston was a few feet away, frowning furiously. "Of course, I doubt that Lady Markston holds the same opinion that I do," he added with a smile.

The orchestra struck up a waltz, and Nigel gazed down at the female clad in the utterly ridiculous monk's garb at his side. "May I see your dance card, Emily? Is this waltz free?" he asked in all seriousness.

Emily stared down at her hands. "I . . . misplaced my dance card," she said simply, and stared at him in abject horror as he took her hand and practically dragged her toward the dance floor. "I'm really an awful dancer," she murmured in complete embarrassment.

As he swept her into his arms, Nigel brought her hooded figure far too close for propriety and whispered, "I think not."

Emily could feel her heart beating a tattoo as he held her next to his firm, muscular body. Her rapid heartbeat, combined with the crowd on the dance floor and the heat of Blackmore's ballroom, began to make her feel slightly light-headed. So she swayed into Nigel, who was now close to making a spectacle of himself.

"Are you feeling all right, Emily?" he whispered into her ear, his breath warm against her skin.

They continued waltzing around the dance floor, and Emily was quite unsure of how to answer. She felt slightly dizzy, yet it wasn't an unpleasant sensation. So in the end, she simply replied, "I think I should have something to drink once our dance is over."

"Your wish is my command my dear," he said, then added, "You look delightful tonight."

A faint chuckle floated out from under the gloomy monk's robe. "Lord Stratford, you're an addlepate. I most certainly don't look delightful dressed as a monk," she declared, a smile appearing on her masked face.

"I hate to disagree with a lady, but I fear I must," he said smoothly. "You do look enchanting tonight, but then you always look charming, Emily," Nigel said in all sincerity.

"Once again you're offering me Spanish coin, my lord. And I must admit that I suspect your motives, since the last gentleman who offered me as much flummery ended up embroiling me in quite the scandal," she admitted, wincing at the thought of Roger Manning.

"The cur should be shot," he declared, bringing her body closer to his.

"I couldn't agree more," Emily said in a voice that was barely audible.

"I want another glass of wassail, Aubrey," Susan commanded, waving her hand toward the refreshment table.

Aubrey glanced at the table, then back at Susan. It was obvious that Susan had drunk more than her share of wassail, and was on the verge of becoming bosky. Very bosky. So he calmly replied, "I don't think so."

Susan's blue eyes lit up in anger. "You will procure another glass of wassail for me or I'll have one of my many admirers do it for me, Lord Langely," she replied haughtily, glancing around the room. They were, for the moment, alone.

"If you drink any more wassail, you're going to disgrace yourself, Susan. Come and dance with me," he ordered, and all but dragged her onto the dance floor.

As they went through the movements of the country dance, she managed to hiss at him, "You'll be sorry. I'm going to be married to Nigel and you'll rue the day you crossed someone of my standing."

Luckily, she didn't hear him mutter under his breath, "Nigel isn't the one you're going to end up marrying."

The country dance did seem to calm Susan, and, as the set ended, a pox-faced young man appeared, begging to lead Susan out. Susan stared at her dance card and realized, to her horror, that she was free.

So the pox-faced young man got his dance with Aphrodite, who in turn glared angrily at Aubrey.

Aubrey smiled at her benignly, and glanced across the room. Lady Markston was staring at Nigel and Emily with a look of disdain. Aubrey checked his jeweled pocket watch, noting that it was approaching midnight. I must speak with Nigel about the sleeping arrangements tonight, he reminded himself with a smile. Susan's plan was going to have consequences that she never imagined.

"Who is that blade she's dancing with?" Nigel asked, craning his neck toward the dance floor. Emily was being partnered by a handsome young man dressed in a dashing, bottle-green domino. He was about Emily's age, and was casting the most ridiculous sheep eyes at her hooded figure, which Nigel found incredibly annoying.

Harriet grinned at him. "I believe that is Lord Richardson. He's quite eligible, and, if I'm not mistaken, spent a good part of the masquerade bringing refreshments to your Lady Susan."

"She is not *my* Lady Susan, and never will be if I have any say in the matter. Must he practically maul Emily while he's dancing with her?" Nigel asked, a frown now etched on his face.

"Zounds, Nigel, they're just dancing. Why don't you try to enjoy yourself," Henry suggested, glancing over at Harriet.

Nigel glared at Henry, patiently waiting for the dance to end.

Before Emily could even move off the dance floor, Nigel was at her side, his hand possessively on her arm. "Is your next dance spoken for, Emily?" he asked in his most charming voice, moving her toward Henry and Harriet.

Emily looked up at him from beneath her monk's hood. "I don't believe so, Nigel," she answered shyly.

Before Nigel could utter another word, the notes of a waltz wafted out to the pair, and Nigel whisked her back out onto the floor.

The music floated around them, and Nigel no longer cared that he was holding an unfashionably tall bluestocking dressed as a medieval monk much too close for propriety. All he could think about was her slim body molded closely to his, and the warmth he felt when she was near.

The pair waltzed in silence, and when the dance ended, Blackmore, from the edge of the dance floor, proclaimed, "It is one minute past midnight in the year of Our Lord eighteen hundred and eighteen!"

"He's going to offer for her," Henry commented, sipping his wassail.

Harriet glanced over at the pair. Nigel was leading Emily out of the ballroom, and from the look of it, toward the library. "Did he say something to you?" she asked curiously, her blue eyes wide with amazement.

Henry adjusted the belt on his costume. "No. A man can tell these things. I'll wager you a guinea that he offers for her tonight."

A smile appeared on Harriet's rosy features. "Every time you wager with me, you lose, Henry."

"Not this time. Nigel is going to offer for our dear friend Emily. I won't wager on her answer, though."

"She'll accept him, of course. Emily is completely besotted with Nigel," Harriet explained, glancing around the room. Susan was still in a deep coze with Aubrey, so she couldn't make any mischief and interrupt the pair.

Henry shook his head. "I wouldn't be so certain. She still doesn't know about the Manning Mermaid, or the fact that Nigel is Roger Manning's older brother," he pointed out.

"Henry, you've heard Nigel in Parliament. He can be brilliantly eloquent when he needs to be, so I don't doubt that he'll be able to explain the situation to Emily logically."

Henry shook his head doubtfully. "I don't know if I can agree, dearest," he said cynically.

The library was a dark, cavernous room lit only by a dwindling fire in the fireplace. Nigel silently led Emily over to the hearth and gently took off his mask, then reached under her hood to dispose of hers.

"I was at Waterloo," he began in a soft voice, taking her two hands in his, "and I don't believe I was nearly as frightened as I am at this very moment."

Emily frowned, confusion written on her delicate features. "You were at Waterloo? Didn't your family object?" she said in a serious voice, her skin luminous in the firelight.

Nigel smiled gently. "Oh yes, my father all but disowned me, but when I actually came back alive, we managed to come to an understanding. My father, the marquess, can be a bit unreasonable at times, but he is good-hearted. You'll see when you meet him."

Her eyes were large as they met his golden-green gaze. One didn't have to be a slow-top to realize that Emily had absolutely no idea what Nigel was talking about.

As she frowned up at him, Nigel couldn't help but smile at her. "I'm sorry, Emily; I am rambling, aren't I? I most certainly didn't bring you here to discuss my father," he said, trying to figure out a way to actually ask her to marry him. He had never proposed marriage to anyone in his life, and it was a bit daunting.

Emily continued studying him, and quietly said, "What would you like to discuss, Nigel?"

Nigel's right hand left hers, and he brought it slowly to her temple and lightly caressed her long, auburn hair. "I brought you in here to offer for you," he said simply, willing himself not to kiss her. Though that was what he wanted to do more than anything else.

"Offer for me?" she asked in confusion, stepping back from him.

"Yes. Will you do me the honor of becoming my wife, Emily?" he asked as her jaw dropped.

"Nigel, Lord Stratford," she stuttered, "I'm sorry, don't you know I'm not eligible? I'm four-and-twenty years old and my family is connected to trade. I'm not a suitable wife for a peer."

Nigel took a step forward and wrapped his arms around her waist, bringing her warm, lithe body next to his. "Yes, well, I play piano, dislike Society, and love you more than I ever thought possible. We all have our faults," he said passionately, drawing her even closer to him.

They were so wrapped up in their conversation that they didn't hear the footsteps coming down the hall. So when the library door burst open and Lord Blackmore and another gentleman walked in, the two broke apart like a pair of guilty school children.

"Nigel, Miss Winterhaven, sorry to interrupt. Gilford wanted to examine one of my illustrated manuscripts," Blackmore said casually, ignoring the fact that he had all but caught Nigel and Emily in an embrace.

"Of course," Nigel replied casually, as Blackmore and Gilford walked through the fairly dark room to a desk in the corner.

"Here it is," Blackmore announced, thrusting a large, ancient manuscript at Gilford, a young, cleric-looking man dressed in a brown domino.

"Thank you so much for letting me see it, Lord Blackmore," Gilford stuttered as the pair joined Emily and Nigel near the fire.

As Gilford began to examine the manuscript, Blackmore glanced over at Emily, as if seeing her for the first time. His eyes were fixed on the mermaid dangling around her neck.

"That's a rather unusual piece of jewelry," he commented, staring intently at the mermaid.

"Yes, it was a gift from my grandfather—he bought it in London," Emily explained, a blush staining her cheeks.

Blackmore continued to stare at the pendant, and finally exclaimed, "Why, it's the Manning Mermaid! Nigel, how did Miss Winterhaven come into possession of one of your family jewels?" he asked, turning to Nigel.

Nigel paled somewhat. He had entirely forgotten about the pendant, the curse, Roger and the real reason he had joined Harriet's house party. He began to get a definite sinking feeling in his stomach.

"Let me guess. Roger, that scapegrace of a brother of yours off and sold it to pay for a gambling debt," Blackmore suggested, completely unaware of Nigel's mortification.

Before Nigel could reply, Emily, who was now almost completely white, asked in a deadly calm voice, "Excuse me, Lord Blackmore, but am I to understand that Lord Stratford is related to Roger Manning?"

"Related?" Blackmore chuckled, in the best of humor. "Roger is Nigel's younger brother. And, if I'm not mistaken, there's something about that pendant that your father told me . . ." he began, then snapped his fingers. "I remember! The Manning Mermaid has some sort of curse attached to it, doesn't it? Your father told me some sort of cock-and-bull story about a curse of ill luck on the family if the pendant is ever sold," Blackmore concluded, smiling at Nigel.

Nigel wasn't smiling. Nigel was more pale than Emily. "Father tends to believe that sort of gammon," Nigel said weakly, trying to catch Emily's eye. She wouldn't look at him and instead focused her gaze on Lord Blackmore.

"Miss Winterhaven, watch yourself or Nigel will try to seduce you into selling the mermaid back to him," Blackmore warned with a chuckle, then turned to the young cleric. "Gilford, I'm not going to let you spend New Year's Eve closeted in my library," he said, taking the book from Gilford. "Let's return to the party and I'll introduce you to Miss Hazelworth," he said, winking broadly at Nigel.

"Miss Hazelworth?" Gilford asked, brightening visibly as he followed Blackmore out of the library.

The silence was deafening in the room once Nigel and Emily were alone. Emily stood staring into the fire and Nigel was at a complete loss as to what to say.

So he moved behind her, put his hands lightly on her shoulders, and quietly said, "You never did answer my question."

Emily turned around slowly, her eyes ablaze. "How could you?" she cried, a single tear running down her cheek.

Thirteen

"I can explain," Nigel said, taking a step toward her.

Emily stepped back, and began to finger the mermaid pendant that was winking at her in the firelight. "I'm sure you can, Lord Stratford, just as your brother Roger told me he could explain. Is this some sort of prank you're involved in? Is that it?" she asked, not meeting his eyes.

"Not at all," he said in a low voice, his pallor almost as ghostly as hers.

"I thought not. This is all about the mermaid, isn't it? That's why you asked me about selling it a fortnight or so ago. It must have pained you greatly when it was returned to me after you stole it," she said, finally looking up into his golden eyes.

"Emily, I didn't steal the mermaid," he said in a choked, desperate voice.

"Of course not. And you never realized that I was the inconsequential female that your brother proceeded to embroil in a scandal several Seasons ago. So, to get back your blasted mermaid, you simply forgot to mention that fact and decided it would be much easier to feign affection for me. That way I would probably give you the pendant back and you wouldn't have to let loose with any of your precious family blunt to get rid of the supposed curse," she explained in a deadly calm voice.

Nigel stared at her, obviously at a complete loss. He noticed how her pale hand had tightened around the mermaid.

"It wasn't like that at all, Emily," he said in a soft voice, staring at the slender figure near the fire.

Emily could feel her heart breaking. It was as if she were going through the entire Roger Manning episode all over again, except that this time it was worse than she ever imagined. Because she did love Nigel. And she had almost agreed to marry him. "Yes, well, your charming brother said the same thing to me," she murmured, staring into the fire, her hand still wrapped around the pendant.

"Emily, I don't care about the mermaid. I want to marry you," he said, his voice husky with passion.

The fire crackled, and Emily stared into the burning embers for a long, long time. Finally, she slowly took the mermaid pendant from around her neck and thrust it at him. "Take it. I don't want it near me," she announced dramatically.

Nigel reluctantly took the mermaid from her outstretched hand and pleaded, "Emily, you have to let me explain."

Emily looked up at him, another tear glistening on her cheek. "I don't require any explanations, Lord Stratford. Lady Markston was right. Members of the nobility don't mix with people of my ilk," she said bitterly, fighting the urge to weep uncontrollably.

"You're wrong, my love. Please let me explain," he beseeched, his voice level and soothing.

"You have what you wanted. Just leave me alone," she said icily, gliding regally toward the door.

Nigel followed at her heels, loosening the collar on his shirt. "Emily, stop being a widgeon. I don't want the damned mermaid, I want you!" he announced, thrusting the mermaid back at her.

As her world crashed around her, Emily stared at him and softly whispered, "I never want to see you again," and quickly rushed out of the library.

Her world had collapsed once again.

* * *

"Emily, what's wrong?" Harriet asked, concern written on her pretty face.

"I want to go home. Now. I've had an . . . altercation with Lord Stratford, and I just want to leave here," she almost sobbed behind her mask.

Harriet put her arm around her friend and led her toward the door. "Of course, dear. Do you want to tell me about it?" Harriet was nothing if not calm in the face of trouble.

As they reached the door and waited for their carriage to be brought, the tears silently ran down Emily's cheeks. "Why didn't you tell me he was Roger Manning's older brother?"

"I didn't want to upset you with talk about that horrible time. And Nigel is nothing like Roger," she added, craning her neck toward the ballroom, apparently looking for Henry.

"Yes, he is, Harriet. He asked me to marry him just so he could have the mermaid back in his family. Grandpapa must have unknowingly bought it from him when he was in London," Emily said between sobs.

"I'm sure there's been some sort of mistake, Emily. Nigel would never offer for you just to get the mermaid back," Harriet said calmly, as the pair walked out the door, toward the carriage. Henry was right, she thought distractedly. Nigel did offer for Emily. And she had obviously refused.

As Emily was helped into her seat, Harriet left word with the footman that Henry was to be alerted that she was leaving early with Miss Winterhaven, and that he should return home immediately.

The drive back was none too pleasant for Emily or Harriet. Emily was convinced that Nigel was the biggest blackguard who had ever lived, and had no honor whatsoever left in his bones.

Harriet tried to appeal to Emily's sense of reason, but to no avail. Emily was still weeping an ocean of tears, and was once again going through a bitter betrayal at the hands of one of the Manning family.

In the end, there was only one solution. Emily was dutifully put to bed and given a small dose of laudanum, so she could get some sleep.

Harriet sat alone, waiting in the parlor. Emily's story was somewhat fragmented, but there were several facts that she was sure of: Emily knew that Nigel was Roger's brother; Nigel had proposed marriage to Emily; Emily knew that the mermaid was cursed; and Emily knew Nigel wanted the mermaid back.

The fire was blazing as Harriet waited for Nigel to appear and to give her some sort of explanation. She had warned him about hurting Emily, and he had assured her that his intentions were honorable. Yet Emily lay in a drugged sleep, her heart broken, while Nigel spent the evening at Blackmore's rout with his family heirloom in his pocket.

Yes, Nigel does have some explaining to do, Harriet thought, sipping a glass of Madeira.

Nigel stepped out of the library and walked down the long, dark hallway toward the main ballroom, in search of Emily. Conviction was written on his stern countenance; any of his fellow soldiers would have recognized the look of determination in his eyes. At that single moment in time, Nigel Manning was a determined man with a goal: to win back the woman he loved.

The ballroom, filled with dancing couples, was also crowded with drunken merrymakers. Since it was past midnight, most of the guests had taken off their masks, so it was a trifle easier for him to search the room for Emily.

How hard can it be to find a female dressed as a monk? he wondered, catching sight of Henry and Lord Blackmore across the room. They hovered around the refreshment table, having what appeared to be a serious discussion.

"Nigel, do you have a moment?" a voice at his side asked, and Nigel turned, only to find himself being addressed by Aubrey.

"Not precisely. I'm looking for Emily—Miss Winter-haven," he explained hastily, still scanning the room and rather ignoring Aubrey.

"Left a bit ago, with Harriet. She appeared to be in a tizzy about something or another," Aubrey offered, sipping his wassail.

Nigel focused his attention on Aubrey. "She left? Do you think she's all right?" he asked with a frown.

Aubrey shrugged. "I have no idea. But I do have another rather urgent matter to discuss with you."

Nigel was completely exasperated. He didn't want to stand in the middle of Blackmore's rout and make polite conversation with Aubrey. He wanted to leave immediately and force Emily to hear his explanation. Finally he muttered, "I really have other affairs to attend to, Aubrey."

Aubrey stared out at the couples dancing, and frowned at the pasty-faced young buck who was leading out Susan. "As you wish. Let me be the first to offer you congratulations, though," he said in a sardonic voice, a slight smile on his face.

The frown on Nigel's brow deepened. "Congratulations?"

"Why, yes. If what my valet learned was true, you will be an engaged man tomorrow morning," Aubrey said simply, his pudgy fingers nervously running up and down his crystal goblet.

Nigel was now truly confused. There was no way that Aubrey, or his valet, could have known that he had offered for Emily. Yet Aubrey was offering felicitations, and everyone knew he was paying court to Emily. Finally he said, "What exactly did your valet hear?"

A relaxed smile appeared on Aubrey's face, replacing his carefully practiced look of sheer boredom. "Tomorrow morning, you will wake up with a member of the delicate sex in your bed. Being a gentleman, you will obviously be obligated to offer for her," he explained calmly.

"And this female isn't Miss Winterhaven?" Nigel asked, the reality of the situation suddenly dawning on him.

"Miss Winterhaven is a paragon, from what I've been able to observe, so the answer is, of course, no."

Nigel shrugged his broad, muscular shoulders. He didn't wish to deal with Susan, not after the Cheltingham tragedy with Emily. "Then I simply won't spend the evening in my suite. I'll have Harriet's staff put me in another bedroom," he replied, trying to catch Henry's attention from across the room.

"That is one way of dealing with it. I have another, more permanent solution in mind, though," Aubrey said, a bit too casually.

"Yes?"

"I propose that we switch rooms tonight, without the knowledge of the rest of the household."

Henry began to walk toward the pair, and Nigel was only half-listening to Aubrey, not really grasping the implications of what he was saying. All Nigel could think about was the look of betrayal that haunted Emily's eyes when she told him she never wanted to see him again. "Yes, that's fine. When we return to the house I'll have my valet see to it," Nigel replied distractedly, walking toward Henry. He had more important matters to attend to before the evening's end.

"I don't wish to discuss Emily tonight, Harriet," Nigel announced, walking toward the staircase to his bedroom.

"Nigel Manning, I have waited up specifically to find out what has happened. I let you join our house party against my better judgment, and you have behaved no better than Roger. I demand an explanation," Harriet insisted, her blue eyes alight with anger.

Henry stood between the pair, obviously torn. On one hand, Harriet was entirely correct. On the other, Nigel looked ragged and definitely unfit to have any sort of conversation. All in all, he reasoned, it could wait until morning. "Harriet, Nigel doesn't seem to be feeling quite the thing. I think this can wait until morning."

Harriet turned to her husband, still very angry. "Yes, well, Emily wasn't feeling quite the thing, either, thanks to this scoundrel," she replied vehemently, her eyes never leaving Nigel.

Nigel leaned against the mahogany banister. "Harriet, the only person I wish to explain anything to is Miss Winterhaven. Since she has already retired, I'll bid you both good night," he said simply, and began to walk slowly up the stairs.

Harriet was about to call up the stairs to him when Henry took hold of her arm. "It can wait, my dear," he said in a soft voice, and Harriet finally conceded.

"All right," she replied, following him up the stairs to their chambers.

"Do you want your hair put up in curling papers, Lady Susan?" Jane, Susan's abigail, asked calmly, studying her employer.

Lady Susan was obviously very bosky. She was in the best of moods, and was thrown into a fit of giggling when Jane helped her into the silk nightgown she had demanded to wear. Her cheeks were bright red, her hair fell down her back like a golden curtain, and her generous curves were more than apparent in the enticing gown.

"No, not tonight," she giggled, then added, "I expect you to wake me at dawn."

Jane frowned. That was dashed unusual. Lady Susan never appeared before the noon hour, especially after a major fete. "Yes, Lady Susan."

Susan giggled again as Jane ran the brush through her tangled hair. "If I'm not in my bed, you must be certain to find me, even if you have to search every room in the house."

Jane raised an eyebrow, and continued combing her hair. Lady Susan expected to be spending the night with Lord Stratford. What she didn't know was that Lord Stratford would probably not be spending the night in his bedroom, so all of her scheming was going to waste. I hope he won't be spending the night in his bedroom, Jane thought, still rhythmically brushing Susan's golden tresses. If he is caught in bed with Lady Susan after being warned, he deserves to be leg-shackled to her, she decided with a slight smile. . . .

"That's fine—you may leave now," Susan ordered, her eyes bright with anticipation.

As Jane left the room, she wondered if that nice Miss Winterhaven might need another abigail in her household, for life with Lady Susan was getting more taxing every day.

The hour was very late, or very early, depending on one's opinion, when Lady Susan padded silently down the hall. She was clad only in her sheer nightdress, but wasn't worried about being seen. Nigel's room was in the same wing as her suite, so she only had a short distance to walk.

The hall was as black as night, save for a few candles, and Susan was smiling in anticipation of the next morning.

Tomorrow morning I'll become engaged and soon I'll be a countess, she thought, silently opening the door to Nigel's room.

Moonlight flooded the room, penetrating the thick curtains. Susan could see the bed, and the figure bundled under a large mass of covers.

As silent as a jungle cat, Susan walked through the room to the far side of the bed. The figure was sleeping as if he were dead, which suited her purpose ideally.

So she simply got under the covers on the other side of

the bed, trying not to disturb the sleeping figure next to her. He'll be disturbed enough tomorrow morning when I announce that we anticipated our vows, she thought with glee, settling under the blankets. She fell into a drunken sleep almost immediately.

A single, blood-curdling scream pierced the early morning light that filtered through the heavy draperies of the Ashton country home.

The response to the obviously feminine shriek was immediate; Henry, followed by Harriet, appeared first. Their butler Coverdail, and Henry's valet Glover, appeared almost simultaneously in the long, winding hallway, trying to find the cause of the disturbance.

The small group stood rooted in their steps, looking up and down the hall. Emily appeared from the north wing, as did Lady Markston.

"I think the scream came from the west wing, my lord," Glover interjected, and Coverdail nodded his head in agreement.

"To the west wing, then," Henry commanded, pulling his maroon velvet dressing robe tightly around himself.

The mass of visitors, all still in various states of undress, moved down the hallway until they spotted Susan's abigail standing at Nigel's door.

Harriet and Emily, who looked a trifle under the weather, exchanged a telling glance.

Lady Markston, her thinning blond hair in a long braid that made her look rather like a very aged Rapunzel, stepped to the front of the group and demanded, "Jane! What is the meaning of this?"

Harriet studied the abigail, who looked as if she were going to burst into a fit of giggles. "Look!" she announced, and pointed into the bedroom.

Lady Markston threw the door open and proceeded to exclaim, "My God!" and promptly swooned into Henry's arms.

As Henry struggled with Lady Markston's enormous limp body, the rest of the party surged toward the door, overcome with curiosity.

"Goodness!" Harriet exclaimed, as she looked into the darkened bedroom.

Lady Susan, who appeared to be suffering the ill effects of being foxed, was standing in her very transparent silk night-dress at the foot of Nigel's bed. Her usually luminescent skin was pale, and she was on the verge of tears.

Curled up in Nigel's bed was a tousled but grinning Aubrey. "Susan dear, come back to bed," he said with a smile, and Susan flew into a fit of rage.

"You! You scoundrel! What are you doing in Nigel's bed?" she demanded, and for good measure, picked up a letter opener off the escritoire and flung it at the prone form on the bed.

Aubrey easily avoided the letter opener and continued to grin at her. "Susan dearest, shall we tell our guests the good news?"

"You vermin!" she shrieked, and began to hurl everything on the escritoire at him in abject anger.

Henry heaved Lady Markston's still unconscious body into Coverdail's arms and stepped into the bedroom. "Lady Susan! Control yourself!" he ordered authoritatively.

Susan flung a small book at Aubrey, then screamed, "What is he doing here? This is Nigel's room!"

Henry glanced over at Aubrey, then back at Susan, who still appeared to be in the throes of a fit of rage. "Aubrey, what happened?"

Aubrey calmly sat up in bed, as if it were the most ordinary of mornings. "I awoke to the scream of Lady Susan's abigail at my door. When I looked over, Lady Susan was sleeping ever so soundly next to me," he explained simply.

"What were you doing in Nigel's room?" Harriet asked, trying to hide her grin.

"Nigel and I were discussing our sleeping arrangements last night, and I mentioned that my mattress was, I'm sorry to say, not the most firm. He said that his mattress was firmer than what he was accustomed to, so he offered it to me. If I found it to my liking, we were going to switch rooms for the rest of the holiday," Aubrey said logically.

Henry looked at Aubrey, then back at Lady Susan, and replied, "My felicitations on your engagement. Will the wedding be in London?"

"Wedding? There will be no wedding!" Susan replied with the voice of a true termagant.

"I'm sorry, Lady Susan, but you have been compromised. Your abigail found you in bed with Lord Langely. It is our duty as your hosts to protect your reputation," Henry explained, much to his delight.

"I will rot in the bowels of hell before I marry you, you grasping fortune hunter!" Susan said as she pushed her way past the crowd at the door and headed toward her room.

Everyone now had their eyes on Aubrey, who looked wonderfully contented. "I think a spring wedding, probably in London," he replied with a slight smirk.

Henry grinned at him. "Once again, my congratulations. We can discuss the matter at breakfast," he announced, turning toward the throng at Aubrey's door. "I believe the Cheltingham tragedy is now over," he said, and motioned for the servants to get about their business.

Everyone headed back to their respective rooms except for Nigel, who was the last to join the onlookers. He silently waited at he door to have a word alone with Aubrey.

When everyone was out of hearing distance, Nigel ran his hand through his thick, black hair and said, "I owe you a great debt."

Aubrey smiled. "Actually, it was Jane, Susan's abigail, who alerted my valet Gable. She wanted to tell your man, but he wasn't available," he said calmly. "It seems that the abigail is a hopeless romantic. She told my man that everyone knew that you should marry Miss Winterhaven, not Lady Susan."

"Well, I concur with her, but at the moment, Miss Winterhaven isn't speaking to me."

"Really? That's a surprise. In any case, someone has to marry Lady Susan, and I suppose it was time to meet Jack Ketch," Aubrey said cordially.

A faint smile finally appeared on Nigel's severe features. "I do believe you're correct, Aubrey. Marrying Lady Susan is akin to meeting Jack Ketch," he pronounced with a smile.

Some hours later, the meeting that Nigel was enduring with Henry and Harriet in the parlor was less than pleasant.

Harriet, clad in a somber Devonshire brown high-necked gown, paced the room, obviously very agitated.

Nigel attempted to relax in the hideous black armchair with gilt ornaments, with limited success. It appeared to be more comfortable than the black-and-gold recamier which Henry was occupying, but barely. He simply sipped his afternoon tea and waited for the peal that Harriet and her husband were bound to ring over him.

Henry, still dazed from the morning's tumultuous events, looked bored with the whole discussion. He stared blankly out the window into the sunny, snow-covered garden, completely oblivious to the fact that his wife was in a fine state.

"Nigel, you promised me you weren't toying with Emily. What, exactly, has transpired between you?" Harriet asked formally, seating herself in the gilt chair next to her very errant relation.

Nigel let out a long, deep sigh and stared at nothing in particular. "Emily and I didn't have any sort of falling-out, per se. We were having a private discussion in the library when we were joined by Blackmore and one of his other guests."

"And?" Harriet asked, her eyes never leaving his disheveled form.

"Blackmore recognized the mermaid. And told Emily about the curse. And mentioned Roger. That was enough for Emily to jump to several erroneous conclusions," he stated firmly, running his hand through his wild hair.

"You should have told Emily about Roger, and the mermaid," Henry added, taking a pinch of snuff from a silver snuffbox.

"Yes, I know," he said, shaking his head. "But to be honest, I completely forgot about the mermaid. Once Emily told me that she wouldn't sell it, the whole curse just slipped my mind."

Harriet raised an eyebrow in disbelief. "You forgot about the primary reason you decided to spend the holiday with us?"

Nigel blushed slightly. "Yes. I realize that I sound like an addlepate, but it's the truth. I was enjoying the time I was spending with Emily so much that the mermaid, as well as her relationship with Roger, never even crossed my mind," he admitted regretfully.

"So what happened?" Henry asked curiously, stretching his legs out in front of him.

"Emily gave me the pendant back and informed me that she never wants to see me again."

Harriet stared at the Aubusson carpet for a long moment before saying, "I do think you owe Emily some sort of apology."

"What for?" Henry asked, sitting up attentively on the recamier.

"Henry, Nigel has been feigning affection for Emily so he could convince her to sell the pendant back. That's a dashed dishonest thing to do!" Harriet exclaimed vehemently.

"Don't be a wet goose, Harriet. Everyone in the household knows that Nigel and Emily are smelling of April and May," Henry replied.

Harriet glanced over at Nigel, her eyebrow raised once again. "Well? Is Henry correct?"

Nigel was none too happy about discussing his private affairs with the family, so he simply met Harriet's eyes and replied, "As I've said, I haven't been toying with Emily. The mermaid means nothing to me and I'd gladly explain it all to her, but she's being devilish stubborn and doesn't wish to speak to me."

"Do you have the mermaid with you?" Harriet asked curiously, and smiled when Nigel pulled it out of his slightly rumpled, black superfine jacket.

"Here, take the damnable thing. I don't want it."

Harriet held the heavy pendant in her hands, and finally said, "First of all, we must find some way to return this to Emily."

The trio all stared at nothing in particular for the longest time, until Nigel finally asked, "Does Duke, her puppy, have a collar?"

Harriet and Henry both frowned. "I don't know," Harriet replied, then asked, "Why?"

A small smile finally appeared on Nigel's somber face. "She could hardly refuse the pendant if her puppy returned it to her, could she?"

"I don't follow you," Henry said with a frown.

"Hughes, my valet, has been helping Emily train her puppy, with some success. I sincerely doubt that she'll sever her relations with Duke because of my digressions. Well, at the earliest opportunity, I'll simply attach the mermaid to Duke's collar and send her in to Emily. She has to accept it back then. And it is rightfully her piece of jewelry," he concluded.

A smile quivered on the edge of Harriet's lush red lips. "She can't argue with Duke—that fact is certain."

"Especially if Nigel's valet—what is his name? Hughes? Especially if he sends the animal into her room, then makes himself scarce," Henry added helpfully.

"And if she still doesn't want to speak with you?" Harriet asked doubtfully.

Nigel shrugged his shoulders. "I don't know. But this situation will eventually be resolved, mark my words."

Much later in the day, a soft rapping could be heard at Emily's bedroom door. Emily had announced to the family that she was indisposed for the day (but promised to appear at dinner) and was curled up in bed reading a rather badly written Gothic.

"Shall I answer the door, Miss Emily?" Eliza asked, popping out of her seat near the window.

"I suppose," Emily replied in a lackluster voice, perfectly reflecting her state of mind.

Eliza trod over to the huge oak door and opened it slowly. Hughes, Lord Stratford's butler, stood there holding Duke.

"Yes?"

Hughes smiled gently at the perky, redheaded servant. "Please inform Miss Winterhaven that Duke is through with her lesson today. I thought she might want to spend some time with her," he said, and purposely put his finger on the mermaid that hung on Duke's makeshift collar.

Eliza raised an eyebrow. "Really?" she said with the ghost of a smile.

"Yes. And the pendant is to stay with Duke or Miss Winterhaven," he said in a hushed voice, and Eliza nodded in agreement.

"Of course," she said, and opened the door wider as Hughes placed the puppy on the floor.

"Go find Miss Emily," Hughes said softly, and gave the reddish-brown puppy a slight push on the behind to urge her toward Emily's bed.

Duke didn't need any encouragement, and moments later was standing next to Emily's bed, her paws on the covers, yapping to be picked up.

Emily looked down from her bed and grinned. "Duke, are you done with your instruction for the day?" she asked, and was rewarded with a yap.

She actually giggled slightly. "Yes, I see that you are. Here, let me help you up," she said, as Duke wagged her tail furiously.

Lifting the squirming puppy up onto the bed, Emily immediately noticed the brand-new collar she was wearing. "What is this you have on?" she asked the puppy, and, as she brought Duke onto her lap, she noticed something else.

The Manning Mermaid was dangling from Duke's collar, its jewels sparkling in the subdued light of the bedroom.

Fourteen

"Lady Markston and Lady Susan won't be dining with us this evening," Henry announced as the now-intimate party sat down at the large mahogany dining table.

Aubrey, clad in a pair of yellow stockinet breeches, a gold-and-Pomona-green-striped waistcoat, and a dark green coat, was in good spirits. He smiled cheerfully at Emily and Nigel, ignoring their obvious discomfort. "I'm sure Lady Susan needs some time to adjust to her newly found status as an engaged lady," he said with a grin, sipping his glass of burgundy.

Henry and Harriet exchanged a grin, and Henry casually added, "You know that word of this incident will never leave this house, if that's what you want."

Aubrey smiled merrily and replied, "And let Susan chase Nigel to the ends of the earth? I think not. Lady Susan has chosen her bed," he said with a cough, "and now she must suffer the consequences."

"So you really wish to wed Lady Susan?" Emily asked in a small voice, momentarily forgetting that she was planning to stay silent for the entire meal, since she was cajoled into sharing it with the awful Lord Stratford.

"Oh yes, Lady Susan and I actually rub together remarkably well. Once she is resigned to the fact that she won't be spending her life as a countess, then a marchioness, she'll calm down," he replied matter-of-factly, much to Emily's astonishment.

She stole a look across the table at Nigel, who looked as dreadful as she felt. Once again his unfashionably long, dark hair was a bit unkempt, and dark circles had now found a home under his glistening golden eyes. He still looks handsome, she thought to herself as she ate a stewed mushroom.

"I doubt if Lady Markston will let your wedding come about so easily," Harriet commented, sipping her burgundy thoughtfully.

"Lady Markston has no choice. Either Susan becomes my wife, or it becomes known in London that she is a fallen woman since she publicly shared my bed. Then no one will marry her," Aubrey concluded.

"Isn't that rather . . . dishonest?" Emily asked innocently, once again glancing at Nigel.

"Not at all," Henry replied. "Lady Susan perpetuated the deception—she should suffer the consequences," he pronounced.

Emily stared straight at Nigel, who had enough morals to turn a slight shade of red.

"Have you tried the fish mottoes, Miss Winterhaven?" Nigel asked, obviously grasping at some sort of conversational topic.

Taking a sip of her burgundy, Emily gave him her most regal glare. "Lord Stratford, I have no wish to discuss the meal or any other topic of polite conversation with you now or at anytime in the future," she said icily.

"Emily, you can't spend the rest of the holiday not speaking to Nigel. It just isn't done," Harriet admonished, glancing from one to the other.

A large tear welled up in her eye, and Emily was certain that she couldn't finish her meal with Nigel sitting across from her, enveloping her in a soulful gaze. So she stood up and faced Harriet, and replied, "I thought you would at least understand."

Before Harriet could deign to reply, Emily murmured, "Excuse me," and left the formal dining room.

Nigel followed her, calling, "Emily, wait a moment."

She was halfway up the staircase when Nigel grabbed her arm forcefully. "Emily, I must speak with you," he said, holding her in her steps.

Emily looked at the glistening wooden steps and said nothing.

Nigel took a deep breath. "Emily, I'm sorry about the pendant, and about Roger. Yes, I originally came here to buy the mermaid back from you, but after you told me you'd never get rid of it, I completely forgot about the matter. I love you and want to marry you. Can't we work this out?"

The tears were now silently streaming down Emily's cheeks. She wanted to forgive Nigel more than life itself, but she had learned about trust from his dear brother Roger. He's just toying with me, just like Lady Markston said, she thought, her face mirroring the anguish of her soul.

"Please, Emily?" he whispered, his face pale and tormented.

Emily looked down at him and softly said, "I'm sorry," before wrenching out of his grasp and slowly walking up the stairs.

It was the right thing to do, she thought, as she walked into her bedroom and flung herself down on the bed. She felt as if her heart was being torn out of her chest.

"Another glass of port?" Henry asked, pouring himself a refill.

"Yes, I believe I need another glass," Nigel replied, gazing at the blazing fire before him.

Henry refilled Nigel's intricately cut crystal glass and took his seat across from his friend. "Did you sort out matters with Emily?"

Nigel shook his head wearily. "No. She looks at me as if I'm the devil himself."

Sipping his port, Henry commented, "Emily was a very trusting person before the incident with Roger. That's why she's avoided the *ton*. You're been the first male she's really . . . befriended since then."

"Thank you, Henry. I now feel even more like a blackguard," Nigel replied sarcastically, his hand white around the stem of the glass.

"I suppose the only solution is to cut and run," Henry replied, his eyes intent on Nigel.

Nigel stared into the fire, his face pale with anguish. "Obviously Emily didn't confide everything that occurred between us in the library to Harriet. I wanted to keep matters private, but I suppose I should tell you that before Blackmore arrived and threw a spanner in the works, I offered for Emily."

Henry didn't flinch. "Harriet mentioned it in passing. Dashed bad luck, you know," he muttered, draining his glass of port.

Nigel gazed into the fire and softly said, "Yes, I know. It couldn't have turned out worse," he lamented, drumming his fingers nervously on the arm of his chair.

"What are your plans?"

Nigel frowned. "For now, I think it's best that I leave for a while. My constant presence is only making things worse for Emily. If she has a few days, she may come to understand what happened."

Henry studied the well-heeled peer sitting across from him. Nigel looked as if he were about to meet Jack Ketch. His shirt and waistcoat were wrinkled, his hair was uncombed, and his boots were scuffed and dirty. It was obvious that Nigel was taking this whole incident as badly as Emily. "Lady Markston mentioned that she was going to be leaving tomorrow morning, since the weather has finally cleared up. It will be a virtual exodus," he commented, then added, "Will you be returning?"

A slight smile appeared on Nigel's face. "Oh yes, I'll be back for the Twelfth Night festivities. But no one else need know that."

"Do you have some sort of intrigue planned?" Henry asked curiously.

The smile became a trifle larger. "Yes, I think so. I do mean to win Emily back, you see. Or, at the very least, convince her that I'm not a heartless blackguard," Nigel announced.

Henry looked toward the heavens and replied, "You'll need a miracle for that, Nigel."

It was a clear, bright January morning and the snow that covered a significant amount of the pastoral English countryside was rapidly melting. The roads were now obviously ready for travel, and, while they were eating their very hearty breakfast, Harriet and Henry discussed that very topic.

"What time did Nigel leave?" Harriet asked casually, eating her kidneys with relish.

Henry, clad in a simple pair of buckskin breeches and a crisp white shirt, pondered the question. "I believe that Jem in the stables said he left before eight A.M.," he replied, picking out the smoked haddock in his kedgeree.

Harriet, her long blond hair bound in a simple maroon ribbon, looked at his plate with disdain. "I can't imagine how you can eat that swill, Henry," she commented with a grimace. "Did Nigel mention if he was coming back? It was dashed odd for him to leave without a by-your-leave."

"I expect we haven't seen the last of him," Henry commented with a broad wink at his wife.

"Seen the last of whom?" Emily asked from the door of the breakfast room, a brave smile on her colorless face.

Harriet brightened immediately. "Emily, good you've made it down for breakfast! Do help yourself," she said, waving her hand toward the mahogany sideboard brimming with food.

"Although I would avoid that awful kedgeree that Cook fixes for Henry," she added.

Emily, looking rather fragile in a high-necked, dove-gray morning gown, sat herself down next to Harriet, a simple sweet omelette on her plate. "Who has left? Is our party finally delivered from Lady Markston and her entourage?" Emily asked, obviously trying her hardest to pretend that there was nothing wrong.

"No. Actually, Nigel left this morning," Henry said, finishing up his meal.

"Oh," Emily said in a small voice that told her friends that the episode with Nigel was far from over.

"We were also talking about the Twelfth Night festivities," Harriet quickly said, and kicked Henry under the table.

"Yes, the Twelfth Night is always a grand celebration. Blackmore and his party usually go mumming, and they're always sure to stop by. Occasionally we join in the festivities," Henry quickly added, sipping his tea.

"Yes, that's always great fun, even if we're not involved. And Cook makes up the most wonderful subtleties for the celebrations, and it's a tradition in Henry's family to play the most ridiculous games that night," Harriet said brightly, staring intently at Emily.

Emily picked at her sweet omelette. "Oh. I'm sure it will be wonderful," she replied in a sedate voice. She radiated the eagerness of one at a funeral.

"We also do have news on Lady Markston. It appears that she is leaving sometime today, but wishes to have a coze with the entire party before her entourage leaves to visit their relations," Henry said, diving into his second helping of kedgeree, the Indian delicacy that he obviously relished.

"Really," Emily muttered, staring blankly at her plate.

Henry and Harriet exchanged a look. It was obvious to the pair that Emily was not recovering from the row with Nigel.

Lady Markston, clad in a bright, apple-green gown adorned with yards of Belgian lace, paced the parlor nervously. She was waiting for that Emily Winterhaven to appear so she could address the entire party (sans Nigel, her trusted neighbor) with her proposition.

Susan, looking radiant in a white silk gown that had just enough flounce to make it daring, sat in the corner, stealing glances at Aubrey. He gazed intently at Lady Markston. Harriet and Henry were seated together on the black-and-gold recamier, prepared for whatever news Lady Markston might give them.

Emily quietly walked into the parlor, and Lady Markston barked, "Finally! We've been waiting for you, miss."

"I'm sorry," Emily said softly, and sat in the far corner on the black armchair with gilt ornaments.

Lady Markston continued pacing the room, the white *coq* feather in her apple-green turban bouncing with every step she took. "As you all know, my daughter and I are leaving today, since the weather has finally cleared," she began, staring out the window into the sunshine. "Before we depart, we wanted to assure you all that the unfortunate incident that happened several nights ago between my daughter and Lord Langely has already been forgotten and never need be mentioned again," she said arrogantly, her heart beating rapidly and faint beads of perspiration appearing on her pale brow.

"It was all a mistake," Susan added, looking at the floor rather than at anyone else in the parlor.

"Then the issue is settled. Susan, we are leaving," Lady Markston announced, heading for the door.

"Excuse me, Lady Markston?" Henry said casually.

"Yes?" she replied, stopping at the large, carved door.

"I'm sure no one wants to forget the incident that happened more than Lady Susan, but you have forgotten that more than one servant in this household witnessed the . . . event. I cannot promise you that they have not already discussed it outside of this house," Henry said calmly.

Lady Markston paled a bit, but decided that she'd best stay

on the offensive. "Are your servants so lax that you can't control their wagging tongues?"

Harriet clenched her hands in her lap in obvious anger. "Lady Markston, our servants are not slaves. If you wished to keep this issue a secret, you should have said something when we found your daughter in bed with Cousin Aubrey. Since you didn't make any sort of request, we cannot guarantee that news of this incident will not follow you to London."

"Posh! No one will believe it, in any case. And you'll support our story, won't you, Lord Langely?" Lady Markston said, her beady eyes boring into Aubrey.

A lazy smile crossed Aubrey's handsome features. "Actually, Lady Markston, I plan on placing a bet at White's on the day Lady Susan is going to bear my child."

"What?" Lady Markston shrieked, clutching her breast. "You told me nothing happened, you lying jade of a daughter!" she practically yelled, her eyes bulging out of her head.

"Mother, nothing happened," Susan said, giving Aubrey a look that could kill.

"So, Lady Markston, I'll be visiting your family once the Twelfth Night festivities have ended so we can discuss Susan's marriage settlement. Is that acceptable to you?" Aubrey asked cordially, as if he were discussing a dinner invitation.

"Yes, after the holiday," Lady Markston managed to mutter as Susan helped her out of the parlor.

Aubrey turned to the rest of the room and smiled. "I am known as a gambler of some repute. Do you think my tactic worked?" he asked with a smile.

Henry chuckled. "Undoubtedly. But do you really want to spend your life leg-shackled to Lady Susan? She does seem to be a termagant at times."

"Once Lady Susan gets accustomed to being my wife, I'm sure we'll manage to get on. She did appear in my bed, if you recall," Aubrey added with a slight wink.

"Actually, I'm sure she was expecting Nigel, but that isn't the point, is it?" Harriet asked, walking toward the door.

"No, it isn't. So offer me congratulations, since I'm going to be caught in the parson's mousetrap," Aubrey observed with a grin, completely oblivious to the look of sorrow that had settled onto Emily's pale features.

A dark cloud of doom followed Emily about the Ashton house like a shadow, casting a somber spell on the rest of the party. Harriet, Emily's closest friend, tried to cajole Emily out of her blue devils, but to no avail. Finally, after a disastrous dinner the evening that Nigel and Lady Markston left, Emily decided that the only solution was to spend some time alone, away from the rest of the family, to think about the situation.

She had been shut in her bedroom for two days, getting daily visits from Harriet and Henry, as well as a short visit from Aubrey. None of it helped to cheer her mood, but she tried to make a good show of it.

Eliza, her abigail, was working on a small piece of needlework when, late in the afternoon, someone knocked on her door.

"Shall I see who it is, Miss Emily?" Eliza asked, lines of worry furrowed into her youthful face.

"Yes. Tell them I don't wish to be disturbed," Emily answered, pulling the bedcovers up to her chin.

Eliza crossed the spacious bedroom and opened the oak door, only to find Victoria, clad in a beautiful blue velvet dress, standing there with Wellington beside her.

"May I please come in and talk to Aunt Emily?" Victoria asked, her deep blue eyes large and pleading.

"I'm sorry, dear, but your Aunt Emily isn't receiving any visitors," Eliza said gently.

"Please," Victoria implored. "I have something ever so important to tell her. Please."

"Let me ask her, all right?" Eliza replied, and partially

closed the door. Turning to Emily, she asked, "Miss Emily, Lady Harriet's daughter is here, and claims that she has something important to tell you. Do you wish to speak with her?"

Emily frowned and sat up in bed. "Yes, I'll see her."

Eliza returned to the door and opened it fully. "Miss Emily will see you now."

Victoria and Wellington walked into the room quietly, as if they were visiting a relation who had taken ill. Which was rather appropriate, since Emily was quite heartsick.

Emily smiled weakly at Victoria and said, "Eliza, bring the chair from the escritoire over so Victoria can sit next to the bed."

As Victoria got settled and Wellington curled up obediently at her feet, she asked curiously, "Where is Duke?"

"Duke is in the kitchen with Cook. You see, she isn't trained for the house yet and shouldn't be up here until we can be sure she won't have an accident," Emily explained patiently.

"Oh. Why are you mad at Uncle Nigel?"

Emily grinned slightly. She will most certainly have to learn to mind her tongue before she comes out, she thought, but replied, "Well, I suppose it's because he took something that belonged to me."

Victoria nodded sagely. "The mermaid pendant."

Surprised, Emily nodded in reply. "Yes, the mermaid my grandfather bought me."

Victoria leaned forward and almost whispered, "Can I tell you a secret?"

Emily finally smiled. Victoria was the most amusing visitor she had entertained. "Yes, of course you can."

Glancing around the room suspiciously, Victoria said, "Before Christmas, I got out of bed when I shouldn't have, and was looking for Wellington. I heard someone in the library and stood at the door and listened."

"You know you shouldn't eavesdrop, Victoria. That isn't right."

Victoria looked at the floor, her face turning pink. "I know.

But I didn't tell anyone what I heard, since Miss Turner said it was wrong to tattle."

"Miss Turner is absolutely correct—it *is* wrong to tattle," she admonished, secretly dying of curiosity.

Victoria squirmed in her chair. "Would it be all right to tattle if the person you were tattling on wasn't here to get in trouble?"

"If what you were saying wouldn't harm them, I suppose it would be all right," Emily replied, her curiosity getting the better of her common sense.

"Aunt Emily, Lady Susan was the one who took your mermaid. She was telling someone about it in the library. She said the only reason Uncle Nigel was here was because he wanted to get the mermaid from you. She said she was going to steal it from you and give it to him so that he could go home instead of spending the holiday with us," Victoria said in a rush, a look of relief on her face.

Emily's jaw dropped open. "Are you sure, Victoria? Lady Susan took the pendant?"

"Honest, Aunt Emily. I was afraid I'd get punished for tattling—that's why I didn't tell anyone. Uncle Nigel didn't take your mermaid."

As Emily pondered that amazing fact, Eliza had moved to the foot of the bed. "Miss Emily?"

"Yes, Eliza?"

"I have something to tell you, too. The day the pendant was returned, Lord Stratford's valet told me that someone wanted to speak with me in the kitchen. But when I went to find out who it was, no one knew what he was talking about. Then I went back to your room and the pendant was there. I think Lord Stratford's man put it back—that's why he sent me to the kitchen," Eliza finished.

Emily's mind was in a whirl. "Why would Lord Stratford give me the pendant back? It doesn't make any sense."

"Aunt Emily, Uncle Nigel wouldn't keep something that doesn't belong to him," Victoria stated innocently.

"Victoria, sometimes adults don't always act like ladies and gentlemen," Emily said calmly, her mind still in a whirl.

"Not Uncle Nigel. He isn't like that."

Emily stared at the wall, her mind still trying to cope with the tidbits of gossip that had been brought to her attention.

"Uncle Nigel came to say good-bye to me before he left. And he told me a story," Victoria announced, a strange gleam in her blue eyes.

"Really?" Emily replied, not really paying much attention to Victoria.

"He told me a story about a puppy he found when he was a little older than me. He said that when he found the puppy, he was half dead, because someone shot him. So Uncle Nigel took him to the doctor, and they made the puppy all better. Except that for the longest time, the puppy was afraid of him, because he remembered the man that shot him. But, after a real long time, the puppy became his friend. Uncle Nigel said people are like that, too, sometimes," Victoria finished.

Emily was frowning. *What is she talking about?* she wondered, and finally replied, "Really?"

Victoria nodded. "Uncle Nigel said that sometimes people get hurt by other people, then they're afraid of everyone else, even people that want to help them. Is that true?"

Emily felt as if someone had punched her in the stomach. Nigel was telling Victoria about her. *I was so afraid that Nigel was treating me like Roger had, that I wouldn't even give him a chance to explain what happened,* she thought, tears welling up in her eyes. And now he was gone. "Yes, Victoria, that's true. Sometimes people have a hard time seeing what's in front of their noses."

Nodding, Victoria leaned close to the bed. "Can I tell you another secret?"

"Of course, Victoria," Emily replied with a confidence she didn't feel.

"When Uncle Nigel left, he asked me to pray that you

wouldn't be mad at him anymore, but I don't think he wanted me to tell you," she whispered seriously.

The tears fell down Emily's cheeks. Her heart was now entirely torn in two. "That's all right, Victoria—I don't think I'm really angry with him anymore," she said in a choked voice, and wanted nothing more than to be left alone to cry.

Victoria brightened immediately and hopped off the chair. "I'm glad, Aunt Emily. Uncle Nigel thinks ever so much of you and I was worried about you being mad at him," the little girl replied as she walked toward the door. "Will you come see me tonight?"

Emily managed a weak smile. "I'll try," she replied without any conviction. She had thrown away her only chance at love because she was too stubborn to listen to the voice of reason.

"You don't mind helping us take down the decorations, do you, Emily?" Harriet asked as she put another bunch of holly into a pile on the brightly shining floor.

Emily stood on her tiptoes and tried to reach another of the dozens of ropes of holly that decorated the ballroom. "No, not at all," she replied, finally grasping the rope and pulling it gently down. "We do the same thing at home every year."

Harriet nodded, bringing a handful of mistletoe to the pile on the floor. "I suppose it is sort of a tradition to burn your holiday decorations on the Twelfth Night."

"At least it is at our house," Emily replied, tackling another rope. "When are Lord Blackmore and his party going to come by?"

Harriet smiled slightly. Emily was obviously coping better with the Nigel situation and her mood appeared to have improved incredibly. "I really don't know. But I'm certainly glad that you're no longer so blue-deviled."

Emily smiled wryly and looked down at her black velvet dress. "Actually, I'm still in the doldrums—that's why I'm in black. But it isn't fair to you or anyone else to have me moping around for the rest of the holiday," she explained.

Harriet frowned. "So you're still mad at Nigel?"

Emily shook her head. "Not really. If anything, I suppose I owe him an apology for being so . . . stubborn. But I'm obviously not going to get the opportunity, since I probably won't be seeing him again."

"Well, you can always join me in London when the Season opens. You'll have a fair chance of seeing Nigel then," Harriet added, the last bunch of mistletoe in her hand.

"I don't think a Season in London will be the solution, Harriet. One does get tired of hearing the words 'ape leader' following one about," Emily replied, a cynical edge to her usually melodic voice.

Before Harriet could reply, a great commotion could be heard in the hall toward the front of the house, and Victoria ran into the ballroom.

"Mama! The mummers are here!" she exclaimed, her eyes shining eagerly.

"Well, let us meet them in the parlor," Harriet said, and they all walked the carpeted halls to the Egyptian-motif parlor.

Once the entire household was seated in the parlor, the festivities began. A light-haired man, dressed as a naval captain, entered the room dramatically.

"I ask your pardon for being so bold, I enter your house since the weather is cold. For with me I bring the man we call king," he proclaimed, and waved his hand toward the door.

A man, dressed in royal fur robes and a crown, entered the room with pomp. Emily immediately recognized him as Lord Blackmore, the host of the disastrous masquerade.

"I am the King of England, I proudly appear, to find my only son, my only son is here!" he proclaimed, looking around the room.

From behind the "King," a man appeared, tall and handsome, dressed as a warrior of old. His ancient silver knight's helmet hid most of his face, but Emily could tell that he had dark hair, rather similar to Blackmore's. The man paused before reciting, "I am Prince George, your valued knight, and I'll spill my blood for my country's right."

Emily's mouth dropped open. Prince George was obviously Nigel.

Fifteen

As Emily continued to gape at Prince George, actually Nigel, the play continued. A gentleman, dressed as a Turkish soldier, joined the company.

"From the land of Turkey I hail, I will cause your women to wail. I come to fight the King of Eng-land, I will challenge you on sea or on sand," the rather thin-looking "Turk" announced, his hand on his sword.

The King strode forward to meet the Turk. "I am the King, as you see. These are my legions standing with me. If you challenge, your life will end, since on them my life doth depend."

Nigel, Prince George, stepped in front of the King and faced the Turk. "I am Prince George, a champion bold, from near and far you will hear stories told. I have slain a dragon and brought him to slaughter, and as a reward was given Egypt's first daughter."

The Turk made a show of looking Nigel over and then laughed in contempt. "You are a fool and a coward to me, it shall take no time to spill the life out of thee," he proclaimed, and men unsheathed their swords and began to duel.

The players were furious, and the swordplay would have been rather terrifying if it had been real. In the end, the Turk "ran" his sword through Nigel, who fell dramatically to the floor, his knight's helmet dropping off in the process.

"What have you done? You have gone and killed my only son!" the King proclaimed in a heartbroken voice.

The Captain who proclaimed the entrance of the party of mummers stepped into the front. "Oh my lord, I know of a way, to heal his wounds and save the day," he announced.

The King turned to the Captain. "Tell me, man, I wish to know, the way to cure my son's mortal blow."

"A maiden we need, one true and kind, will help your son out of his deathly bind," the Captain replied, and the King and the Captain began to obviously scan the room for a maiden.

The King walked over to Emily and asked, "You, young lady, will you help me? My only son's death I do not choose to see."

Emily was mortified. The entire room was staring at her. "What must I do?" she said in a soft voice, her embarrassment very apparent to everyone in the room.

The King took her hand in his and coaxed her out of her seat. "Come, my girl, come to the place, but do not be afraid to look death in the face," he said, leading Emily over to the place where Nigel lay prone on the floor.

"You, young maiden, are you still free?" the Captain asked, and Emily nodded yes, since he appeared to be asking if she was unmarried.

"There is only one way to restore his sad life, with a kiss and a promise that you will be his wife," the Captain announced with a slight smile on his face.

Emily paled slightly. This was not any play that she had ever seen performed on the Twelfth Night. And she could obviously not kiss Nigel in front of the entire household.

To Emily's horror, the King dropped to his knees and appealed to her. "I beg thee, my friend, his life should not end. Please give the kiss so a life he won't miss," he said, clutching her hands in his.

Emily looked out at the audience, who now began to chant, "Kiss him!" Turning a deeper shade of red, she said,

"Oh, all right," and knelt down to kiss Nigel gently on the cheek.

Nigel looked into her hesitant green eyes and smiled gently at her as he stood up and faced the King. "Her kindness and love has brought life into me, whatsoever shall her eternal reward be?" he asked the King.

The King took a small box out of his pocket and opened it for the audience to see. It was a large diamond-and-emerald engagement ring. "My son, I do ask, before I give you this ring, will your heart be true, no matter what luck will bring?"

"My heart will be faithful through thick and through thin, it is her heart that I live to win," Nigel recited, his eyes boring into Emily.

Emily was still a deep shade of red. The audience, though, was leaning forward, eager to see the outcome of this very unconventional St. George play.

"Very well, my son, the ring you shall take, and I only hope that your heart doth not break," the King said, handing the ring to Nigel, Prince George.

"Will you take this gift to seal the rift that has broken my heart and torn my very sorry life apart?" Nigel asked softly, handing the ring to Emily.

Before Emily could make any sort of reply, Victoria cried, "Take the ring, Aunt Emily! Uncle Nigel wants to marry you!"

Emily giggled as she felt the love swelling inside her. She took the ring from Nigel's outstretched hand and he put his arm around her waist, bringing her next to him.

"It is time to go, we must be done," the entire party began to recite, "The play is over, we have had our fun. We hope we have spread some Christmas cheer, and wish to sample your holiday beer!"

As the entire household began to applaud, Nigel took Emily's hand and led her through the house, out to the garden.

The crescent moon shone overhead, and Nigel let go of her

long enough to walk over to the cobblestone wall that encircled the edge of the garden. He returned almost immediately, holding her pelisse and his Polish greatcoat. He wrapped the pelisse around her shoulders and led her to one of the trees at the far end of the garden.

"If you'll notice, we're under Henry's holly tree. Didn't you learn about the holly tree at Miss Haversham's school?" Nigel asked softly, taking her cold fingers inside his warm, large hand.

Emily frowned. For the life of her, she couldn't recall one single thing that Miss Haversham told her about the holly tree, or anything else, for that matter. "No, I can't say that I do," she said in a breathy voice that she didn't quite recognize as her own.

Nigel smiled in the darkness. "Well, traditionally, anyone who has quarreled will settle their disagreement peaceably under the holly tree. And we certainly have quarreled," he said softly, his thumb tracing invisible designs on the palm of her hand.

Emily looked up into his dark eyes. "I'm sorry, Nigel. I know you didn't take the mermaid, and I'm sorry I didn't give you a chance to explain." But she really didn't want to explain, either. She simply wanted to reach over and kiss the handsome peer who was making her blood course wildly though her veins.

"Will you give me a chance now?"

Emily nodded and moved closer to his tall, masculine figure.

"I think I fell in love with you the first day I met you, when Wellington upset my horses and you ended up haring around the grounds retrieving my small clothes," he began with a chuckle, wrapping his arms around her waist. "I didn't expect you to be Emily Winterhaven, since Roger was rather . . . inaccurate in his description of you. In any case, I agreed to come to Harriet's Christmas party to meet you and see if you would sell the mermaid. And I did ask you about it, not long after we met. Do you remember?"

"Yes, I told you it was a gift from my grandfather and that I wouldn't sell it," Emily replied, gazing up into his dark eyes that danced in the moonlight.

"And I immediately forgot about it. I never really believed in the Manning Mermaid Curse in the first place, and had no affinity for the pendant at all. So how could I convince you to sell it back when it obviously meant much more to you than it ever did to me? That's why I let the matter drop and tried to enjoy the holiday."

"But you did end up with the mermaid," Emily replied, oblivious to the damp wind running through her loose auburn hair.

"Yes. I suppose you know that Lady Susan was under the misguided notion that if I had the mermaid in my possession, I would leave here and spend the holiday with her. That's why she stole it and gave it to me," he explained, wrapping his arms around her and pulling her close.

"But why did you give it back? I would never have known that you had it, or that Lady Susan had taken it."

Nigel chuckled slightly. "Dearest Emily, I couldn't keep your mermaid, knowing how much you treasured it. That's why I had it returned to you as soon as I could."

"It was your valet who returned it, wasn't it? While we were at church."

"Yes," Nigel admitted. "Hughes did my dirty work so you could have the pendant back, since it is rightfully yours. After that, I rather forgot about it. I know I sound like a slow-top, but there it is. I was enjoying our time together so much, that everything else just became . . . unimportant," he said in a slightly desperate voice.

Emily paused for a moment, then softly said, "But you had to know about my unfortunate alliance with your brother."

"Yes, I knew. The reason I didn't mention the connection is

purely selfish. I wanted to get to know you better and I was certain you would have nothing to do with Roger Manning's older brother."

A sigh escaped Emily. "You're right. I wouldn't have given you the time of day."

"There you are. I had no choice," he said passionately, dropping small kisses onto the nape of her neck.

Emily curled up into his warm Polish greatcoat and murmured, "Your family will never accept me."

Nigel laughed merrily. "I think I should worry that your family won't accept me. I'm sure that your father will be none too pleased when the Earl of Stratford comes calling to beg for his daughter's hand in marriage."

That made Emily smile. "Oh, I think my father will be much easier to convince than your father. I met the marquess once while I was in London. You might find yourself permanently disowned for taking up with a cit bluestocking."

The smile on Nigel's face continued to shine as brightly as the crescent moon above them. "My love, if I remember correctly, my father, who is the most difficult man in England, actually liked you. That's why he was so disgusted with Roger when he heard about his prank. So I sincerely doubt that he will be anything but pleased with our connection." He continued kissing her velvet-smooth neck, and murmured, "You never did answer my question at the masquerade."

Emily was still silent. Her heart was beseeching her to proclaim "Yes" for all of the universe to hear, but a part of her wanted a little more. For all of her four-and-twenty years, she'd wanted a romantic proposal. Nigel had all but bungled the proposal in the library, and she wanted him to be . . . romantic.

When Emily didn't reply, Nigel gently pushed her away and, to Emily's utter delight, fell to his knees in the ice and snow.

Taking her hand in his, he softly said, "Emily, I want nothing more in life than to have you as my wife. Will you accept my hand in marriage and accept my promise to love and protect you until the end of both our days?"

The tears of joy began to stream down Emily's pale cheeks. "Yes," she said softly, and pulled him off his knees. "I was going to say yes when you asked me in Lord Blackmore's library," she said, throwing herself into his strong arms. His lips met hers and proclaimed that their passion was almost hot enough to melt the winter snow.

After a very long time, Emily determined that Nigel was quite accomplished at kissing. And that she enjoyed kissing Nigel probably as much as he enjoyed kissing her! Finally, Nigel released Emily and took something out of his pocket. It was a folded paper, and he explained, "Before Blackmore and I rewrote his Twelfth Night play, I managed to procure this."

Emily squinted at the papers in the moonlit darkness. "What is it?"

"It is a special license. We can marry whenever you wish, my dearest. Or we can publish the banns and have a wedding that the *ton* will not soon forget," he said, his hand running through her luxuriant auburn hair.

Emily smiled up at him. "I must commend Lord Blackmore on his creative talents. The play was very impressive," she said, reaching into her pocket and holding up the ring he had given her.

Nigel took the ring and gently slipped it over the third finger of her left hand. It was a perfect fit. "It's quite real, you know. I couldn't go home and bring you the Manning engagement ring, so I had this one made. It will have to do for now."

Emily smiled up at him. "It will do perfectly. You know, you really had no chance, Lord Stratford," she said with a mischievous grin.

"And why is that, my love?"

"Well, I decided that this was the year I was going to follow every Christmas tradition I knew to find a husband. I put rosemary and thyme in my shoes, and then I dreamed of you. That was the first sign."

Nigel chuckled and lightly kissed her forehead. "There's more?"

"Much more. On Christmas Eve, if you go into the garden at midnight and pick twelve sage leaves, you'll see the image of your husband. I had just finished picking my sage leaves when you came out and attempted to seduce me," Emily explained in a soft, seductive voice.

Nigel ran kisses through her hair. "Yes, well, I am rather enamored of you, dear Emily. I wasn't going to ravish you, though, if that makes you feel any better."

"Much better. Do you remember Mass on Christmas Day?"

Nigel began to lightly kiss her neck. "Yes, you were wearing some sort of half-dead flower so I bought one from a flower girl and gave you a new one. That's hardly extraordinary."

"Another Christmas legend. That was a rose I picked on Midsummer's Day. If an unmarried female wears the rose to church on Christmas Day, her future husband is supposed to come and take it from her," Emily explained patiently, quite enjoying Nigel's attentions.

"And finally, the last Christmas legend. All quarrels should be settled under the holly tree. Everything is settled, isn't it, my love?" Nigel asked, his eyes wide with love.

"Yes, Nigel, everything is settled. Are you sure you want to marry an aging bluestocking cit?" she asked softly, pressing her lithe body against him.

"Oh, yes. If you can somehow learn to live with the fact that you're eventually going to be a marchioness, and your children will have the tainted blood of a peer running through their veins," he replied, and kissed her lightly on the lips.

"I do love you," Emily whispered, almost afraid to say the words out loud.

"And I will love you to the end of our days, and I'll make sure you never regret our marriage," he said in a voice thick with emotion, then added lightly, "Of course, you really must marry me, for Duke's sake."

Emily smiled. "For Duke's sake?"

"Yes. She's quite an affectionate thing, but rather on the stubborn side. I think the only person who can possibly train her is Hughes, my valet. So to save her from a life in the kitchen, or worse yet, in the stables, you'd best marry me, Miss Winterhaven."

Emily giggled. "Yes, I suppose I can't just hire Hughes away from you, can I?"

Nigel shook his head. "Hughes has worked for the family for ages. You'll simply have to marry me so your puppy can be house-trained," he said in a somber voice.

"Yes, I suppose I'll have to, for Duke's sake," she said, and lightly kissed him on the lips.

"By the by, Duke isn't the only Christmas present you've given me," Emily said in a breathless voice.

"Well, there is that rather impressive ring you're wearing . . ." he said with a slight smile.

Emily smiled up at him. "Yes, there is that. But do you remember when you asked me what I wanted for Christmas, weeks ago?"

"Yes, you seemed hard-pressed to answer."

"More than anything else, I want a family of my own," she said in a soft voice.

Nigel was grinning ear to ear. "I believe I can help you with that, Miss Winterhaven. Would you like to get started on that right now?"

A rich giggle escaped Emily. "We should go back inside, shouldn't we? Before Harriet comes out looking for us."

"Your wish is my command," he announced, and the pair began to slowly walk toward the house.

"Do you think your family will be very upset that there is

no Curse of the Manning Mermaid?" Emily asked curiously as they trampled through the snow.

Nigel put his arm around her waist as he led her toward the glass door. "I believe from now on it should be referred to as the Christmas Mermaid, and that the curse, if there ever was one, should be laid to rest. If anything, the mermaid is good luck, since it was what led me to you," Nigel replied, holding her close to him.

Emily smiled up at him. "The Christmas Mermaid. I think that has a nice ring to it," she replied, as they opened the door to Henry's house.

And the rest of their life together.

Thrilling Romance from Meryl Sawyer